A [illegible]

"Well, my dear Charlotte, it is time for you to think of your own needs."

She glanced back and saw that the groom was far enough behind not to hear the conversation. "Actually, I have none."

"Nonsense! A beautiful young woman should spread her wings."

"Wings? I have hoofs!" she exclaimed, sending Prince into a canter.

Sir Roland was only a couple of strides behind her. They crossed a field, sailed easily over a hedge, and drew up at the far side of a second field.

"How could I do that in London?" she demanded, hardly even breathless.

"Well, you could not," Sir Roland admitted, "though you could swoop over ballroom floors with great effect."

"Are you pushing me to London again?" she said. "How superficial Society sounds!"

Sir Roland was smiling, yet he spoke decisively. "Sydney will be going there before long," he reminded. "You must be in a position to guide him. How much better to be acquainted ahead of that time!"

She frowned. "Of course. Syd's *sister* will invite all the bonniest girls to a party. And you must come to ogle with the rest."

"One need not do that," he replied huskily, "if one has already seen perfection."

Charlotte turned slightly pink. Could he be implying *herself?*

WATCH FOR THESE REGENCY ROMANCES

A Proper Match

Dorothea Donley

Zebra Books
Kensington Publishing Corp.
http://www.zebrabooks.com

ZEBRA BOOKS are published by

Kensington Publishing Corp.
850 Third Avenue
New York, NY 10022

First Printing: January, 1998
10 9 8 7 6 5 4 3 2 1

Printed in the United States of America

One

A great oaken door of Heritage Castle stood open to the fresh summer air. The sky was bright blue and the lawns, flowing gently down toward the pale yellow stone and shingle roofs of a village, were rich green. Yet the young woman standing in the doorway noticed no colors or zephyrs. She waited impatiently for the distant figure of a young man to reach her. He was coming, she could tell, not from the village, but from the Dower House of Heritage, which was partially visible in a clump of oak trees near the manor gates.

The watching lady was of slim and graceful form, with brown hair drawn back to a smooth knot. A slight flush tinted her cheeks. Her brown eyes were serious, their aspect softened by long, dark lashes, and her mouth was modeled with a slight, appealing lift at the corners. From time to time she pursed those lips, and had she been a dragon would have breathed some fire to relieve her inner tension.

Obviously the young gentleman saw her, for he waved, but he did not hurry his pace. They were too far apart for him to read her mood, though the fact of her waiting boded ill for him. He could expect a lecture.

Not that a gentleman of sweet nature could ever be caught in serious error. It was simply a question of his health, which had not been good when he was a child, and his sister had never accustomed herself to the idea that he was not only well, but now grown to manhood. He was nineteen.

She was twenty-four and for nine years had devoted herself

to the nurture of the fragile duke. When he came closer she would see that his color was good, that he stood straight (if not above medium height), and that he was well fleshed. But in her mind's eye he was still a delicate youth. While he called her Mother Hen and endured her attentions amiably, she, for her part, was not very successful in turning him loose . . . though she might have done so, were it not for that minx, Cleone, living at the Dower House.

The duke was in no hurry for another lecture. He walked steadily but slowly, and when a curricle caught him halfway home, he halted to greet a neighbor warmly. Lady Charlotte, at the doorstep, ground her teeth at the delay.

But the baronet was taking up her brother, and they reached Lady Charlotte sooner than Sydney might have done had he continued to walk.

"Charlotte!" called Sir Roland March in his irrepressible way. "I have brought Sydney to you." Having known brother and sister all their lives, and being twenty years older than Lady Charlotte, he did not hesitate to call the late duke's offspring by their first names. He was large and fair, without facial lines, and exuded an admirable self-confidence.

"You are always welcome, Sir Roland," she said. "I am sure it must be time for tea."

"I had tea with the Beechams," the young duke mentioned.

A stable boy came running to take Sir Roland's vehicle, and the three went into the castle by the oaken door to the family wing of the building. Another stately entrance on the east facade was approached by a long and artistic driveway from ornamental gates at the turnpike, but neighbors, like Sir Roland, found this way more convenient.

Lady Charlotte led them to a parlor.

"Sydney Held, I thought you were never coming," she said as she rang for tea.

"But you see that I *was,*" he replied, unruffled. "The Beechams have an unexpected visitor, and there were many expressions of astonishment and introductions. A niece has arrived to visit, and nothing must do but she must be presented to her uncle's 'benefactor.' "

"Mr. Beecham's niece?" Charlotte exclaimed. "This is the first I have heard of his having one."

Sydney shook his head. "No, actually Mrs. Beecham's. No kin to us, Charlotte."

"That is merciful," his sister said. The late duke in an excess of goodwill had invited an impoverished kinsman to come as his chaplain, only to find his fulsome gratitude extremely boring. When the Dower House became vacant, he had, with some relief, there established Mr. Beecham's family with several servants, including a cook, which made his own dinners more digestible. "Did you stop there, Sir Roland?"

"No," replied Sir Roland, "for I did not know about the visitor."

"How strange that Cousin Maude never mentions her. What is her name?" asked Charlotte.

"Mercy," said Sydney wryly. "From Mercillia. A very young lady. Perhaps seventeen, and very retiring."

"No competition for Cleone, then." She was about to add "more's the pity," but Sir Roland gave a small shake of his head, and she bit off the words.

Tea arrived and Lady Charlotte set about pouring cups. She was a handsome young woman who gave little thought to her looks. Family pride kept her neat and elegant; her focus, however, was always upon Sydney.

There was a momentary lull.

Sir Roland warmed his tongue with a sip of tea, then said tranquilly, "Tell us about the addition to the Dower House, Sydney."

"I know very little," the duke responded, "though as much as anyone else. Miss Pope, you see, arrived before the letter announcing that she was to come."

Charlotte said, "Upsetting for everyone. Surely she did not travel alone!"

"No, there is an elderly watchdog who does not smile. The

young lady was dismayed, I think, but quickly explained that her mama and papa had gone suddenly to Greece, after sending her off to the care of her dear auntie. She promised that she would not be a nuisance, for she is accustomed to be of use to her mama."

Charlotte said tartly, "Oh, yes, Mrs. Beecham will be sure to make use of her, and very likely Cleone will turn her into a slave."

The young duke frowned and Sir Roland sent Charlotte a warning glance. "Perhaps the girl will enjoy meeting all the local beaux who visit the Dower House regularly," he said mildly.

Thus gently reminded that other young males besides Sydney danced attendance upon Cleone, Charlotte sipped her tea before venturing to say that they must ask the Beecham group for dinner soon. "The three are here at least once a week. It will be no trouble to add a fourth."

"That would be kind," Sir Roland said, confident that she understood his subtle warning not to impel Sydney into greater attentions in that quarter by thwarting him.

"We must include Sir Roland, too," Sydney said, remembering that it was Sir Roland's influence which had made it possible for him to have two years at Harrow.

"Yes," said Charlotte. "It is difficult to say who depends upon him most, you or I." She was laughing, but the two gentlemen knew she was speaking truth. Neither she nor her brother could manage without the kind mentor who was her father's friend, Sir Roland March.

They discussed a probable date.

"Cousin Maude is sure to bring the niece for a duty call. Tomorrow, very likely. I will engage them for Thursday or Friday, if that is agreeable to you, Sir Roland," Charlotte decided. "Shall I invite any others?"

But Sydney said oh, no, eight was just congenial. He was, of course, counting the sweet and timid septuagenarian, Aunt Emilie, who was a ghostly chaperone to Charlotte. Soon he went off on business of his own, leaving the two old friends to talk comfortably.

"I am afraid Sydney thinks only of having Cleone's company without sharing her with other beaux," Charlotte said regretfully.

Sir Roland nodded. "Possibly. But if you will agree for him to go off to Oxford, he will soon be thinking of *that.*"

"Oh, must I permit him to go?"

"Yes, you must, Charlotte. What sort of duke will he make if he sees nothing but Shropshire, and has half an education?"

"I employed a very good tutor!"

"Yes, but a tutor isn't the same as male friends. What sort of larks and challenges can he enjoy alone at Heritage?"

She was silent for a moment, adding fresh tea to her cup. "More?" When he shook his head, she said in a flat voice, "I suppose I must listen to you."

"I am not a tyrant, Charlotte," he reminded gently. "Harrow did Sydney good. Were you so lonely then? Why not show yourself in London for a change? Heritage will not fall apart. Why not travel?"

In a way she knew he was right. At least about Sydney. But London *alone* or travel *alone* sounded grim. Self-pity Charlotte considered shameful, so—although she felt her eyes sting—she said briskly that she would give the matter some thought.

After a brief silence which somehow seemed companionable, Sir Roland said, "I may have a visitor, myself, soon."

"Oh?"

"My sister Katherine is coming down from the border. I expect her to make a stay of a month or two. She hasn't visited for three years."

Charlotte said, "I have never understood why Katherine March went so far away."

"Why did you not ask me? Like you, she needed a change. When a cousin who was home-bound after an illness invited her for a visit, she went off to be helpful and ended by finding several congenial friends and a cooler climate. I have not been able to lure her home permanently—only for rare visits."

"Is the cousin still an invalid?"

"No indeed. Hale and hearty. Raises collies, which are as interesting to Katherine as people."

Charlotte smiled. "Papa was the same about his spaniels. I am glad we are not overrun by them now! A well-schooled dog is nice enough, but yapping kennels I cannot like."

Laughing, the baronet said, "*Kennels* don't yap."

They continued in easy conversation for a time, and nothing more was said about Sydney's infatuation with the minx at the Dower House, but Cleone lingered in Charlotte's mind—a pretty chit with bouncing gold curls and teasing eyes. A real threat to Charlotte's peace. Saucy Cleone might have numerous beaux, but Charlotte knew none could compare with a duke in the aspirations of a chaplain's daughter.

Just as Charlotte had foretold, the next morning brought Mrs. Beecham and her niece to call. Cleone not being along to overshadow this new cousin, Mercy appeared quietly attractive. She was small, not over five feet in height, with gentle gray eyes that did *not* immediately assess the richness of Heritage, and soft brown hair that clouded about her shoulders; her clothes had the look of Paris without being unsuitable to her age. A faint blush touched her cheeks.

Supposing the girl to be uncertain of her reception, Charlotte said kindly, "We are not a very active society here, Miss Pope, but will hope you enjoy our simple pleasures."

"Oh, call her Mercy," said Mrs. Beecham. "Family, you know. Must not stand on ceremony. I have told her to call you Cousin Charlotte, as the rest of us do."

Charlotte had a strong feeling that a very young girl could wait until invited to call her that, but as she could discern some embarrassment on the girl's part, she took pity on Mercillia and said she must follow Cleone's custom.

Mercy breathed, "Thank you, my lady. My mother said my aunt's acquaintances would be sure to befriend me."

Poor child! What did her mama know of Mrs. Beecham's friends or patrons? Thinking it must be difficult for such a gentle young creature to be thrust upon virtual strangers, Charlotte unbent to say she was sure Mr. and Mrs. Beecham were happy to welcome such a pretty niece. Even Cleone, secure in her popularity with the local swains, would casually accept the girl, she thought. But what sort of parents would cast off a child in such a harum-scarum fashion?

When several sentences had been exchanged between Charlotte and Mrs. Beecham, establishing that Mr. Pope was a student of antiquities and had taken his wife (also a Grecophile) off to Greece to follow in Lord Elgin's footsteps in case his lordship had overlooked anything, Charlotte concluded that Mr. Pope was a gentleman of artistic curiosity and independent means. This was all very well, but somewhat hard on his daughter.

"I am hoping you and your husband—and Cleone—and Mercy will come for dinner with the duke and me," she said to Mrs. Beecham. "Would Thursday or Friday be best for Cousin John?"

The polite fiction of the chaplain's work being maintained, his wife chose Friday.

"This is a kind thought, Cousin Charlotte, but there is no necessity for you to include Mercy. *We* are your kin, not Mercy. She is only a child, after all. I can have my cook heat up a little something for her—"

Seeing Mercy's stricken face, Charlotte interrupted harshly: "Pray, permit me to choose my own guests! It is my wish to make Mercy welcome at *my* home. The duke, who has spoken kindly of her, would expect her to be included."

"Whatever you wish—the duke wishes—" fluttered Mrs. Beecham. "I am sure Mercillia—" here a sharp look at the girl "will be pleased to do—accept—"

"Then we will expect the four of you on Friday," her hostess said firmly. "Are you rested after your journey, Mercy? I did not hear from where you came."

"From Portsmouth, my lady," whispered Mercy. "My parents embarked there."

"And you are missing them already, I'll be bound."

"But she has three relatives to make her welcome at the Dower House," inserted Mrs. Beecham quickly. "I am sure she will enjoy the beauty and—er—society of Heritage."

"Why did Cleone not come with you this morning?" asked Lady Charlotte, shifting ground pointedly.

"Oh, a headache, a wee headache, and I thought it best for her to linger in bed. She is always so—vivacious, overly vivacious, and I would not want her to overextend her strength."

"If ever I saw a girl with strength, it is Cleone," asserted Charlotte with a side glance at Mercy, in whose eyes she detected a very alert look.

"Oh, so true, Cousin Charlotte, but even hers has *limits*. Now that we have a dinner with you and the duke to look forward to, I particularly wish Cleone to be at her best."

"Your daughter, Cousin, is always at peak performance."

As Mrs. Beecham judged this to be a compliment, she accepted it as a favorable sign. "Too kind. Come, Mercillia, Mr. Beecham will wonder what has become of us. He does like an early nuncheon. Then he takes a little nap. And then—back to his studies."

What the studies were, no one seemed to know.

"Yes, of course," said Charlotte, rising. "He pursues serious matters. So exhausting."

Mrs. Beecham saw that she could linger no longer. She lunged to her feet. "Yes, yes. His studies are so *deep*. I do not try to understand. Come, Mercillia."

With Charlotte herding them like a border collie, they moved across the room and down the hall. As Mrs. Beecham afterwards reported to her husband, Charlotte was all graciousness, making a special point to congratulate her on a delightful niece, and to tell Mercy she must come sometime for a private coze.

"You must not think," Mrs. Beecham explained to her niece

as they returned to the Dower House, "that Lady Charlotte means you to come alone to call. Why, she would be astonished to see you! Even Cleone—as long as she has lived here—would not impose upon Lady Charlotte in such a way. That was only parlor talk."

Mercy looked perplexed.

"She said 'for a private coze—' "

"That did not mean a thing," her aunt insisted.

Two

Guidebooks might describe Heritage Castle as being located near the village of Fallford, while actually the castle came first and the village grew up near it as various trades settled conveniently at hand. The castle also expanded when successive dukes added to it. There was, therefore, some mixture of styles, though the whole was imposing. The present duke, his sister, and Aunt Emilie preferred the private comfort of a wing which was only seventy years old, while servants were obliged to be content with quarters scattered throughout various attics; *they* took pride in showing public visitors the splendors of the state apartments.

Like a small city, the castle was maintained by Audley wealth, of which no one knew the exact amount—that is to say, none but an army of conscientious managers, bankers, legal gentlemen, and Lady Charlotte, to whom all were courteous, being rather surprised at the extent of her understanding.

Her ladyship was beginning to introduce her brother to the complexities of his estate and outlying manors, but still held the reins until he might be of age to take them. She loved Heritage Castle and had met no man to lure her away. How could she have left it? The delicate health of her brother and her duties to the estate took all her time, beginning six years before when her father had died and she was only eighteen.

Sydney was grown now and showing some interest in the inheritance of which he must take charge in another two years.

Charlotte's work was almost done. Sir Roland was right. She should turn herself in a new direction.

Dinner was served on Friday evening to the guests from the Dower House in the family dining salon of the "new" wing. Perhaps Mrs. Beecham would have preferred the state dining chamber with its linen-fold paneling and emerald draperies; even so, Charlotte knew that lady was pleasantly flattered to be entertained by a duke.

"This is charming," she said to His Grace, to whom a family meal was nothing unusual.

"We are delighted to have your company," Sydney responded graciously, but Charlotte saw with dismay that his eyes were upon the glowing Cleone, and he meant *her.* Something must be done about Cleone—or about Sydney, as Sir Roland said.

Actually, little Miss Pope, though younger and less sophisticated than Cleone, seemed perfectly poised. Who could know? Perhaps she had learned demeanor from more critical persons in the company of her parents. Her white muslin dress was ruffled about the neck and little puffed sleeves with fine lace that was unmistakably French. Her manners were dainty.

Cleone, seated between Sir Roland and Aunt Emilie, sparkled and sent teasing glances at her host so often as to limit her to small bites of food. To watch such coy antics was galling to Charlotte, who was obliged to converse with the gentleman guests on either side of herself. Aunt Emilie, as usual, was quiet as a mouse, but Mrs. Beecham found plenty to say to the duke, beside whom to her satisfaction she was seated.

When Cleone was plainly heard to say "La! What a tease you are, Cousin Sydney" and little Miss Pope looked up in obvious surprise, Sir Roland favored Charlotte with an amused wink. Yes, a wink! Fortunately the chaplain was too intent on his meal to notice.

Oh, thought Charlotte, something would have to be done about Cleone. It was obvious that Cleone, abetted by her mother, was out to capture the young duke. Could he not see that he was a target? Or did he enjoy being pursued?

At least Mercy was no threat. Too young to cast out lures, or too well bred . . . or perhaps too inexperienced to take advantage of introduction to a prime *parti.*

Charlotte's eyes met Sir Roland's. She had the distinct feeling that his thoughts were the same as hers. He nodded slightly. Yes, she would have to send Sydney to Oxford, though she dreaded temptations to which young men were said to be exposed at that place. Their father, and his father before him, had studied at Oxford, so she did not consider Cambridge, since Sir Roland was an Oxford man also, and *he* was certainly an educated gentleman.

The tinkle of Mr. Beecham's fork coming to rest upon his plate called Charlotte's attention to the fact that he had finished eating. Unobtrusively she signaled her butler to clear for their next course. One entertains primarily to give pleasure to one's guests. Looking down the table she found that the main course had been well received. How many times had she sat with the Beecham family? And how many times lay ahead?

Cousin John Beecham, who had read for Holy Orders under a scholarly rector at Manchester, was a man with scriptural virtues of faith, patience, and goodwill toward all men. For what he lacked in aggression he made up by a sort of universal tolerance. It must take something like that, Charlotte thought, to remain serene with a wife who always thrust herself forward and a daughter who was a tiresome coquette. It was no mystery where Cleone had learned her encroaching ways.

Perhaps it was better to have the dinner table enlivened by the Beechams than to dine with only her brother and timid Aunt Emilie, who had no more conversation than a spoon or fork.

But then there was her father's friend, Sir Roland, who was always ready to come for a meal and who added verbal zest to the hour. When she looked his way now, he rolled his eyes and she knew he was thinking the company a dead bore.

"This is pleasant," he said, as if to prove her wrong. Then he asked Cleone, on his right, how many young ladies there were in the neighborhood for Miss Pope to meet. This was deliberate needling, as Cleone had little concern for local competition and none at all for mousy cousins.

"Well, I daresay there are several, but they are always having sewing parties and tableaux and things of little interest to me. Besides, we have so many callers at the Dower House that I do not have time to waste on gossip."

"Perhaps they gossip about you," Sir Roland suggested mildly. "Or perhaps they do not gossip at all, but discuss books—and—er gardening and—"

"Gardening!" exclaimed Cleone. "That is ruinous for one's hands!"

"Well, then," he persisted, "flower-arranging? Surely that is a genteel activity for ladies."

Cleone admitted she sometimes helped her mama with flowers, but she did not say that her help generally consisted of carrying vases to the parlor, or setting bouquets in water when her gentlemen callers brought them.

Sir Roland learned nothing that he did not already know, although he did succeed in blocking her overtures to Sydney for a short space.

Having heard all, Lady Charlotte bit her lip to keep it from twitching. Obviously Cleone did not think it worthwhile to spend her charms on a gentleman who had silver hairs showing in his sideburns. Cleone tossed her head and presented a smile winsomely to the duke, who smiled in return.

After they had eaten, Lady Charlotte led the four ladies away, and the duke, who gave himself no airs, moved to take her place between Sir Roland and Mr. Beecham. They circulated the port without much enthusiasm, although it was a very good vintage. Sydney was not fond of port, and Mr. Beecham's taste buds were not discriminating. If Sir Roland thought the duke's cellar was being wasted this evening, it was because he, at least, could recognize a very smooth wine that Sydney's father had laid down some years ago; Charlotte offered it to him from time to time.

So presently they went along to join the ladies and found Mrs. Beecham delivering a monologue to Lady Charlotte, whose jaw was rigid from fighting yawns. The girls' eyes were glassy.

"Servants do not serve as they used to do," Mrs. Beecham was saying. "I cannot see why my sister sent This Woman with Mercillia, for she—oh, there you are, Sydney. Do come in and enliven us. Your chef gave us an excellent meal, as usual, but now we are craving intelligent conversation. Three such lively gentlemen must have interesting things to tell us. I know you, Sydney, are out and about locally and see so much that we stay-at-homes do not have a chance to see, and you, Sir Roland, are so often at Bath and London that there must be titillating things you could tell, and as for my own honored husband—well, I daresay you can expect *me* to find him exceedingly knowledgeable?"

If the last was a question, her hearers were too numb to answer. Cleone looked simply bored, and Mercy's expression was one of slight bewilderment.

Charlotte spoke into the gap. "I find gentlemen want only to tell ladies what they should be doing that they are *not*." She tossed Sir Roland a saucy look that made her seem not much older than little Mercy.

"I, for one, would not dare to tell any lady her business," declared her brother humorously.

"Something else for a leader to learn," said Mrs. Beecham.

"But books come first," insisted Charlotte.

Seeing that Sydney recognized himself to be the focus of this exchange and was chagrined, Sir Roland came to his support, saying, "Charlotte has decided that it is time for you to apply to Oxford, *haven't* you, Charlotte?"

"I say!" cried Sydney, his face taking on a sudden glow. "Is this true? Oxford!"

Charlotte rolled her eyes heavenward, but allowed that she was almost agreed.

"Almost! If I know my sister, 'almost' means it's settled."

"Well, agreed, yes. But there is still an application to be made," she said. She noted with some pleasure that Cleone and her mama were looking annoyed, for both must realize that a duke out of sight was a duke at risk. Sir Roland had given her sound advice. Of course, Sydney might meet other predatory females in Oxford—more numerous than in a small place such as Fallford—but the danger here was real and must be dealt with. Charlotte shot Sir Roland a meaningful look which he returned blandly.

Mrs. Beecham did not notice, being intent upon establishing eye contact with her husband. He, however, felt no nuances and calmly gave his opinion that his young cousin must certainly follow in his father's footsteps.

"His Grace—the late duke," he said with all due solemnity, "was well schooled at Oxford. Had a creditable record there, I believe, although afterwards he displayed more interest in his land than in his books."

Sir Roland said, "Audley was an excellent landholder. Also, his father before him. He did not learn debauchery at Oxford, if that is what anyone fears."

Looking shocked, Mrs. Beecham turned to her husband for censorship of the *awful word,* but he was murmuring, "Yus, yus. We know our Sydney is a sound young man."

Seeing Cleone and Mercillia were wide-eyed, Sir Roland said suavely that he was making a joke. "Sydney did well at Harrow. With the right don, you may be sure that books will keep him busy. Are you game, Sydney?"

"Yes, I am," said the duke. He did not, for the moment, notice Cleone's chagrin.

Then little Mercy astonished them by volunteering that her

papa said more than once that if she were a son, he would certainly send her to Oxford.

"Are you studious, my dear?" asked Mr. Beecham kindly.

Coloring, she admitted that she liked to read.

"Then you are welcome to any of my books," he returned, "and I daresay Sydney will make you free to use the excellent library here at the castle."

Being unwilling to give even a modest young girl like Mercillia the run of Heritage Castle, Charlotte frowned slightly and pursed her lips, which was a cue for Sir Roland to say, "Now, now, can't have young ladies burying their noses in books when the weather is so pleasant. Do you ride, Miss Mercy?"

"Yes, sir," said Mercy, "but Papa does not permit me to take jumps."

"Time for that when you have grown a bit," he responded, for he obviously considered her little more than a child.

Mercy volunteered nothing else, and Mrs. Beecham seized control of the conversation again, saying, "I cannot allow Cleone to take chances with *horses*—unreliable beasts!—and risk broken bones or worse." To date, no one had offered Cleone a saddle horse. She and her mother were satisfied with occasional use of the chaplain's gig. For jaunts into the village, when they had business there, they walked, as it was almost at their doorstep. All the young men within ten miles of Fallford had discovered Cleone. What need had she of going anywhere?

Conversation had now veered from Oxford, and although the duke would have liked to talk more of it, good manners kept him from harping on the subject. He said mildly that he enjoyed a good gallop, but allowed Mrs. Beecham's protests against "unreliable beasts" to silence him. It required no subterfuge for him to dream of Oxford while she expatiated on all sizes and sorts of horses; he had only to maintain a courteous expression.

Since Charlotte had had the foresight to order tea brought half an hour early, the evening soon drew to a close.

"You," she said to her brother when the guests had gone, "have the joys of college to anticipate, while I can only expect repeated evenings like this."

"Oh, Charlotte," he said, chagrined. "I am a selfish pig to think only of myself."

She smiled a whimsical half-smile. "How can a pig be selfish about anything except, perhaps, the swill? Sir Roland thinks you must increase your knowledge. I hope you will let him advise you what to study."

Sir Roland, though neither knew it yet, had formed the intention of escorting Sydney to Oxford to investigate rooms and enroll him under a suitable don. Meanwhile, there were some weeks of summer to be lived through, and Mrs. Beecham's schemes to be foiled.

Charlotte remained uneasy about the threat from the Dower House, but what more to do she did not know. As many times before, she was relying on Sir Roland. He said nothing of writing to contacts at Oxford, and then, on Monday, Katherine March and her abigail arrived from Scotland via a post chaise, followed in two hours by a dusty traveling coach with lathered horses.

It was Wednesday before Sir Roland came after an early breakfast to find Lady Charlotte poring over household accounts.

"I must appeal to you!" he said, taking a ledger from her and setting it aside. "Katherine came late on Monday—"

"Oh! Is she well?"

"Yes, well, if you mean her health, but singularly uncommunicative. She has been followed by a chap who wants to wed her—he told me that at once—and Kate will not say if she means to have him."

Amazed, Charlotte asked, "Why not?"

"It is unclear. All she has said so far is that she is too old—do you think thirty-four is *old?*" Sir Roland, who was forty-four himself, did not wait for an answer, going on to say, "I suspect the gentleman may be a bit younger, but if that does not matter to him, why need it bother Kate?"

"Well!" said Charlotte, her hands dropping to her lap as she sat back in her chair. "This is all very astonishing, but who am I to advise you? I hardly know Katherine. There are ten years between us, and she would not be interested in any opinion of mine. In fact, she might resent my even knowing her—your—dilemma."

"Yes, but you are female and may be able to explain to me how her mind works."

"Well, do sit, Sir Roland. What exactly does this gentleman say?"

"That he is well-to-pass and can support her in comfort. I shall verify that, of course. He claims he would have brought a good character report from our cousin, but left in haste the day after Kate, as soon as he found her gone. By changing horses often and setting a hot pace, he reached here only two hours behind her. That would indicate his earnestness, don't you think?"

Charlotte thought it would. "How *is* Katherine?" she asked. "I mean, in truly good health?"

"Yes, blooming. Bonny."

"Could she," asked Charlotte slowly, "could she have made this dash to bring him to the point?"

"Well, he *is* to the point and she evades him."

Charlotte said, "Perhaps she is uncertain about herself. Does he look younger? Are his manners brash? Does she fear he will regret an older wife in time to come?"

"Questions! Questions!" said Sir Roland, dropping finally into a chair. "I came to you for answers."

"Then here is another question: does Katherine insist upon his leaving?"

"No," said Sir Roland, his expression changing. "I see what you imply. Make Mr. Macnaghten welcome? All right. I have already done that and will continue in that way. But there are no ladies in this village—except Mrs. Beecham, and I do not consider *her* suitable to advise Kate. Will you help me?"

"After all the help you have given us? How can I refuse?" replied Charlotte. "But I have no experience with romance, and Katherine will not think me a useful confidante."

"But you are intelligent. Don't demur. You have a sound head and a generous heart. Kate will recognize that at once. Keep open, Charlotte. That is all I ask."

"I will do what I can," she promised.

"Good," said Sir Roland. "There is something you can do at once—come for dinner tonight, you and Sydney. I suppose Lady Emilie will not, but you won't fail me? Imagine what my dinners must be with only Macnaghten and Kate!" His expression was ludicrous, though he meant every word.

Charlotte agreed, even if she doubted Kate would welcome her. Then, having her promise, Sir Roland resumed his usual savoir faire and said, "Good girl."

Three

"Shall we go by the turnpike or the village?" asked the duke, as he and his sister took their places in a tilbury for a jaunt to Sir Roland's manor.

"If we go through Fallford, Cousin Maude will be sure to see us pass and will guess our destination," Lady Charlotte answered.

"Does that matter?"

She frowned. "Not really. She will find out sooner or later where we have been. I *do* tire of surveillance. Well, go the short way."

Sydney flicked his reins and they rolled forward toward the gentle slope to the Dower House and village. All was serene at Heritage. No servants were to be seen, though a great army of house servants and grounds-keepers kept glass sparkling, knockers gleaming, gravel raked, twigs gathered, faded blooms plucked, horse droppings whisked away.

Nearly two hundred were employed at the Duke of Audley's seat; they were quiet and unobtrusive. Lady Charlotte directed all through such intermediaries as an excellent butler, housekeeper, steward, chief groom, and bailiff. She doubted Sydney even knew the number of his servants, and if he did not, it was her fault for shielding him from any serious thoughts.

"Before you go to Oxford," she said now, "you must learn some details of your staff and establishment."

"Must I?" he asked lightheartedly, looking toward the Dower House for a glimpse of a flirt.

"Yes. Must. Your butler, for instance, is aging and will soon be retired. Whom shall you appoint in his place?"

"Whom? The under-butler, I suppose," Sydney said.

"Yes. In this case, he will be the right choice, for Milton has trained him well. But Ponde is already in his forties, and you will have to have another understudy coming along."

Sydney said he had not thought of that.

"Perhaps I am to blame that you haven't thought," Charlotte admitted. "I have usurped—taken hold of everything—"

"For which Heritage and I thank you!" averred her brother, sending her a fond glance.

She smiled slightly. "Well, someone had to make decisions. You won't always have me."

"Why not?"

"Perhaps I shall run away to Greece—like the Popes."

He laughed and said he did not believe he had ever heard her speak Greek.

They passed through Fallford's main street, where few persons were seen as evening had sent shoppers and shopkeepers to their homes.

At Sir Roland's pretty Georgian manor house they were welcomed warmly; even Katherine March seemed glad to see them. She was smiling, poised, and gracious, though Charlotte felt a certain reserve, a gentle wall, or perhaps only a *distance.* The stranger, Mr. Macnaghten, beamed amiably and said he was happy to meet them, which his open manner indicated to be true. Charlotte did not think he had ever met anyone he was not ready to accept as friend.

Macnaghten had a well-balanced face, if not a handsome one. His eyes were bright blue and his hair nearly auburn. His eyebrows, strongly defined, were expressive, rising or knitting in accompaniment to his speech, which had a very slight and pleasing burr. He might be a bit younger than Kate, though he did not seem so, as he was taller by a head than she and had a sure presence that spoke of maturity.

Charlotte drifted to Kate's side to rebuke her lightly for

having stayed away so long, which was not clever conversation but often heard in polite discourse. There was little to show the ten years' difference in the two girls' ages. While Kate's honey blond hair was cut fashionably short to riot youthfully about her ears, Charlotte wore hers drawn back into a severe knot low upon her neck in a no-nonsense manner. Both ladies were quite pretty, and neither being vain, each could admire what she saw in the other.

Mr. Macnaghten, who was clearly an extrovert, promptly said, "If I had known about the ladies of Fallford, I would have come south sooner!"

This sentiment startled the young duke, who was accustomed to think of his sister as a Very Good Sort, neither male nor female.

"If possible, we keep our ladies secret from border shires," Sir Roland replied. "Will everyone have sherry?"

A footman offered glasses, and they all accepted, it being the usual way to set guests at ease when they were not well acquainted. Charlotte might have known Sir Roland would deal smoothly with such assorted guests. He merely held his wineglass without drinking and spoke teasingly of Mr. Macnaghten's arriving in a cloud of dust.

"That I did," said Macnaghten. "Very likely brought billows into this house." As he was immaculate now, either he had bathed or liked to exaggerate. "Do you think I set a new record from Carlisle?"

Charlotte was interested to examine Kate's face when Kate was watching that gentleman's face (if he was not watching *her*). Katherine's expression was not easy to read. It was serious without being sober, and her eyes slid away whenever Mr. Macnaghten's head began to turn in her direction.

Mr. Macnaghten, having reached his target, and being ready to acquire new friends, seemed unintimidated by a duke's presence. He soon won them all by his naturalness and affability. Why had Katherine fled from him?

"We are only five," Sir Roland said when they were summoned to dinner. "I thought a small table would accommodate us more congenially."

They found a round table set in a pleasant green parlor that looked out upon a small garden which Kate claimed as hers.

"It *was* yours," her brother conceded, "but who has kept out the weeds these last several years?" He seated Charlotte to his right, Mr. Macnaghten to her right, Katherine next to him, and then the young duke between his sister and himself.

The visitor from Carlisle told them that they should see what Miss March had done with her cousin's languishing garden in the north. "She has a true gardener's touch," he said, smiling at his Object.

"I hope you do not mean dirt under my nails," she said lightly.

Sir Roland exchanged a quick and comprehensive look with Charlotte. They were glad to see that Kate was not oppressed by being followed from her cousin's home. Evidently Mr. Macnaghten felt the thawing, for he said to her quite easily, "What a race you gave me! Why no warning of your departure?"

"I had talked of coming sometime soon," she answered with a very slight retreat of manner.

"But you set no date," he protested. "I would have been glad to escort you."

Seeing his sister's unease, Sir Roland said quickly, "You the same as brought her, coming so close behind."

"There was that," Macnaghten agreed. "I was able to verify her safety and discover the accommodation that was made for her at inns, though I was obliged to find space myself elsewhere, coming along at different times. The nearer we came to Fallford, the closer I was upon her heels—er, wheels." He chortled good-naturedly.

"Well, I thank you," said Katherine's brother. "When she goes back—if she goes back—I will certainly see that she is properly escorted."

"My cousin expects me," she said faintly.

"And I," said Sir Roland, "intend to keep you a while."

The clash of wills (and wishes) was palpable, Charlotte thought. To diffuse the tension she said calmly, "We have waited so long for this visit. Do let us not think of ending it yet."

After dinner Katherine expressed a desire to go into her garden, and as there was still light and the air was balmy, they strolled through French doors to grassy paths. Somehow, Lady Charlotte found herself walking with Mr. Macnaghten, while Sir Roland pointed out blooms to his sister and the duke.

"It's a bonny place," Macnaghten said. "Not at all like my place at Carlisle, but I do not think my Kate spurns mine. I am next to Kate's cousin, which has been very convenient."

Evidently there was to be no secret of this gentleman's intentions!

Groping for suitable topics, Charlotte asked, "Do you farm your land, sir?"

"Not best suited for that," he returned frankly. "But grazing is good. I raise horses."

"Oh? What sort?"

"Racers," he replied. "They are what take me from home a great deal. Keep me from seeing Kate as much as I would like."

Feeling that she might be treated to details that she would prefer not to hear, Charlotte said, "We had a wet spring, which was something of a nuisance but has served the gardens well. Ours at Heritage, across the valley, are extensive and keep a number of gardeners busy—but such a pleasure to the eye."

Mr. Macnaghten regarded her with an amused side glance.

"Now, lass," he said, "do na be evasive. I am hoping for your help with Kate." He took her hand and placed it on his arm. "Let us stroll this side path. Can you not say a good word for me to Kate?"

Already half-won by his personality, she went along as led,

wondering where Kate had found the power to flee away from such a charmer.

Before she could think of a suitable rejoinder, he was saying, "Too late. We are seen. I shall call privately one day soon."

Charlotte had turned her head, and sure enough, Sir Roland was leading Katherine toward them, as the duke stood aside to give them passage. She released Macnaghten's arm and whispered, "Best come by the turnpike and knock at the main door so that Cerberus won't see—"

"Ah! Dear Miss Kate," Mr. Macnaghten was interrupting as he moved to transfer Kate from her brother's arm to his own, "Lady Charlotte and I are enchanted with what you have built here. How interesting it would be to see what you could make of *my* summer garden."

After a very slight hesitation, Kate responded, "You must remember that your seasons are a bit later and cooler than ours."

"Whatever you advise is sure to please me."

"And there is the question of *soil,"* she persisted.

He chuckled. "Will you be wanting new soil?"

"Now, Macnaghten," interposed Sir Roland, "I refuse to let my sister even think of Carlisle. She is here to enjoy a time in her own home with her brother and old friends."

Kate had flushed rosily, and looked to Charlotte for some support.

"Mr. Macnaghten will have to meet my cousins," Charlotte said obligingly. "It will be interesting to see what he makes of Mrs. Beecham—"

"And of Cleone," inserted Sydney. "She has grown into the most charming girl, Miss March."

Obviously glad to have a new subject introduced, Katherine asked, "That small girl with curls like an angel and enormous blue eyes?"

"The very one!" said the young duke, beaming. "Only, she is a belle of the county now, I warn you."

Sydney's sister thought he might be indirectly warning the visiting gentleman that Cleone was his own interest. Charlotte did not suppose a man of Macnaghten's age and experience would find the local belle as alluring as did young cubs, yet she wanted nothing to trouble Kate. Mr. Macnaghten's showing the slightest attraction to Cleone could kill Kate's interest in him, if she *was* seriously considering his suit.

"Cleone Beecham is still half child," Sir Roland said flatly, with authority that Charlotte admired.

It was Sydney's turn to flush with annoyance and chagrin.

Kate, on Mr. Macnaghten's arm, recovered her composure then, and led him down a new aisle, speaking of some most annoying beetles in the area. He, on his part, was willing to hear about beetles if his Kate wished him to do so.

"Let us sit upon this low wall until the others have had their stroll," said Sir Roland, whipping out a handkerchief to spread for Charlotte. "They will not be long, as the light is failing fast."

They settled on the wall, Sydney, somewhat disgruntled, sitting two or three feet from the others.

Four

When Katherine March and Mr. Macnaghten rejoined their host and the Helds, it did not seem that anything earthshaking had transpired during a circuit of the garden. Neither did their relations seem strained. Even so, with Mr. Macnaghten treading carefully, Kate evasive, and the young duke somewhat flattened by Sir Roland's setdown of Cleone, a sort of gray cloud hung over the garden.

Soon Lady Charlotte was saying that she did not suppose the travelers had fully recovered from their tiring journey and that, in any case, she and her brother must drive home before darkness closed in.

"Will you come to us for dinner Saturday?" she asked. "Sydney and I would welcome your company, would we not, Sydney?"

Not being one to mope, Sydney was beginning to recover his good spirits. He said, "Oh, yes. Do come." Not having seen Kate since he was an awkward youth of sixteen, he was uncertain just how to address her and compromised by saying, "Marches will always have a place at our table—and any friend of theirs."

Looking amused, Mr. Macnaghten said, "Kindly spoken, Your Grace. Then are we promised for Saturday, Sir Roland?"

They were.

The tilbury was summoned, and the Helds wheeled off, all five persons—going or staying—feeling that the evening had passed off tolerably well.

At the castle the duke decanted Charlotte. While she went inside, he took the tilbury around to the stables and was able to enjoy a chat with his chief groom who was still awake, "puttin' abed" the duke's horses and checking to see if his boys had done their chores properly.

This was one employee whom Sydney knew well.

"Evening, Pucket," said His Grace. He strolled along the stalls, expecting to see perfection (which of course he did) and making noises of approval. Several lanterns lighted his way. Every enclosure was fresh and clean, as though just mucked out. By now Sydney knew that Pucket never sent his boys to rest without a final "sweetenin" of the stalls.

"Looks spanking," he said.

"In course," returned Pucket. "Lady Charlotte is one as likes things tidy."

His Grace chuckled to think his sister should be commanding stables as well as castle. "So do I. Remember that, Pucket. So do I." He did not for a moment think Charlotte was interfering in his domain; he knew Pucket valued her opinion because he was her slave, like all the rest of the servants.

"Her Ladyship reigns here," the duke added. "I cannot say what we would do without her."

"Aye," growled Pucket. "I'll just put Moxie and the tilbury to sleep."

Feeling mellow, His Grace helped to unhitch Moxie, after which he went into the castle to look for Charlotte, but she was in none of their usual sitting-rooms, so he assumed she had gone to bed.

Upstairs in her room, Charlotte was undressing slowly as she thought about the evening just spent. It was good for Sir Roland to have his sister home, she thought. Without a wife to be his hostess, he never had visitors, or at least not ladies. What a waste of that beautiful house! And now he had Kate with him . . . and that irrepressible Macnaghten about whom they knew nothing. Sir Roland would be sure to find out all pertinent facts of the man's background, finances, and dependability. But what of Kate's emotions? Was she more interested in the stranger than she revealed? She was, Charlotte thought, more beautiful—more blooming—than Charlotte remembered her to have been three years ago.

She looked critically at her own reflection. *When I am thirty-four, will I,* she wondered, *look as lovely as Katherine March does?*

Charlotte climbed into her bed and pulled the covers to her chin. It was a bad question for a lady to ask herself, if she had any hope of falling asleep.

She speculated on when Mr. Macnaghten might appear at Heritage Castle. Undoubtedly not before Cousin Maude Beecham!

Mrs. Beecham appeared at ten in the morning, bringing a little pot of chives. "Raised from seed, my dear! From seed! Such a handy way for your chef to keep them in the kitchen."

Charlotte thanked her solemnly, and was rewarded with advice to *dry* some.

"Did you have a pleasant evening at Sir Roland's, Cousin Charlotte? I saw you and the duke pass, and I knew you must be headed there, for there is nowhere else you might visit at that hour—but with his sister and that Other Person present it was perfectly proper for you to dine with—"

"Yes," said Charlotte patiently (or perhaps impatiently), "Kate has come for a visit at last."

"But who is the Other Person?"

"A very kind Mr. Macnaghten, a neighbor of Kate's cousin, who followed her carriage in his own to be sure she reached Fallford safely." Every word was true, though there was none for Mrs. Beecham to sink her teeth into for a tasty bite.

"Will he be staying long?" asked Mrs. Beecham eagerly.

"I really cannot say," Charlotte answered coolly. "How is your niece adjusting to Fallford?"

"Oh, nicely. Such a quiet little creature. Cleone has been very good about introducing her callers to the girl, and the young gentlemen are most civil, but of course it is *Cleone* that they come to see."

"She must miss her parents," Charlotte reminded.

"Well, I daresay she does, though maybe not so much as one might fear. She reads a lot. Your Cousin John says she is so quiet that he scarcely notices when she is in the room with him."

Charlotte exclaimed, "She must be lonely indeed!"

"Oh, no," replied Mrs. Beecham calmly. "John says she enjoys quietude."

Lady Charlotte frowned, impelling Mrs. Beecham to add, "I asked that nurse—chaperone—whatever she calls herself. She says 'Miss Pope is accustomed to be quiet.' "

"It is one thing to be quiet, and another to be neglected," Charlotte reminded.

"Very true," agreed her visitor who did not relate the implication of the word to herself. "I am accustomed to my husband, who is always a bit withdrawn. Some people are like that. It is very *useful* of Mercillia to amuse herself when I am busy chaperoning my daughter. Dear me! Such a parade of beaux! It will be a relief when she is suitably settled in marriage and has an establishment of her own."

"Surely you are in no hurry to lose Cleone!"

"Lose? Indeed not," returned Mrs. Beecham. "I hope to have her settled near at hand."

Settled in my place, thought Charlotte. Aloud she said, "If you do not exhibit her in London or Bath, she is sure to accept a local man." Well did she know that Mr. Beecham's salary could not cover such places as those. Perhaps she should increase his stipend with just such end in view . . . but it all came back to the fact that Mrs. Beecham's eye was upon Sydney and a dukedom, not some lesser light in a watering place.

"Oh, la! I am in no hurry to lose our sunbeam," declared the visitor archly.

Charlotte, who had seen the sunbeam become a thunderclap when thwarted, said, "No, indeed. She is full young."

At this point a footman entered to say, "Beg pardon, m'lady, Mr. Macnaghten is enquiring if you will receive him."

"Yes, indeed," she said with some relief. "Ask him to come in." She had had enough of Mrs. Beecham's insinuations.

In the time required for her footman to return to the state apartments and lead Mr. Macnaghten to them, she repeated in a carefully disinterested manner that he was a neighbor of Miss March's cousin and had kindly followed Katherine's chaise to see that she traveled without mishap from Carlisle.

In a few minutes Macnaghten had joined them, and she presented him to Mrs. Beecham, who eyed him with interest. This morning he was immaculately garbed in a well-fitting brown riding coat and buff breeches. His manner to Mrs. Beecham was so gracious as to win her favor immediately. Charlotte had suggested he come to the State Entrance, for the purpose of his avoiding Mrs. Beecham's scrutiny, but his being announced at just this worst possible moment defeated that.

Having become immediately alert to a possible new beau in the neighborhood, Mrs. Beecham nodded and smirked and said, "At Sir Roland's, are you? Very welcome there, I am sure."

"Oh, yes," Macnaghten returned with a slight questioning look at Charlotte who invented glibly:

"Mr. Macnaghten has asked to see how we stack and age manure to enrich it. I must beg you to excuse us, Cousin Maude."

Only a *business* call!

"I see," said Mrs. Beecham, disappointed to find this well-looking man was there on business. "Yes, of course I will not delay you." Manure! Not a social call at all. She got to her feet and allowed Charlotte to escort her to the hall, where a footman was waiting.

"Thank you, again, for the fine pot of chives," Charlotte said, handing her over to the footman before returning to Macnaghten's side.

"Cerberus?" he asked sapiently.

"Exactly," said Charlotte, pleased that he had caught her hint last night. "Mr. Beecham is a relative. When Papa first installed him as chaplain, they lived with us in the castle. I was a child then. But Papa lost patience with Mrs. Beecham's curiosity and moved them to the Dower House. Things are tolerable now, no unpleasantness—even so, we cannot make a move that she does not know."

He nodded. "I see. You did not wish her to observe my coming here, and I have given all away by arriving at exactly the wrong moment."

"That is no error on your part," Charlotte returned with a smile. "Shall you mind walking out to the barns with me to make me truthful?"

Mr. Macnaghten said, "Not at all."

"I thought it might be best to put your call on a business basis," she explained. "Soon you will be seeing the Beechams on a social level—in fact, I shall be obliged to include them for dinner Saturday—but your coming *now* might be misunderstood."

He proved his sharpness by saying, "You mean *Kate* might misunderstand?"

Charlotte blushed slightly, and he did not miss it.

"Never mind. Might be helpful."

She hoped he was not going to ask her to set herself up as a rival, to spark Kate's interest, and he did not.

Through a series of halls of diminishing charm they reached the stable yard, barns, and at last a modest heap of manure.

"I see no signs of curing," Mr. Macnaghten said with a laugh. "Well, your truthfulness is established. Now let us go back to the stables, so I may see the duke's horses."

"We have no racers," she said apologetically.

As they neared the stables Pucket came out to meet them, and Charlotte introduced him as being of great use to Sydney.

"Aye," said Pucket modestly. "Like to see our horses, eh? Just step inside, sir."

Soon Mr. Macnaghten had proved himself sufficiently knowledgeable to satisfy Pucket and was invited to look at teeth and examine hocks. Charlotte found an overturned bucket on which to sit while various horses were led out of their stalls for closer consideration. The men quite forgot her. When Sydney came on the scene, she realized she was superfluous and so slipped away to the castle.

She did not think *Kate* would have been forgotten, which was logical as Kate was Macnaghten's reason for being in Fallford. She was not offended.

Aunt Emilie was mending heirloom table linens in their favorite parlor. She smiled affectionately at Charlotte, but said nothing when Charlotte settled nearby with a book. Sometimes people assumed Aunt Emilie was deaf, because she spoke so little. No, merely timid, and content with her thoughts. Oddly, Mrs. Beecham talked too much, Aunt Emilie almost never.

Though Charlotte held an open book and intended to read it, she sat wrapped in her thoughts, not turning a page. The castle was quiet. Wasn't it always? The walls were so thick, the floors generally spread with carpets. She was wondering if Sydney and Mr. Macnaghten were finding some common ground besides horses. It would do Sydney good to have a friend with more maturity than the several youths who frequented the Dower House. Or would Mr. Macnaghten have no interest in *him?*

She could not suppose that Kate's suitor really cared for anything beside Kate. He had come to Heritage for the purpose of asking her help with his suit, or finding some clue that would unlock Kate's heart. Kate was a mystery. Or only being cautious? After all, she must know Macnaghten better than anyone in Fallford could do so soon.

The door opened and Sydney entered, smiling.

"Good chap," he said, as if he and Macnaghten were equals in age. "Said there ought to be some races in the county and asked if I would like to go. Well, I would. You do not object, do you, Charlotte?"

Why would she?

"He is Sir Roland's guest. It really must depend on commitments to him. I see no reason for you not to go, if Sir Roland agrees."

"Yes. Well. We will see." He dropped a kiss on Aunt Emilie's cheek and exited, leaving the door ajar.

She was glad to see his good spirits and did not mind rising to latch the door properly.

Already it was Thursday, and if her dinner for Kate's guest was not to be perfectly flat, the number of persons must be increased. If she invited the Beechams, her number would grow to ten, although conversation would scarcely be scintillating. Who could be added on such short notice? It would have to be the local squire, Mr. Guinn, who could be counted upon to discuss horses with Macnaghten. He had a pleasant wife and two sons who were satellites of Cleone.

Aunt Emilie looked up at her sigh.

"I shall send a note to Mrs. Guinn. It will have to be the Guinns to make up our group. At least they are presentable and the sons, if I seat them on either side of Cleone, will solve *one* problem," she said aloud, to which Aunt Emilie nodded agreement.

"You would think," Charlotte muttered, moving to a desk, "that a duke could command more distinguished company."

Perhaps when Sydney reached his majority and took his rightful place in Society, things would improve. Sir Roland would undoubtedly say *she* should have made a bow and been presented at Her Majesty's Drawing Room long ago.

After she had penned a note to Mrs. Guinn, she handed it to a servant for delivery, took a straw Gypsy hat from the cloak room, and sallied forth not very enthusiastically to the Dower House.

It was another sparkling day, and Charlotte enjoyed her walk down the hill. She was received with an overwhelming welcome by Mrs. Beecham, just as though they had not already met that morning, and by her own brother, who was entertaining Cleone with some sort of nonsense. Mercillia, Charlotte was glad to see, was in attendance.

Cousin Maude was delighted by an invitation, verbally extended, to meet Sir Roland, Katherine, and their guest at dinner on Saturday, and Sydney looked pleased that Cleone and Mercy should be included. Almost immediately Peter and Alexander Guinn arrived to hear that an invitation was on its way to them and their parents.

I should entertain more often, Charlotte thought. Why had she not? Inertia? No, disinterest . . . and preoccupation with her brother's castle. Perhaps, when Sydney was at Oxford, she would make an appearance in London, as Sir Roland seemed to think she should do.

She looked at Mercy, standing on the fringes of the group. "Walk back with me for lunch, my dear," she said to the girl, and was rewarded with a blushing smile of pleasure.

Five

If Mrs. Beecham was displeased that Mercy had been singled out, there was no way she could interfere with Lady Charlotte's wishes, except to say tightly, "You must wear a bonnet, child."

This Mercy ran off to fetch, while Charlotte, who had come carrying a hat without putting it on her head, ignored the implied criticism of her freedom to do as she wished on her own estate. Was Mrs. Beecham's lack of tact deliberate? Charlotte had long wondered about the background of Maude Beecham. Perhaps Mercy, in telling of her own parents, would reveal something of her mother's sister.

"Would you like to see something of the park?" Charlotte asked as she and Mercy strolled up the carriage way.

"Oh, yes," returned Mercillia eagerly. "Indeed I would. I enjoy walking—and Nature."

"Good. Just beyond that next tree is a path that leads past a pond. There is a little brook that feeds it, but no one can explain why the pond never overflows, for there is no outlet."

"I expect Papa would say it is a matter of evaporation," Mercy said.

Surprised, Charlotte asked if Mr. Pope was a scientist as well as an antiquarian.

"Oh," returned Mercy, "everything interests Papa. Mama says he is better than any governess she could hire."

"Indeed? Has he taught you himself?"

"Well, not sewing—and mending—and curtsies—and watercolor painting—and things like that. Mama was in charge of *those.* I did have a governess once, but Papa said she was a fool who thought keeping one's gloves clean was more important than knowing one went *south* to France and *west* to the Americas."

Charlotte smiled and said she must agree with Mr. Pope. "Are you missing your parents very much, my dear?"

"I did for a day or two," admitted Mercy, "but it is so beautiful here, and I am glad—really glad to know my Beecham kin. I had not seen my aunt since I was three, and certainly cannot remember that."

"How old are you, Mercy?" asked Lady Charlotte.

"Almost eighteen, my lady."

"Indeed! I had not supposed you that ancient!"

Mercillia put on a pixie look. "It is because I am small. Cleone is only two months ahead of me, but taller, and so much more experienced in talking with—beaux."

"Oh, yes," agreed Charlotte, "she talks trivialities very well. See, here is the pond. Let us walk around the right side so as to have shade from trees."

The dappled shade was pleasant, and when they reached a rustic bench, Charlotte suggested they sit. "Let us get acquainted," she said. "Tell me: do your parents travel often?"

"Yes," replied Mercillia. "But never before so far as Greece. I went with them to France—and Switzerland—and Belgium. Oh, yes, and Ireland, though I do not remember much of that. We once spent a winter in Oxford, where the duke is to go. That was when I think Papa wished I were a boy, so he could enroll me there."

"I wager he no longer wishes you to be anything but a very dear daughter," said Charlotte, beginning to recognize the gentle charm of this creature. She, herself, felt a million years older than she actually was, having been in command at Heritage for so long. But twenty-four was not old, was it? There must be much in life that she could still welcome with surprise and enjoyment.

Mercy was saying, "I hope I am not a burden to my aunt. She does not seem to like my poor maid, who has been with me forever. I could not turn her away!"

"Does Cousin Maude suggest that?"

"Not exactly. She has hinted that another mouth to feed . . . Indeed, Betty tries to be helpful with dusting and dishes and things like that, and I do not think she eats very much—"

"Certainly she must eat!" cried Charlotte. "If you are worried about your Betty, you can send her up to me, but I really think your parents meant her to watch over *you.* Pray tell her she can eat as much as she wants, for the Dower House kitchen is well supplied by the home farm! Perhaps I should have a word with Cousin Maude . . ."

Mercillia said, "Oh, no! I do not mean to complain. Papa says one must always *adjust.*"

"In a sense, I agree," replied Charlotte. "Life is a series of compromises—although a *duke* can command all sorts of attention, but that is not always wise."

"His Grace does not seem the least demanding," Mercy said.

"Well," admitted Charlotte, "he need not be, as his wishes are generally interpreted in advance. I do not think Cousin John would want you to do without your maid, and *he* is the head of that house."

"Oh, dear. I was wrong to complain." Mercy looked mortified. "My mama says one learns useful things from *any* experience. Sometimes on trips we have had to wash with cold water, but if you let it stand a while in a wide shallow bowl, it becomes bearable."

"I do hope," declared Lady Charlotte vehemently, "you have warm water at the Dower House!"

Mercy's lips twitched. "Oh, yes. My Betty sees to that."

"Good. Are you becoming hungry? Let us go on to the castle. Aunt Emilie will be waiting to lunch with us. Do not be surprised if she says nothing." Charlotte got to her feet.

"Perhaps I talk so much that Aunt Emilie has lost all inclination to do so."

Aunt Emilie was still in the parlor when they entered the castle, although she had laid aside her mending and was nodding peacefully over a newspaper. She looked up at the sound of Lady Charlotte's voice.

"See Aunt Emilie's dainty stitches?" said Charlotte, lifting a damask serviette for Mercillia to examine almost invisible darning.

"Like the finest of French needlework," said Mercy admiringly. "Mama had undergarments embroidered for me by nuns at a convent near Tours—so beautiful, with only me to see."

"Yes, but I daresay they make you feel like a princess," Charlotte pointed out, and Mercy noted with some surprise that Aunt Emilie's eyes twinkled. Her mind was clearly active, though for some unknown reason she did not like to talk.

Then Lady Charlotte rang to indicate they were ready to eat, and presently they were conducted to a luncheon of cold meats and salads colorful with red, yellow, and green vegetables. There were hot, crusty rolls, with curls of fresh butter.

At the luncheon table, Lady Charlotte asked if Mercy's parents had considered bringing her Out some season.

"Mama spoke of that a year or two ago," Mercy replied, "but Papa always had plans that must come first. Before they sailed, he did say perhaps they must think of a *debut* when they returned."

This cheered Charlotte, who felt Mr. Pope's considering such a thing might indicate that the Popes had better connections than a very tenuous one to a duke not yet on the town himself.

His Grace did not appear to eat with them.

The Duke of Audley, much to Miss Cleone's annoyance, had gone off with Squire Guinn's boys to see their father's champion pig, which would be defending its title at the next county fair. While the three were just old enough to dangle after the local beauty, they had not outgrown an interest in any sort of competition . . . and probably never would. Squire Guinn certainly had not.

Cleone, deserted, and not asked to lunch with Cousin Charlotte, flounced up to her bedchamber to examine her face in a mirror.

Mrs. Beecham, who was equally annoyed, comforted herself with intentions to entertain Sir Roland March, his sister, and their guest. Any invitation would have to wait until she had been reunited with Katherine March on Saturday, but nothing prevented her from concocting plans.

Chaplain Beecham, had he been the least aware of his wife's annoying habits, would have defended her, for he was excessively tolerant and did not notice anyone's foibles. His wife was capable, nearly handsome, and never interfered with his hours in his study. He asked nothing more. They rubbed along together fairly well.

When Cleone, bored alone in her room, descended to await luncheon with her mama, she asked, "Mama, will Sydney's going off to Oxford ruin our plans?"

This was the first outspoken mention of "plans," and both understood what was meant.

"It's a nuisance," said Mrs. Beecham slowly. "Sydney certainly admires you. I think you could bewitch him, but in Oxford there will be other girls—living there or sisters of the new friends he may make among the other students. A pox on Sir Roland for pushing this! . . . However, there will be several weeks before His Grace leaves home. You will have to make more effort. I mean, *tantalize* him."

"But how, Mama? The local chaps fall all over themselves for a smile and a batting of lashes. Well, for that matter, Sydney does, too. But his attentions are all superficial, I fear, Mama."

Mrs. Beecham said, "Umm," and studied her daughter's face. "You are very pretty. Certainly the prettiest girl in the neighborhood—if one excludes Charlotte Held—and she cannot really be considered a girl at twenty-four. Anyway, she is his sister."

Cleone waited patiently through this ramble.

"There will never be a *parti* equal to Sydney Held. You will have to manage more time alone with him. Oh, I do not mean anything clandestine. It is absolutely vital to keep your reputation untarnished."

"Then how—"

"I mean strolling in plain view, little whispers when seated near him, alluring upward glances when walking or dancing, distinguishing attention to what interests him. You understand what I mean?"

"Yes," sighed the manipulator's daughter. "It will not be easy."

"No. But it can be done successfully."

Cleone considered her mama's face, which was almost handsome, and her manner, which was purposeful. "Is that how you captured Papa?" she asked boldly.

Mrs. Beecham was torn between anger and self-satisfaction. "You understand what matters, I think," she replied. "I will help you when I can, but in the end your future will depend upon *your* cleverness."

Nothing was spoken of affection for the duke.

The minx at the Dower House that Lady Charlotte had disparaged was alive to her opportunity. She did not see Sydney on Friday, and only for a few minutes Saturday morning when he stopped by to say he would send a carriage down so that the Beechams would not have to walk up the hill in evening finery. Then, though Cleone cast him alluring glances alive with unspecified invitations, he soon went away, saying he was off to a meeting with Sir Roland.

This had an ominous ring to the Beecham ladies, so they comforted themselves by planning their ensembles.

Meanwhile, at the castle Lady Charlotte was designing what she hoped (and had every reason to expect) to be a festive evening. Fourteen to dinner were more than she had entertained for a long time, and she wished to make it as lavish as possible. The state dining room was chosen for the event, food discussed with the housekeeper, and a profusion of flowers ordered from the head gardener. There was no premonition of disaster.

But disaster it was.

Mrs. Beecham was insufferably condescending to the squire's wife, who babbled inconseqentials in embarrassment. Cleone batted her eyes excessively and cooed at the duke, who unfortunately seemed to enjoy it. Peter and Alexander Guinn were tongue-tied, Kate remote. As usual, Aunt Emilie said nothing, though Mr. Macnaghten tried to draw her out, but finally gave up and endeavored to talk with Cousin John Beecham with equal lack of success. Thereafter he tried a few friendly overtures to Mercillia, who was so subdued as to be monosyllabic.

It remained for Kate, Sir Roland, and the squire (who was never without words) to maintain some sort of accompaniment to the acrobatics of silverware. At least the dining room was mellow with the light of many candles, and a profusion of colorful flowers filled the air with sweetness.

Charlotte was not sure that candles or flowers could offset the effects of guests determined to be difficult. She was very nearly sure she would never again attempt such an entertainment . . . until she caught Sir Roland's eye. He raised one brow and made a slight gesture with his wineglass to indicate sympathy and respect.

After dinner things were somewhat better, as the guests rearranged themselves more congenially. That is, some did. Mr. Macnaghten attached himself to her side, saying she was an "unusual" woman. Charlotte was not sure in what way he meant the word, but was grateful for his attention and glad to believe the word indicated approval.

Out of the corner of her eye she saw Kate talking with Mr. Guinn with every sign of serenity, so Charlotte was thankful to assume she was not conscious or jealous of Macnaghten's seeking out his hostess. It was a natural thing for a guest of honor to do, she reminded herself.

Cleone had captured the duke, and Mrs. Beecham held Sir Roland with a stream of chatter which was impossible to interrupt. But the general mood of the drawing room was better than it had been in the dining room. *If only,* Charlotte thought, rubbing her forehead, *the dreary evening would end!*

Sir Roland caught her gesture and immediately deserted Mrs. Beecham to come to her side, as Macnaghten drifted away.

"Hold hard," he whispered. "It will soon be over."

She murmured, "Disaster."

"Not quite," he replied softly. "The squire is enjoying himself and—" with a nod toward Sydney and Cleone "—alas!—so is Syd . . . and I also, as I always do at Heritage Castle."

"You surely cannot be doing so tonight," she said.

The baronet said crosscurrents were challenging.

"To a salmon," she quipped with a slight smile.

"There!" he pounced. "Your sense of humor is intact. Do you want me to send everyone away?"

She asked how he could do that.

"Use your head, my girl. After Sydney, I have the superior title. If I leave, the others must follow. It is not often that I have this power! Shall I withdraw?"

"A show of strength? Yes, let me see it."

He bowed and went into the hall to request his carriage. Then he joined his sister, tucked her hand through his arm, whispered it was time to go, and led her to speak adieu to Charlotte. Mr. Macnaghten was quick to follow. The babble of voices increased.

Sir Roland's carriage came promptly from the stable yard, with the squire's following, and the duke's coming just behind it for the Dower House passengers. Leave-takings were enthusiastic, Charlotte thought wryly, more so than her reiterated mumble of having appreciated their coming (a negligible distance) for a simple meeting of friends. If the meal had not spoken for itself, she did not intend to do it. She knew her kitchen had served them magnificently, and she told herself firmly that the guests should realize it.

When the last guest had gone, Sydney kissed his sister fondly and thanked her for planning such a pleasant evening.

"A *what?*" she drawled.

He drew back, genuinely astonished. "A congenial gathering of friends. Why, Cleone said how much she enjoyed it."

Charlotte wanted to shout, "That chit will enjoy anything that can advance her ambitions." But seeing the danger of putting Sydney on the defensive, she bit her tongue and muttered that she was tired.

"Of course you are," he agreed immediately like the devoted brother that he was. "To bed with you!"

They went upstairs together and separated in the upper hall. As her maid helped her to undress for bed, she wondered if she was making a dustbin out of a mote. No! She was not. That minx at the Dower House was surely determined to entangle the duke. She would have to think of a way to stop it!

Six

Chaplain Beecham took his duties seriously. It was his custom to spend a quiet time in the chapel of Heritage Castle on early Sunday mornings, so on the day after Charlotte's misbegotten party he went there to kneel a few moments before the altar and then retreat to a pew for meditation. Although he was a man without humor and dominated by his wife, he was true to his calling. Twice a month, in the afternoon, it was his custom to conduct a vesper service for which he regularly sought Divine Guidance.

Fallford was too small a village to have a church of its own. For many years, decades, the Duke of Audley's private chapel had been open to villagers and employees of the manor. It was not part of the original castle, having been added late in the seventeenth century. Walls and floor were of dressed stone, much like that used in the village and aged to a mellow beige. The ceiling was vaulted with great oak timbers, and furnishings were carved of the same material. Light from narrow windows was dim, on rainy days forcing Mr. Beecham to have a candle beside the papers of his message.

At the end opposite to the chancel, a gallery intended for the privacy of the Held family hung partly over seats available to villagers and servants, and from its rail was draped a scarlet banner with the ducal crest. It was entered from an upper hall of the castle.

Mrs. Beecham was not invited to sit upon the balcony. With her mouth set in a grim line she regularly took a place beneath its shadow, though if Cleone captured the duke, her mama was certain to consider herself entitled to an elevated seat.

The chaplain sighed. He had prepared a little homily on the subject of Vanity, but did not suppose the villagers really needed it, for they had so little about which to be vain. Their hearts, he thought, were kind, they worked hard, and were trustworthy. He hoped he was not vain himself. Did one ever know? Perhaps it would be better to speak clearly of Abominations . . . or the folly of Deceit. But he had prepared Vanity, and that would have to be his subject at four o'clock.

Having settled this in his mind, he walked home, dawdling until it was only an hour till Sunday luncheon.

His three ladies were in the parlor, all quite pleasing to the eye, but two of them alarmingly confident of manner. He chose to address Mercy: "Did you often attend a church with your parents, my dear?"

"Oh, yes, sir," she responded. "Whenever we were within walking distance of one—any sort—large or small."

"Church of England, I hope," snapped Mrs. Beecham.

Mercy smiled ruefully. "Not always, Aunt. At least, not when we were on the Continent."

Her aunt sniffed, and the chaplain reminded her gently that there was no Church of England in the first century Judea.

"We," said his wife, ignoring so frivolous a comment, "have the privilege of worshipping with the duke in his private chapel at four o'clock. You will find your uncle very edifying."

The truth was that Mr. Beecham wrote wise sermons and delivered them with gentle passion, being convinced that few of those gathered in the chapel at Heritage Castle *really* understood their spiritual condition. His own was very good, but he was doubtful of it also.

After the midday meal Chaplain Beecham retired to his study to receive any new thoughts that might be headed his way; and his wife and daughter went up to rest on their beds to contemplate on His Grace, the Duke of Audley, Cleone shivering with delight at the prospect of being a duchess, while her mama focused on the improvement in her own status if her daughter could nab the young gentleman. Mercy thumbed a picture book of the Cotswolds.

A little before four o'clock, the four of them walked up to the chapel so as to be in advance of villagers. Mr. Beecham took a seat in a dark oak chair half-concealed by a stone pilaster. There was a faint sound of carriage wheels, and presently Sir Roland, his sister, and Mr. Macnaghten entered to take seats across the aisle from the Dower House ladies. Quite a crowd gathered, very likely as much to see little Miss Pope, and Miss March, and the stranger from Carlisle as to hear what Mr. Beecham had so earnestly prepared.

The duke and his ladies were not visible, even to over-the-shoulder peeps at the balcony, but surely they were there, for they always were.

Somewhere a chime sounded. The chaplain rose to his feet and went forward to begin the simple service without music or parade of cross or flags. His gentle manner and mild voice, which carried surprisingly well, stilled shuffling feet and last furtive whispers.

" 'Verily,' " he said to each attentive ear, " 'every man at his best state is altogether vanity.' "

It was remarkable, Lady Charlotte thought, how Mr. Beecham came into his own when he was behind a pulpit. Though she did not realize it, this was because his whole message was pure Scripture. Without hurry, yet not causing unrest, he led them through Book after Book, reminding them through Job that the wicked especially are characterized by vanity, and winding up at last with Proverbs—" 'Wealth gotten by vanity shall be diminished, but he that gathereth by labor shall increase.' "

His hearers liked that. Most were laborers. They knew hard work. And the chaplain had comforted them to face another week.

Charlotte wondered if Mr. Beecham's own daughter had listened—heard—taken to heart what her earnest papa had distilled for her benefit.

When the vesper service had ended, Aunt Emilie slipped away, and Charlotte and her brother went down to greet their neighbors, great and small, on the steps of the chapel. The Beechams, having sat well back, were early into the pleasant afternoon air and soon able to monopolize the brother and sister. In fact, Mrs. Beecham so thoroughly attached Charlotte that Cleone was free to work her charms upon His Grace.

Presently he said to his sister, "I will walk down with Cousin Maude," and a delighted Cousin Maude immediately said, "Oh, you and Cleone will have a lot to say to each other. Go along. Mercillia and I will follow."

Charlotte clenched her teeth and turned away to greet Kate March cordially.

The duke, at nineteen, was certainly conscious of enticing femininity and delighted in the lures Cleone cast his way. However, he was overjoyed to be going into the man's world of Oxford, and talked happily of this as they walked, not noticing at all that Cleone did not share his enthusiasm.

Cleone's mama was slow to follow with Mercy, allowing the couple as much time together as possible, but as others from the village were going the same route at various speeds, there was no occasion for privacy. The chaplain was last to reach his home, and when he did so, Mrs. Beecham urged Sydney to take tea with them. But Sydney was already saying that Sunday supper (as she perfectly well knew) was served early at the castle, and he must go. And go he did.

No one commented to the chaplain on the quality of his little sermon, Mercillia thinking it was not her place to judge—and praise—a minister of the Church of England, and Mrs. Beecham and Cleone because they never did so.

They took tea, after which the chaplain strolled about the lawn of the Dower House until he had come down from ecclesiastic heights and was ready for a simple, cold supper.

The duke and his family were, of course, his chief concern, yet the villagers were also in his heart.

At Heritage Castle the evening meal was tranquil, although Charlotte's mind spun. "What plans have you and Sir Roland made for visiting Oxford?" she asked her brother in a manner intended to be casual.

"We have not settled anything," Sydney replied. "He cannot leave home while Mr. Macnaghten is visiting there."

"True. He cannot leave Kate without a chaperone. Will he write to make enquiries?"

"He has already done so. Oh, Charlotte, dearest Charlotte, I am so happy that you have given permission." It had not occurred to him that he could choose for himself.

"I was pressed into it," she said, but she smiled and added, "I have always known it was the perfect plan for you, but—I shall miss you."

"What shall you do?" he asked, helping himself liberally to slices of roast chicken in an excess of good spirits.

"If I were your brother, I would go also. To be female is to miss much. Women count for little."

Sydney frowned in reflection. "I don't know that. Does not all of Heritage dance to your tune?"

Aunt Emilie cleared her throat.

"So they would have me think," Charlotte said. "If there were no Lady Charlotte, our bailiff would manage all perfectly for you."

"But he would not be as lovable as my sister!" declared Sydney triumphantly, and their aunt beamed upon them.

Charlotte thrust herself back from the table. "Oh, already you have mastered sophistry! What will you study when you escape from Heritage?"

"Sir Roland suggests I begin with a sample of different disciplines, in order to have some basis for a choice of the direction in which I would prefer to go."

"Perhaps he can tell you what studies he enjoyed most," she suggested.

Sydney said, "I did ask that, but he says I must choose for myself and not let his—or anyone's—interests choose for me."

Charlotte nodded. "That sounds like Sir Roland. He is wise, isn't he?"

"Yes," agreed her brother, "though I might say clever. If he let me depend entirely on him, I might blame him if all became dull. He would not like that."

She mentioned the tutor that had spent some months with them. "Mr. Oglevie was supposed to have given you a general basis of Great Minds."

"Yes. He did. Some seemed dull to me, but I rather liked Machiavelli. Confounded devious, but made good sense!"

"Perhaps you would like to go deeper into the Classics."

"Perhaps . . . though Socrates did not convince me that it was virtuous to drink poison."

"Certainly not!"

Turning serious, he said, "What does it take to be a duke on the scale of Father? I have no inclination to be a Corinthian. It is *Heritage* that matters, isn't it? I have to take charge some day, and I hope to do half as well as you. Don't protest! Everyone knows you have been an excellent duke, but it is really up to me to step into Father's shoes, isn't it? Brrr! Scary!"

But Lady Charlotte was frankly laughing. "Papa was more than nineteen when he became Duke of Audley. And so will you be. Sir Roland is right. You do need some edges rubbed off and some dignity added—only, please, when you get to Oxford, do not do such things as swill Blue Ruin, thinking it will make a man of you!"

Sydney began laughing, too. "Silly girl! I have already tried Blue Ruin."

"You have! Where did you get *that?*"

"At the pub in the village. Coomes gave me a sample."

"Oh!" she cried, even though rumbles of laughter were coming from Aunt Emilie. "I would never have thought it of Coomes!"

"Don't be alarmed," said her brother, who seemed suddenly to have grown larger and surer. "I did not like it at all. You need not worry that I will spend my days at Oxford in drunkenness. I love Heritage as much as you do, and I know my duty to it."

Charlotte was silent for a moment, wondering how much it was safe to say. His mood was certainly not hostile.

"I have great expectations of you, dearest," she said, "and—like a devoted mother—apprehensions. I hope you will enjoy your studies—concentrate on them—and not rush into entangling r-relationships too soon."

"Word of a Held," he replied, reaching to take her hand and squeeze it.

She had to accept his word, but she could not forget the determination that she had recognized in Cleone and her mama. It would be fatal to mention the name of either at this point, so she smiled blindingly and said she supposed he was practicing on *her* the earnestness that he would need to impress his instructors.

It was difficult to let go of him. She was beginning to feel as bereft as a mother might have been, but of course Sydney was her brother, not her son, and all the years of caring for him, worrying over his health, and sharing his pleasures had not made him anything but an adored brother. She had to turn him free . . . though he had never been hers to bind.

Would their father be proud of him if he could see him now? She thought he would. Yes, of course he would. She did not think of their gentle mother—so long gone. Their father had been both parents for many years, until she was old enough to share the load.

If only there were not a beautiful, spoiled girl at the Dower House!

Sydney was speaking to Aunt Emilie, now, in his affectionate way. Really, he had a wonderful disposition. Too good a nature to waste on a spoiled chit who did not understand that there was more to being a duchess than wearing pretty frocks, wheedling for *bijoux,* and ordering servants about.

Briefly, Charlotte toyed with the idea of working some sort of magic in Cleone while Sydney was away, molding her into a lady suitable to be a duke's wife. She was quite beautiful already; her looks would pass muster at Court and anywhere else, but if one believed that Beauty was as Beauty *did,* there was a good deal to change in pert Miss Beecham. Charlotte could visualize her ordering the servants imperiously and causing rebellion in the ranks.

It was a difficult situation. A man simply employed by the Helds as chaplain could be sent away with a generous gift of money, whereas a *cousin* could not. It might be possible to explain the situation tactfully to John Beecham, but his wife was another matter; she would be sure to vilify the Held family far and wide—in the village—and wherever in England she might go. The prospect made Charlotte shudder.

It was impossible to speak to Sydney of these things.

Seven

On Monday morning, after a debate in her mind between ten o'clock or eleven, Mrs. Beecham chose ten-thirty to set out in the chaplain's gig for a call upon Katherine March. She took Cleone with her. There was no room for Mercy, and—anyway—Mercy did not matter, a mere child, only on a visit until her parents returned from travel to Greece.

She was fortunate enough to find Katherine, Sir Roland, and Mr. Macnaghten just rising from breakfast. Since the gentlemen were preparing to ride out to Sir Roland's fields, she issued her invitation immediately.

"A luncheon party on our terrace," she explained. "The shade is on that side at that hour, and really the weather has been delightful, do you not think?"

Nothing was said about Mr. Macnaghten's leaving any time soon. The invitation was accepted by Sir Roland on behalf of all three of them.

Mrs. Beecham rather thought a formal dinner would be beyond the capabilities of her servants, but believed she could provide a tolerably pleasant midday meal. She would have liked to plan a larger gathering, but spurned the Guinns, and no other family close by would suit at all. There were two or three young men who called upon her daughter; their families were *respectable,* yet hardly persons she wished to invite with her ducal connections.

When Mrs. Beecham, Cleone, and the gig returned home, they were just in time to see the duke reining his curricle at their door and hoping to take Cleone for a little drive. With much more enthusiasm than she had shown for the brief trip to Sir Roland's manor, Cleone was instantly down and reaching for Sydney's hand to draw her beside him.

"*Such* a day," said the duke. "Must not let it go to waste. We won't go far. I'll have her back in good time for luncheon. One o'clock?"

The delighted mother waved them away and continued to the castle, where she issued her invitation to Charlotte, civilly including Aunt Emilie who was sitting with her niece, though she did not expect Lady Emilie Held to accept, and she did not.

Mrs. Beecham fished a bit: "Mr. Macnaghten does not seem in any hurry to return to Carlisle."

"No," agreed Charlotte, not taking the lure. "He does not come this far south very often and is not in any pressing hurry to return, I suppose. Sir Roland has said crops are no concern for him. He raises horses. I believe he has suggested Sydney attend some races with him."

Since Charlotte did not mention Macnaghten's attachment to Katherine and Mrs. Beecham had not detected a partiality, the chaplain's wife suspected nothing of the tensions at Sir Roland's home.

"What are the girls doing for amusement?" Charlotte asked to change the subject.

Her visitor swelled slightly. "Sydney has taken Cleone for a little drive before lunch. Shall I keep him to eat with us?"

Lady Charlotte replied that she did not know his plans. "You have not told me how Mercy is occupied. Perhaps some of the local swains are entertaining her."

Mrs. Beecham said, "Oh, I do not think it likely. I saw no horses or carriages waiting. The young men are looking for Cleone, you know, and she was with me—and now with Sydney."

"How dull for Mercy! Can you not introduce her to a few girls of the village? I know some are perfectly respectable."

She watched the play of expressions across Maude Beecham's face.

The chaplain's wife repressed a frown. "I do not encourage village girls to hang about Cleone," she answered stiffly.

"Do you not? Several are very well behaved. The squire has two young daughters. I should think they might be pleasant company for your daughter and Mercy."

As Mrs. Beecham could not say that the only company she wished for Cleone was a *duke,* she made some comment about beaux being underfoot most of the time.

"Well, we cannot wish your sister's child to be lonely. I shall take her with me the next time I go shopping at Hays. Tell me, is Mercy like your sister?"

This distracted Mrs. Beecham, as it was meant to do. "In some ways," she said. "Their coloring is similar, and Mercillia is a small person like my sister, but her nature—well, I can only say studious like her father. He is a bundle of energy, of course, whereas Mercy seems to be tranquil. He is also quite serious about odd things like antiquities—and books of philosophy (which are no good at all for everyday life), and my sister says he is curious about *everything.* Fanny does not find him tiring, but I am sure he would exhaust me!"

"You are describing someone with a bright mind," Charlotte noted.

Mrs. Beecham allowed that to be possible.

"Is it not likely that Mercy is also bright?"

The chaplain's wife admitted that Mercy might be, but as she did not consider intellectual power to be anything to appeal to eligible young gentlemen, she put a period to the discussion by saying, "Well, that is her parents' problem. *We* do not have to find a husband for her. I daresay Mercillia will not be here more than a month or two."

"Will your sister and her husband come here to collect their daughter?" Lady Charlotte spoke casually, but she was beginning to be curious about Maude's sister. "We would like to know your family."

"They may or may not. It is something they will decide at the last moment, I am sure. Fanny is not a bit like me—" Mrs. Beecham hesitated and being unable to resist unburdening herself added "Not my sister, only my half sister. Her mother was the daughter of Viscount Bruton."

Much had immediately become clear. Mrs. Beecham, though envious of a half sister with noble roots, could not resist claiming the connection. No wonder that she, Charlotte, heard herself incessantly called Cousin Charlotte. Much of her irritation with John Beecham's wife was swept away by sympathy.

"If your sister comes to Fallford, perhaps you will permit her and her husband to stay here at the castle with me? Two more persons and their servants will surely crowd you at the Dower House."

Cousin Maude quite spilled over with thanks, which Charlotte thought ruefully might be a new source of irritation.

"I believe I see Sydney's curricle stopping at the Dower House," Charlotte interrupted gently.

Her visitor, who had not been facing the window, turned quickly to see for herself the curricle's rear wheels disappearing into the trees. "Sure enough! I must hurry down to see if Sydney will stay for lunch."

Charlotte, meanwhile, hoped he would *not* and was relieved when his curricle appeared again as he started homeward, slowing only when he encountered Mrs. Beecham on her way down. Evidently he declined any invitation for a midday meal, for after a brief exchange of words he continued homeward.

"There is not enough," Charlotte told Aunt Emilie, "to keep Syd busy. I must ask our bailiff to take him on his rounds of the manor and lecture him a bit."

Her aunt nodded in agreement.

It was not necessary to send for Mr. Lewis, for he came just as they were finishing lunch to say he had found plowman's cot where they kept a bucket beneath a roof leak in case of rain, and did Her Ladyship wish to verify this before he set men to repair the roof.

"His Lordship will go with you," Charlotte said. "Just take a look, Sydney, and order whatever is needed."

Sydney, not loath to enjoy any sort of entertainment, went off happily with the bailiff to see the threatened roof and spend a pair of hours determining that other cottages were sound. He came home breathing satisfaction with his bailiff, his chief carpenter, his tenants, his manor, and the whole day and season.

Meanwhile, a note had come from Mr. Macnaghten saying he had located races to be held twenty miles east on the morrow and he would pick up His Grace at eight. His team, he wrote, brought on slowly by his men, was well rested and would think nothing of twenty miles. Better bring duds; very likely they would stay overnight.

Seeing how pleased her brother was, Charlotte could only be glad for him. Also, it would take him from Cleone's orbit for a time.

She slept well that night and welcomed a visit from Kate about two hours after the men had set out.

If she had expected Kate to discuss Mr. Macnaghten, this did not happen. They met on pleasant terms, the ten years between them having shrunk.

"I hope I am not keeping you from duties," Kate said.

"Not at all," returned Lady Charlotte. "While there is no one to overhear our female chatter, I *must* tell you that you are looking charming with that cropped hair. I would like to copy it, but fear my hair would not curl so enchantingly as yours."

"One cannot tell until the awful deed is done," Kate said. "My cousin had begged me to ply the scissors, but it took me two years to dare. I seem to remember that your hair rioted on your head when you were a little tot. Shall I dare you?"

Charlotte cried, "No, no! I shall insist on two years for me to decide. Does your brother approve your new style?"

"Roland looks at me at with the eyes of a fond brother. He is never critical of me, although he has said that he thinks hair dressed as yours is regal."

"Heavens!" exclaimed Charlotte. "I do not want to look so unapproachable as that."

Kate replied quickly, "I hope our two families are always on easiest of terms. Do you think me wrong to live so far away? Is Roland lonely? He would never say so."

"I think your brother is not one to mope. I am sure he misses you, for he mentions you often. From time to time he goes off somewhere—London—or Brighton—or someplace in the lake district—"

"Yes, he has an interest in a sheep farm there. I encourage *that,* for he will sometimes come on to Carlisle for a visit. My cousin, I must tell you, thinks Roland is quite perfect."

"Sydney and I are always very dull when he is gone. The society of Fallford is certainly flat, you know . . . virtually nonexistent. Is that why you stay away?" Charlotte asked then.

To be polite Kate could say no such thing. When she hesitated, Charlotte said, "Sir Roland insists I must travel or do something tedious in London while Sydney is at Oxford. Perhaps I will have to find a Carlisle of my own."

Kate laughed lightly and said she must come for a visit in the north. "You would like the cousin with whom I stay. She is twice my age and three times as lively."

"Perhaps . . ." Lady Charlotte replied vaguely, her mind being on problems at home. It was not her own situation that troubled her, but Sydney's, and there was a limit, she felt, to how much she should reveal of that.

Then Katherine said astutely, "You think always of the duke, do you not? Roland says you have been a wonderful parent to him, but the time has come for him to spread his wings. He thinks a university will do Sydney no end of good."

"Yes," said Charlotte. "So he has been telling me. It is a way of getting Syd away from—" She broke off, not knowing how much Sir Roland may have told Kate, and never wanting to be disloyal to her brother. It did not seem right to be exposing the duke's affairs, when Kate was so close about her own.

Charlotte had never had a female confidante except Aunt Emilie, who only listened and never advised. She quite *longed* for such a person and wondered if the nameless cousin in Carlisle was this to Kate. Charlotte had only Sir Roland to lean upon, and while he was always understanding, he also knew her flaws and did not hesitate to point them out—tactfully, of course—when what she wanted most was to be thought flawless. That, Cousin John Beecham would say, was Vanity!

Changing the subject, Charlotte said, "Mrs. Beecham has invited you to lunch on her terrace?"

"Yes."

"It will be pleasant enough. I am sorry we cannot make things truly festive for you and Mr. Macnaghten at Fallford. When Sydney comes into his inheritance, in two years, things should become more—more *ducal.* In fact, even before then, I daresay Syd will be bringing friends from Oxford to house parties here at the castle."

"If so, it will give you an opportunity to judge the friends he acquires," Kate pointed out.

Charlotte said rather dolefully, "Sydney should have been Papa's firstborn, not I."

"Roland says you have been superior in rearing your brother."

Surprised, Lady Charlotte exclaimed, "You do not mean it!"

"Yes. He also said you have managed Heritage in a masterful manner."

Flushing, Charlotte said, "Oh, surely not. *Someone* has to make decisions. I have listened to hundreds of Papa's—enough to know how he looked at most problems. Mr. Lewis is an excellent bailiff. He has always asked my opinion, but it is simple to recognize what *he* thinks important and just tell him 'go ahead.' Really, I trust him completely. I cannot like to be thought masterful, Kate."

Katherine suggested that perhaps she used the wrong word. "Will you allow me to say capable?"

Charlotte made a little moue. "Dull, but say whatever you please to me. Perhaps I shall kick up my heels when Sydney has gone."

"Well, you need not think you can do anything outrageous, because Roland will have his eye on you."

Charlotte pursed her lips and rolled her own eyes. "Almost you tempt me to make a scandal on the Town."

Her visitor merely laughed and changed the subject. "Shall we wear hats to Mrs. Beecham's luncheon?"

"Well, perhaps carry one. I do not know whom Cousin Maude has invited, but there cannot be many. She disdains most of the neighborhood."

Nothing was said of Cleone, although she was not far from either lady's mind. Nor was anything said of Mr. Macnaghten, who very likely was also lurking in both of those places.

Afterwards, Charlotte said to Aunt Emilie, "Kate did not reveal a thing about their visitor from Carlisle. I am perishing of curiosity. What keeps him here if he is receiving no encouragement? It does no good to ask Sir Roland, for he does not know either. Maybe Sydney will have some clues after spending time with Macnaghten at the races."

It was the evening of the third day before Mr. Macnaghten's carriage dropped a beaming Sydney at Heritage Castle. His sister restrained herself from falling on his neck and even became chill when he announced he had seen "great sport" and was of a mind to stock some horses "for the turf."

Her heart sank to think he might have exchanged an obsession with Cleone for one with thoroughbreds.

"Not at this time," she protested. "You cannot go off to Oxford and expect me to nurse highbred racers!"

Sydney planted a kiss on her forehead and promised not to make a jockey of her. He did not even ask if he had been missed, assuming his sister coped with his absence as easily as she did with his being under foot.

"It is fortunate that you stayed away no longer, you and Mr. Macnaghten, for both of you are expected at Cousin Maude's *alfresco* luncheon tomorrow," she said flatly.

"Are we? Oh, good! Chances are that Cleone has never seen a horse race. She will be interested to hear about them."

Eight

As Lady Charlotte dressed for Cousin Maude's luncheon, sleeking her hair back and twisting it into a knot, she wondered what would happen if she took scissors to it, as Kate advised. Small hairs about her ears had an unruly tendency to curl. Suppose . . . suppose all her hair was short . . . would it become more lively? It seemed a dreadful risk to take. Suppose it did not hold a curl—even stood out all which way like prickles on a hedgehog! She was not ready to take that chance.

For one thing, her mind was still occupied with the future of her brother. Would he stay interested in horse racing? He could afford a few racers, but would he be satisfied with only a few? Then there was the matter of a trainer, someone who knew how to bring them to peak performance, which Sydney certainly did not. And who would ride the horses in races? For a duke to set himself up as a sort of gentleman jockey was unthinkable!

She almost wished he was a small boy again, in delicate health and needing to be coddled.

When she had donned a willow green garden dress and kid slippers that laced about her slim ankles, she hung a straw bonnet from her arm and went down to join Sydney in a walk to the Dower House. Here they found an unexpected guest, Mr. Todd.

Charlotte supposed her hostess had wished to even the number of her group to ten and had hit upon including Mr. Todd, who had the virtue of being essentially unknown, and therefore no one knew anything unsavory about him.

This gentleman (one imagined he was a gentleman) had settled in Fallford three years previously, leasing a quaint stone cottage on the green. His age could be thirty-five, or perhaps fifty-five. No one knew. His hair showed very little gray and his face was unlined; he was generally thought to be scholarly, because he spent long hours indoors. Mrs. Beecham gave him the benefit of all doubts, for his manners were impeccable and he rounded out her table.

At the appearance of Charlotte, Mr. Todd attached himself to her side and treated her with such deference that she could not dislodge him without being rude. To her side he hung. She shot Sir Roland a silent plea, but he only bit his lip, as if amused, and remained across the terrace. She quite lost her patience with both gentlemen and looked about for other help.

Sydney was, of course, glued to Cleone; likewise Mr. Macnaghten attended Kate. Only Chaplain Beecham was unattached, and Charlotte could not feel he would be an improvement over Mr. Todd, so she said brightly, "Let us congratulate Mrs. Beecham on this pleasant idea." With a dazzling smile she drew Mr. Todd toward their hostess, only to find that Mercillia was hovering behind that lady.

"Mr. Todd," said Charlotte gaily, "I do not believe you are acquainted with Mrs. Beecham's niece, Miss Pope, who is here to visit. Mercy, my dear, let me present Mr. Todd who, from all I hear, is a scholar like your papa." She could not have said anything more fortunate.

"Oh!" exclaimed Mercy, her eyes sparkling. "Antiquities?"

Mr. Todd said, "Er—yes, in a small way, though I have not been able to travel as I would have liked."

"Papa is traveling to Greece now," Mercy replied happily, and both promptly forgot the beautiful Lady Charlotte Held while they compared archaeological sites.

Charlotte caught Sir Roland grinning at her. As he had not

come to her when needed, she gave him a darkling glance and drifted toward Kate and Mr. Macnaghten.

"Mr. Macnaghten," she said, "I shall hold you responsible for any racehorses that Heritage suddenly acquires."

He was not alarmed.

"Do not worry," he replied. "I have heard your brother expatiate for several days about a new life at Oxford, and I believe that will come before horses." He turned to Kate. "His Grace is full of youthful enthusiasms. I was glad to see him enjoy races, for I am addicted to them myself, as you know. But help me reassure his sister that the lure of independence—well, semi-independence—at college holds the greatest attraction for someone who is—what?—twenty."

"Nineteen," supplied Charlotte.

"Mr. Macnaghten spent several years at a college himself, even with racers waiting in his father's stables," said Kate.

"At what age did you become horse-mad?" persisted Charlotte.

He was not to be disconcerted and insisted he was not so horse-mad, even now, as to overlook the charms of young ladies.

"Oh," exclaimed Charlotte, "I think you must be half Irish!"

"Who is half Irish?" asked the duke, bringing Cleone to join them. "No one here, surely."

"Not anyone of Fallford," said his sister. "Mr. Macnaghten is suspect because of speaking blarney."

"Which we ladies enjoy," Katherine said quickly, "do we not, Cleone?"

As Cleone was not sure she should agree to this openly, she said, "Gentlemen like to tease." That, from a practiced teaser of the opposite sex, Charlotte thought ridiculous.

"You mean," she asked, "that all teasing is empty froth?"

Not wanting to agree her own conversation was trivial, Cleone did not reply. Mr. Macnaghten rescued her by declaring that it did not matter what pretty ladies might say, because gentlemen liked best to *look* at them.

"You can look at statues any time," Charlotte pointed out. "Flesh-and-blood ladies like—"

"What?" said a voice behind her. It was Sir Roland, but before she need reply, Mrs. Beecham had called them to be seated.

How to distribute her guests about the table had kept Mrs. Beecham awake several nights. The duke, of course, must be beside her. Cleone would want (and she herself would want) the daughter of the house next to him. But what of Sir Roland's sister? Ambition won over protocol; Cleone's wishes were gratified. Mr. Todd could ogle Lady Charlotte from across the table. This put an end to his conversation with Mercillia, but he would be happy enough between Kate and Cleone. Mercy was then stationed between Sir Roland (who was at his hostess's left) and Mr. Macnaghten, who thus had Charlotte on his left and who had the manner of being happy anywhere.

The more Charlotte saw of Mr. Macnaghten, the more she admired his good nature. Of course, she thought, one did not choose a husband simply because he was amiable, but surely it must be a trait that would contribute to domestic harmony. Good nature, such as Mr. Macnaghten's, must first attract a lady's notice; then other attributes, such as charm, easy conversation, humor, and social graces must reinforce the lady's opinion.

He was saying to her now, "This is so pleasant. When I return to my home, I must see about extending my terrace around the corner of the house, where it will have more shade and be comfortable for dining."

"You enjoy this?" she asked. "Heritage, being a castle and rather heavily built, does not lend itself to informality. You understand, I love my home and would not change it, but I can certainly appreciate another setting."

"At the castle," he said, "you have broad passageways and

lofty ceilings, and I daresay a tranquillity that spaciousness brings."

She said, "Oh, yes! I had not thought of it that way, but you are exactly right. What is the nature of your home?"

"It is a rambling, country house with a step up here or down there that could trip you if you are not careful, but I know it so well that I never take a fall. My father added a glass room with flowers planted colorfully outside and potted ones inside, so that the two masses seem to flow together and one has no feeling of being in or out. It is pleasant, is it not, Miss March?"

The table, being a makeshift arrangement, was smaller than one in a formal dining salon. Kate could hear every word they spoke.

"Like a bit of magic," she replied.

At the other end of the table, Sir Roland was describing to Mrs. Beecham the effect of current weather upon planted fields about which she cared nothing, so her attention was only enough to seem polite, and she caught the word magic.

Immediately, she said, "Magic is nonsense."

Leaning forward slightly to catch her eye, Mr. Macnaghten corrected kindly but firmly, "Miss March said *like* magic. If you could see my Garden Room, you would enjoy the feeling of openness, dear lady."

Mrs. Beecham, not recognizing a polite setdown, conceded his point with a slight nod and asked the duke at her side when he would be going to Oxford.

The duke said he was not just sure.

"I am awaiting answers to enquiries," Sir Roland put in evasively, so Mr. Macnaghten would not be made to feel he was an impediment.

Mrs. Beecham had no idea when new students enrolled, but felt it must be during the coming Fall. Her wanting to know how much time remained for Cleone to snare the duke had prompted her question, and the answer was no help. Fortunately, a servant came between her and Sir Roland at that point to offer biscuits.

Her husband serenely opined that Oxford would be a splendid experience for Sydney, which silenced his wife as surely as it annoyed her. Mercifully, several small conversations broke out.

Emboldened by the informality of the occasion, Mr. Todd spoke across the narrow table to Mercy:

"Will your parents visit any of the Greek islands, Miss Pope?"

"I do not know, sir," she replied, breaking her customary silence. "They hope to reach Delos. I do not know what others. All must depend on their finding boats."

"Ah!" he returned. "I would wish to be with them."

Then Greece was drowned out by a spirited discussion of horse racing that was launched by Sir Roland, Mr. Macnaghten, and the duke. The foot of the table lapsed into silence, although Macnaghten politely tried to include his host by asking if he had an interest in racing.

The chaplain said, "Not my cup of tea," and went on eating. Charlotte and Kate, on either side of him, did likewise.

The topic of horse racing could not charm Mrs. Beecham. However, as she could see it appealed to Sydney, she let it flow unchecked. Cleone, though bored, knew to put on a face of spurious interest, until a bee threatened attack and the duke sprang up to drive it away. Fortunately, the bee, which had a mind of its own, scented a nearby blossom and went off busily to sip.

Presently there was served a large and luscious fruit compote, which was something Mrs. Beecham's cook—a village woman—did well, and the meal ended on a high note. Finally, there were small cups of coffee. Cousin John Beecham, though he enjoyed a glass of wine when it was offered to him, did not think it becoming of a serious clergyman to serve wines, so his wife was obliged to content herself with coffee to end her meal. She had for so many years been accustomed to this that it no longer irked her; it had the additional advantage of being less expensive.

When they rose from the table, Lady Charlotte was gratified to see that her brother's good manners (or was it his good nature?) led him to seek out Mercillia for a small exchange of words. The girl glowed with pleasure, yet was poised enough to draw Kate March, who was momentarily alone, to join their conversation.

The duke explained, "I have discovered that Miss Mercy likes to ride—"

Mercy added, "Gently!"

"Yes. Gently. What would you say to a ride with us, Miss March? Do you remember the view from Audley Knob? Shall we show it to Miss Mercy?"

"Indeed I do remember that," said Kate. "We are not so hilly here as to the west, but Audley Knob commands a fine outlook."

"Then we must go there tomorrow. Will eleven o'clock suit? Shall we meet here? I will bring a mount down for Miss Mercy."

Cleone, who was hovering so as to hear some of what was said, knew perfectly well that His Grace knew perfectly well that *she* did not ride, and her lower lip began the suggestion of a pout; storm clouds would have gathered had not Mr. Todd come up and captured her attention by asking if she realized she looked like one of the flowers in the border of the terrace.

This was conversation more to her taste. She dimpled delightfully and, switching her pink frock, led Mr. Todd to the nearest flower bed to receive a blossom plucked by her dainty fingers.

Mr. Todd accepted the gift gracefully. He had dallied around the less expensive watering places enough to know what attentions young ladies welcomed and how to flatter them gently. As he led her along the terrace, she accepted his arm for a resting place of her little soft hand and tossed her head, chattering with animation, even while peeking to see if Sydney noticed.

He did not, but Sir Roland was watching. He caught up with the strollers and contrived to place himself so as to block Cleone's view of Sydney. Was this done consciously? Who could tell? He held the couple in a conversation which required answers from first Cleone and then Mr. Todd. Was she warm enough? Too warm? Was Mr. Todd looking forward to the fall season? Which was Miss Cleone's favorite season?

When, from the corner of his eye, Sir Roland noticed that the duke had left Mercy's side and was expressing polite thanks to his hostess, he drew his watch from its pocket for a quick peek, muttered something that sounded like "By Jove!" and left this oddly unmatched pair to fumble at conversation.

"Come, Kate," Sir Roland said, collecting his sister, "our carriage is leaving. Ready, Macnaghten?"

Final goodbyes were said, the Marches drove off with their houseguest, and the duke and his sister walked leisurely up the hill, while Mr. Todd, presumably, made his way to his cottage in the village.

"You will ride with us, won't you?" the duke said to his sister as they walked.

"Yes. I have not been up to the Knob for a long time. Do you realize that Cleone is left out of the plan, Sydney? She will not be pleased."

"Oh," said Sydney, "Cleone prefers houses and gardens. I will take her on a stroll around the pond one day." His attitude did not seem loverlike to Charlotte, which she found encouraging. "Did you know there is a rumor in the village that trout have been seen in the brook? Do you think Cleone would walk as far as that?"

A good countrywoman like Charlotte often tramped for miles. Even Aunt Emilie sometimes accompanied her, and Katherine March had a reputation for walking stoutly. But Cleone? Charlotte did not think the chaplain's daughter would welcome such exercise . . . unless—possibly—invited by a duke.

"I hope you will pick a gentle mount for Mercy," she said. "We do not know how experienced she may be."

The duke said, "Oh, of course. Which horse do you want?"

"Prince, I suppose."

"Then I will take Floral for Mercy. She will prefer a mare, don't you think?" When his sister nodded, he added, "It is steadily uphill, you know. We must take it slowly, so that Mercy will be comfortable. We do not know how long it has been since she spent any time on a horse. As for our return, it is naturally all downhill, but a gentle slope and not at all difficult. You will not mind going slowly, will you?"

"No," said his sister with a faint smile. "Prince and I are game for anything."

Sydney frowned. "You sound roguish. No sudden tricks or starts, mind!"

Nine

"It is another fine day," the duke said to Charlotte when they met over breakfast. Charlotte was wearing a well-tailored riding dress of bronze velvet with frogs of gold braid; he looked at her approvingly, saying, "You are very smart today."

She took this as another sign of his new maturity, for he seldom noticed her apparel.

"I am looking forward to this expedition," she said, setting down her emptied coffee cup. "Are you sure the trail is in good condition and will not cause problems for Mercy? We do not know how experienced she may be."

Sydney said she was not to worry. "I was up there only a week or so ago. All was clear and smooth then, except for a tiny trickle after the last rain, which may be dried by now. If it is still running, the horses will very likely step over it with ease."

Having finished eating, Charlotte collected hat and gloves from the hall and went out with her brother through the passages down which Charlotte had taken Mr. Macnaghten to the stable. Sydney tossed her to her saddle on Prince.

"I think I will have Andy bring up the rear of our line, in case we need him," said His Grace, nodding at a young groom, who dodged back into the stable for another horse. Then, with Andy leading Floral for Mercy to ride, they proceeded around the end of the castle and down the driveway to the Dower House.

Not to be left out, Sir Roland and Mr. Macnaghten had accompanied Katherine and were waiting with her.

"Oh, very good! You all came," said Sydney.

Sir Roland, having stood down to help Mercy mount, passed his reins to Mr. Macnaghten, and tossed her to her saddle on Floral, where she settled herself neatly, cooing to the mare and then saying, "What a beauty!"

The duke looked around for Cleone, but she was not visible.

Mrs. Beecham watched from the doorway, unsmiling, as they rode away. She had no more liking for horses than did her daughter, yet sensed that Cleone was missing something desirable. Her niece looked very stylish in a royal blue habit, close-fitting in the jacket, with a matching hat and small plume. Her sister, Mrs. Pope, had certainly sent Mercy with clothes that were not only proper, but up to the nines. Although there were not many dresses in Mercillia's luggage, they were exactly *right.* She could be proud of Fanny's taste, but since Cleone was not one of the party, this was cold comfort.

As the cavalcade circled the pond, Sydney kept his eye closely on Mercy, and was relieved to see that she sat with perfect posture and sure hands on the reins. From the pond they went up a slope beside the small stream that fed the pond, presently crossed the stream on sturdy planks, and entered a pretty woodland where the trail widened.

Charlotte discovered Mr. Macnaghten beside her.

"That is a fine gelding," he said.

"Thank you. Papa bought him for me when he had decided that I could ride to his satisfaction," she responded with a twinkle that dared him to say Prince was too much horse for a lady.

"I expect you pleased him in many ways," he said.

She snapped a look at him, halfway expecting a leer, but he was watching Kate March who was just ahead of them, and her tension evaporated when she realized he was only being polite.

"Next you will say he spoiled me," she challenged.

"No. A good rider deserves a good mount."

Ah, thought Lady Charlotte at once, *his interest is in horseflesh.* Aloud she said, "Does Kate do much riding at Carlisle?"

"Not a lot," he answered. "She cares for her cousin very much in the way you have cared for your brother, and shares her interest in dogs. I think she is devoted to the lady. Indeed, they are mutually fond, Mrs. Glengower having no children and viewing Kate somewhat in the light of a daughter. I can see—well, Kate does not have a particular place here—I can see she enjoys a mother-daughter sort of relationship." He cast Charlotte an inquisitive look. "Would you not think she would welcome a marriage that will keep her next door to the cousin of whom she is so fond?"

Their horses had slowed, forcing the groom behind then to drop back tactfully.

"Mr. Macnaghten!" Charlotte said severely. "You must not expect me to discuss Kate's private business!"

He managed to look both chastised and determined at the same time. In fact, he had a bonny countenance, unruffled disposition, and, she felt, a genuine interest in everyone he met. But it was Kate he wanted, and she could not understand how Kate withstood his courtship.

Shrubbery was closing on them. Mr. Macnaghten slowed, and Charlotte went ahead. When the trail widened again, she drew even with Kate. Sir Roland was just ahead, turning back now and then to be sure they were keeping up the pace Sydney set. Sydney had Mercy beside him.

Presently, they passed the point at which a side trail led down to the bridge just north of Fallford, where the brook that was alleged to have trout crossed the road to Hays. After that, their trail grew steeper, though not difficult. Sydney led, Mercillia followed gamely, then Sir Roland and the others came along single file. Once in a while one of the horses would comment with a snort. Otherwise, they rode quietly, only to burst from the trees to confront a glorious panorama of hills through which their brook made its way to join the Severn River.

"Why, this is beautiful," whispered Mercy. She eased her reins to allow Floral to crop some delectable wildflowers. Blooms were gone—it was too late in the year for them—but the leaves seemed to please the horse.

Sir Roland dismounted and stood enjoying the view. "I have not been here for nearly two years," he said. "I had forgotten how splendid it is."

Beaming as if he had created the landscape, the duke said, "Whenever things get out of proportion, I come here."

His sister was astonished at such an admission from him. Astonished and pleased. Sydney, she thought, was beginning to mature in a way that could only be good. She glanced around her and saw that Mr. Macnaghten had brought his horse beside Katherine and was having a low-voiced conversation with her. For a moment she felt a sting of envy for the admiration—the love—of which Kate was the object. She could not begrudge this to Kate, who was an admirable person. And, of course, Sydney was devoted to herself, as was Aunt Emilie. Only, it was not the same. In her mind, she reproved herself, calling herself selfish, wanting the moon, without ever having looked at it.

She heard Sydney ask Mercillia if she wished to dismount.

"Oh, no," said Mercy. "I am quite comfortable. This is a perfect horse for a lady."

"Charlotte rides her sometimes," Sydney said.

"Oh, have I taken your mount, Lady Charlotte?" Mercy asked, looking chagrined.

"Not at all," said Sydney, before Charlotte could answer. "Prince is her favorite; Father bought him especially for her."

"I ride Floral sometimes to keep her exercised," Charlotte added. "I am glad for you to enjoy her. You must feel free to ride her any time."

Mercy colored becomingly and thanked both brother and sister with sweet earnestness.

"Shall we circle the Knob?" asked Sir Roland, remounting. "Kate—Macnaghten—are you ready to explore further?"

Those two indicating willingness, Sir Roland took the lead and conducted them around the Knob on a narrow track which gave views in other directions, though none so splendid as westward toward the hills.

"Someday," said Charlotte for all to hear, "I shall climb to *sit* on the very top of the Knob."

When they had completed the circuit, they descended, Sydney and Mercillia this time in the rear, with Sydney's groom somehow sandwiched in the group. The stay on Audley Knob had not been long, and Sir Roland's pace taken on the downward track was cautious for the ladies' sakes, the descent being thus slower than the climb. From time to time they were able to remark on lesser views that could be glimpsed through breaks in foliage.

When, at last, they reached the level path around the pond, general conversation broke out, all agreeing that it had been a fine expedition. At the Dower House they found that Cleone had not missed them at all, having been entertained by the Guinn boys and another chap from a manor out the Hays road. She was not at all interested in views of familiar westward hills.

"Oh, Aunt Maude," exclaimed Mercy, flushed with pleasure and exercise, "we had the most magnificent view."

Those in Mrs. Beecham's parlor regarded her with some surprise, for she was seldom so effusive.

"I fear you are overheated, child," said her aunt tartly. "Do go up and wash your face and hands to rid them of aromas from the stable."

Mercy colored even deeper, murmured, "Yes, Aunt," and fled up the staircase to her room.

Kate and Mr. Macnaghten had continued to Sir Roland's manor, but the three who had entered Mrs. Beecham's parlor—Charlotte, the young duke, and Sir Roland—were in various conditions of indignation.

"I must compliment you, Mrs. Beecham, on your niece's skill at riding and her ladylike grace both in and out of the saddle," said Sir Roland with a strong note in his voice that quite took Mrs. Beecham's speech away.

"Yes," said Charlotte quickly, "you must be proud of her! Such competence! Such poise!"

A series of dismayed, indignant, puzzled, and angry expressions flowed across Cousin Maude's face. "Er—" she said doubtfully. "But too much attention to someone so young can cause—"

"No younger than I was when I took charge of my brother and his castle," Charlotte reminded. "Nearly eighteen, is she not?"

"Well, yes, I suppose she must be something like that," admitted Mercy's aunt. "But not out, you remember, and rather immature, I feel."

"On the contrary," drawled Sir Roland, "I found her sweetly poised. Cleone has only to give her a few hints about beaux."

Cleone's mouth fell open.

"I am sure," continued Sir Roland, "your daughter will know tips to share."

"Miss Mercy is delightful the way she is," added Sydney gamely. "We can all watch over her. Be happy to steer her right, if there is ever any doubt!"

The Guinn boys and the other young gentleman listened enthralled, and Mrs. Beecham, remembering their presence, hastily said, "Oh, yes. To be sure . . . Cleone, I expect the gentlemen would be willing to stay for whatever lunch Cook has prepared for us. Charlotte, are you free?"

"So kind," said Charlotte without much enthusiasm. "But Sydney and I are expected by Aunt Emilie."

"And I must go also," added Sir Roland.

They went out to their horses together, while the three very young beaux remained to try whatever Mrs. Beecham's cook could send out of the kitchen. They were dazzled by Cleone to the point of not caring much what they ate, as long as she was there to tease and flatter them.

Andy had taken Floral with him to the castle's stable. The other horses were waiting peacefully, tied to the Dower House fence. While Sydney boosted Charlotte to her saddle, Sir Roland mounted, touched his crop to his hat, and rode off toward the village.

Brother and sister turned homeward, not talking, somewhat subdued by the ending to their small adventure to Audley Knob.

Finally, as they neared the stable yard, Sydney said soberly, "Why has all suddenly gone flat?"

"I think," returned his sister hesitantly, "that Cousin Maude was angry that we did not include Cleone. I had warned you, you remember."

"But Cleone doesn't ride," he protested. "It was impossible to take a carriage up that hill!"

"Her mama does not think of that—only that she was *left out.*"

Andy was waiting to take their horses.

The duke slid down glumly and held up his arms for his sister. As they walked toward the castle, he muttered that he would take Cleone to look for trout soon. Charlotte rather thought she heard him say under his breath, "Spoiled chit!"

Perhaps it was too soon to expect his recovery from thralldom. He had known few young ladies, and this one had such long lashes and full bosom. *What parents of sons must go through!* thought Charlotte, giving little heed to the anxiety of parents who must struggle to find husbands for their beloved daughters. She did not think about herself at all, being content as mistress of Heritage Castle.

She went in search of Lady Emilie to pour out her troubles.

"Heritage used to be a place of peace," she complained. "I do not understand what has happened. One cannot blame Mercy, who is a very sweet and biddable girl. Cleone has always been pert—so pretty that one excuses her excesses. I am afraid the problem is that darling Syd is . . . oh, amiable as ever, but now growing beyond my control."

Aunt Emilie cleared her throat and clicked her knitting needles, but said nothing, letting Charlotte voice her uncertainties.

"Perhaps I should not say control. I promise you I do not mean—and never meant!—to live his life for him. Yet who does he have to guide him but me?"

Lady Emilie did not reply, for the answer was obvious.

"He has grown up," Charlotte admitted. "At least, almost. His manners are perfect, and his instincts good. I suppose I should trust his good sense, but—Auntie!—what does he know about the wiles of calculating females? The university will get him away from the tricks of Cleone—oh, would that Papa had never brought that Beecham family here! Poor Cousin John is unable to control those two ambitious females." She looked wryly at her aunt. "I hope you do not think I am horrid. Wherever Papa is, I know he depends on me, and I am so uncertain how to proceed."

Finding a temporary solution, she said, "I shall go up to my room and wash my face with very cold water, and then, perhaps, I will be able to think more clearly."

When the luncheon gong sounded a half hour later, the little family of three met in their dining parlor, and both Charlotte and her brother were restored to their more natural selves. Aunt Emilie never changed. Charlotte had calmed, at least outwardly, and Sydney was over his grouch. Indeed, he was practically never out of sorts, and his having been so was what triggered alarm in his sister.

Just as they finished eating, a message came from the stable that Floral had got a scratch on her foreleg that morning. Lady Charlotte immediately dispatched her brother to see about the matter, knowing he would not only take an interest in Floral's welfare, but also could very well judge the chief groom's treatment of the injury.

At the stable, just as in the castle, Lady Charlotte's orders were regularly accepted. She realized, however, that participation of the young duke in any area of the estate was always welcomed by the staff.

The good weather seemed likely to hold. Charlotte pleased herself by composing a letter to Mrs. Beecham, requesting Mercillia's company on a shopping tour to Hays two days later. She knew this difficult and jealous cousin would like to be included, and she took a shameful pleasure in leaving her out. Sir Roland might think her horrible. Still, she knew he would understand.

The reply came from Mercy herself, Mrs. Beecham presumably being too annoyed to write. Mercy would "dearly love" to make a trip with Lady Charlotte.

When Sydney heard they were going, he begged a seat in the carriage. "If I will crowd you, I will be happy to go on the box with our coachman. I have been meaning to visit a bootmaker to see about new tops."

Charlotte was not sure she wanted the added complication of Sydney. Then she swiftly determined he would be useful to amuse Mercy while she herself had a fitting at her modiste's.

"Yes, you may go," she said. "Perhaps you will lunch with us at The Grenadier."

She hoped Mrs. Beecham and Cleone would not be watching when Sydney handed Mercy into the carriage, but they would be sure to be doing so—if not from the open front door, certainly from the shelter of a window curtain.

I never used to worry about what the Beechams did or did not see, she thought. Why need she worry now? Oh, yes! Sir Roland was wise! It would be judicious to send Sydney as far away as Oxford. She would miss him sorely. Yes, and she and Aunt Emilie would be lonesome in the castle, but Sydney would be safer if removed from Cleone's small orbit.

Eight-thirty was set as the time of departure, and Lady Charlotte went to bed the night before, tolerably satisfied with the one-day plan of escape.

Ten

When Charlotte's maidservant drew back the curtains of her chamber on the day set for travel, only a very weak sun was showing. It did not spill into the room, and her ladyship sat up, saying, "Bleak day! Is our little trip to be ruined?"

"No, m'lady," replied the girl cheerfully. "It is quite early and the ground mist hasn't burned off."

"Are there rain clouds?"

"No, m'lady, just a lot of wispy white ones. My pa would say it is going to be cooler."

Lady Charlotte yawned and arose. "Perhaps that is just as well. One can be uncomfortably hot in a carriage if the windows must be closed. Pray, lay out a light cloak in case there is rain by the time we reach Hays."

Sydney was in good spirits when she found him at the breakfast table. He said, "Pooh! What is a little sprinkle?" when she mentioned the possibility. "Do not give it a thought. There are even fewer clouds to the north. If it rains here, we will be running away from it."

"I am not so poor-spirited as to mind a few drops," she said. "I am thinking about the spoiling of Mercy's escape."

"What escape?"

"From the doldrums of the Dower House."

He looked astonished, and sat back in his chair to examine her face to see if she was making some sort of joke. "The Dower House strikes me as a welcoming place."

"It welcomes a duke," his sister agreed, "but surely you do not think Mercy's reception there has been warm."

Sydney put a bit of kipper in his mouth and chewed it reflectively. "I will admit," he said slowly, "that Cousin John has his head in the clouds—or in a book. Cousin Maude sometimes snaps before she thinks. But certainly Cleone is the soul of good nature."

When you are there, thought Charlotte. She changed the subject. "You must come inside with Mercy and me if it rains."

"It won't. If I ride on the box with your coachman, he might let me handle the horses a bit . . . and you need not be afraid I will ditch you. Any one who likes horses does not take risks with their hurting a leg or something."

"Oh," laughed Lady Charlotte, "So it is the *horses* that concern you—not the safety of your sister and her guest!"

Sydney also laughed heartily and said, "Just so!"

Already the sky was clearing somewhat, and by the time Mercillia had been taken aboard, there was some evidence that the weather was going to turn fine. Mercy's piquant face was aglow. They traveled north through the village at a gentle pace, and when the bridge over the brook had been crossed, the coachman flicked his team into a good trot, which did not excite the duke, but kept the ladies from bouncing uncomfortably. On one level stretch the groom permitted his lord and master to demonstrate his ability to tool a four-in-hand. The ladies, inside, did not suspect potential danger, for they were deep in a discussion of French laces, of which Mercy knew a great deal, having made several visits to France.

When Mercy's mama had been quoted more than once, Charlotte easily found openings for simple questions about the Pope family. Mama and Papa, Mercy confided, had met at Bath, near which Mama and Aunt Maude had lived. They fell into love. It was like a novel! Papa had brought his father there to try the waters, in hopes that they would improve his poor health.

Grandfather was *very well off* and might have opposed a marriage, but he quite doted on Mama, just as Papa did.

"Was that not romantic?" Mercy concluded.

"Oh, very," agreed Lady Charlotte. "Do you resemble your mama?"

Mercy said she did, and Charlotte felt that she had the answer to all that puzzled her. No wonder Maude Beecham was jealous of this girl and so ambitious for her own daughter!

Where, exactly, Cleone got her pretty face was not clear, although both Cousin Maude and Cousin John did have normal faces which may have combined fortuitously in Cleone. Cleone's calculating ways (yes, that was how Charlotte thought of them) stemmed undoubtedly from her ambitious mother.

She became conscious that Mercy was waiting for comment from her, looking at her expectantly. She said, "Er—yes. Acquaintance with *you* makes me think that I would find your parents most delightful."

"Well, they really are loves," said their daughter. "Mama is quite as enthusiastic as Papa about ancient ruins. She makes beautiful little sketches of ones they visit."

"Do you draw, too?" asked Charlotte.

Mercy shook her head. "No. I cook."

"Cook!"

"Yes. I create interesting dishes for Mama and Papa. At least, they seem to like them. Mama says it is wise to take advantage of learning things wherever one goes—like cooking the French way in France. We have had several very artistic cooks there, and they have been wonderfully kind in showing me little secrets of sauces and cakes. Cooking, you see, is an art in France."

Lady Charlotte mentioned that she had heard French chefs were temperamental, waving cleavers and such things, but Mercy went into trills of laughter.

"They like to be thought so. The chefs are very susceptible to admiration. One has only to say '*oo*-la-la' when tasting something—which is always good, so one need not pretend. They are always willing to share their secrets, though sometimes a bit impatient if one confuses a *rouelle* with a *rouget,* or some such thing. Papa is very fond of French food."

"What about good roast beef?" asked Charlotte.

"He orders that in England."

The time passed quickly as they talked, and both were surprised when the carriage swung into the yard of The Grenadier. The duke himself opened the door for them to step down, Mercy saying no more and leaving all talk with him to Lady Charlotte.

"I have a fitting with my modiste," Charlotte said. "She is expecting me. Can you spare us a bit more time, Sydney? Mercy would be bored while I am being pinned up. Can you take time to point out things of interest while I am busy?"

"Yes, indeed. I will be happy to escort her up and down the main street to see which shops are promising."

He and Mercillia accompanied her to the doorway of her fashion establishment and arranged to rejoin her in forty-five minutes.

"I do not know if you will be much impressed with what Hays has to offer—not after travels with your parents," the duke said, offering his arm.

Coloring faintly, Mercy placed her hand upon it. "Sometimes the smallest villages have unusual items," she said. "Mama used to say 'touch with your eyes,' and if I discovered something special, I had only to tell her, and she or Papa would buy it."

"Why are you not spoiled?" Sydney asked, for he thought her not the least demanding.

She blushed more deeply. "I do not mean they satisfied every whim. Neither would buy anything they thought foolish. They encouraged me to learn about values."

By virtue of always having the best of things—because it was customary for a duke to do so—Sydney had a fair sense of values. He was interested in her comments as they examined shop windows along the main street of Hays.

Just as his eyes were drawn to a passing red curricle with gilt paint on its wheels, he heard Mercy give a little gasp. Her eyes were fixed upon a modest window in which was displayed a Hat, a singularly beautiful Hat. It was a straw bonnet with brim neither so broad as to impede a wearer's view, nor so narrow as to be insignificant. About the crown were artfully twisted gossamer lengths of fabric in several shades of green, with a single one of blue intertwined to lend interest to all. The lengths were gently knotted at the back to float downward past a wearer's shoulders.

Sydney was inclined to look less at hats and more at the females wearing them, especially if they were young and pretty.

"You like it?" he asked.

"It is splendid," she breathed.

"Then you must buy it. Let us go into the shop."

"Oh, I could not! It must be very expensive."

"Why do you think so?" he asked.

She said, "Because it is the *only* hat in the window."

Sydney thought about that for a moment and agreed that could be a sign. "But this is Hays—a small town—not known to be fashionable. You have money? I don't think this will be exorbitant."

Mercy, well supplied by her papa with crisp notes, allowed herself to be led into the shop, where a woman came forward to offer them seats.

"Miss Pope would like to try on the bonnet in the window," Sydney said firmly.

"Certainly. Is it not beautiful like the lady?" said the shopkeeper in a faint accent, which Sydney would not be surprised to find assumed. But Mercy began at once to prattle in French and the woman responded volubly in the same language.

The hat was set upon Mercy's head, and Sydney said "Parfay!" in his imperfect French, which made both ladies laugh.

All three knew Mercy would buy the bonnet, but first she must examine herself from every angle with a mirror.

"Mademoiselle was made for my *chapeau,"* said the proprietor. "I should give it to her, but—*helas!*—it is my bread and butter."

Sydney, studying her, thought she might be younger than she endeavored to look. It seemed a poor way to earn a living, one hat at a time. Perhaps there was an unseen "benefactor" in the wings . . . but he could not suggest such a thing to Mercillia. "Buy it, Miss Pope. Charlotte will be wondering what is keeping us."

So Mercy paid, and the bonnet was tucked tenderly amid tissues in a box. They said "Goodbye" and *"Adieu"* and hurried up the street. Lady Charlotte was just saying farewell to her dressmaker.

"We bought a beautiful bonnet," said Sydney.

"A *chapeau,"* corrected Mercy, laughing, and looking particularly pretty in her happiness.

Charlotte said, "Let me guess. From Mlle. Galatoire?"

"How did you know?"

"Because no one else in Hays can fashion such a thing. I am glad you bought something from her. She needs help, for she came as a governess to Viscount Dacrond's daughter, but the viscountess turned her off in a fit of jealousy."

"I should think London would be a more profitable place for a shop," the duke said.

"Yes, but also more expensive to establish. Here she at least has the support of several families who know the horrid propensities of Dacrond." She smiled reassuringly at Mercillia. "Have nothing to do with him, Syd. Are we keeping you from your new boots? Will an hour be long enough for you? Good. Then meet us at The Grenadier."

Sydney turned back to his bootmaker, whose shop they had passed, and Lady Charlotte led Mercy down a short side street to visit a small lace shop, where they could compare laces and ribbons with French ones that Mercy had seen on her travels.

There were no clouds at Hays, no suggestion of rain. When they had visited all the shops that might interest a lady, it still being early for meeting the duke, they strolled around the town green and peeped for a few moments into the village church, part of which was heavy masonry that dated from Norman times.

"How far away does the horrid viscount live?" asked Mercy. "Is Mlle. Galatoire free to worship here?"

"I expect Mademoiselle is a Catholic, being French. As to Dacrond, his place is five miles further along, nearer to Market Waddel. I doubt that he ever comes here . . . even for the bootmaker that Sydney thinks is so fine."

"His Grace always seems splendid," Mercy said admiringly.

Charlotte looked amused at this tribute. "He is no dandy, but a perfect gentleman, I hope."

"Yes, indeed," agreed Mercy hastily, remembering that her mother had warned, "Make no personal remarks!"

During their meal at The Grenadier, Mercy was quiet, answering when addressed and looking in good spirits, yet not putting herself forward in any way. It seemed, to Charlotte, quite a change from Cousin Maude or Cleone.

All three ate heartily, for somehow travel seemed to have increased their appetites. Or perhaps it was the stimulation of new surroundings—or The Grenadier's excellent food. No Viscount Dacrond came to ogle the ladies or snatch away Mlle. Galatoire's box with the precious bonnet.

On the way home Sydney again rode beside their coachman. The ladies, inside, though drowsy from fresh air, sunshine, and an excellent meal, chatted companionably. Mercy, who had been so silent during the threesome at lunch, conversed easily, and Lady Charlotte was forced to the conclusion that she had been intimidated by the presence of a duke. No conversation could be heard from the driver's seat.

Rumbling of planks, as they passed over the brook at Fallford, aroused everyone, and the carriage slowed to avoid the slaughter of dogs and children as it rolled through the village and turned into the Dower House yard.

Sydney jumped down, like a good servant, to open the carriage door and assist Miss Pope to the ground.

"Here is your precious box," he said, receiving it from Lady Charlotte, and handing it to the girl.

She thanked her benefactors, adding a smile for the coachman who was looking down from his perch.

"A sweet girl," Lady Charlotte said to her brother, when he had climbed in beside her for the last lap up the driveway. "Did you have difficulty making her talk?"

"Not at all," he replied.

"She was so quiet at lunch."

"Perhaps you intimidated her, Charlotte."

"I? Why, she spoke quite freely to me in the carriage!"

Sydney chuckled. "I tell you what it is: been taught to hold up her end of a conversation, but not put herself forward in company. Restful!"

Charlotte decided he was right, pleased that he could appreciate another sort of girl from the one he knew so well. She concluded that she must make some effort to introduce him to a variety of acceptable damsels; she would call upon neighboring families, some farther afield than the Guinns, to see what daughters might be invited to visit at the castle. Being both mother and father to a comely duke was more complex, *difficult,* than she had ever stopped to consider. Would Sir Roland be able to advise in this? He was no parent! Was, in fact, somewhat at a stand in dealing with his own sister and her suitor. She must remember to ask if he had made enquiries about Macnaghten. How did one go about this?

Even with such worries troubling her mind, she was able to feel that it had been a satisfactory day and a pleasant one, which is what she told Aunt Emilie when Sydney had gone off on affairs of his own, and the ladies were able to share a quiet teatime.

"I am certainly curious to meet the parents that have reared such a charming daughter as Mercillia," she said. "She does not thrust herself forward as one or two I might name, and she has such—such sense of decorum. Why must the girls that flutter their eyelashes and pout be the ones to attract young gentlemen?"

Auntie made rumbles to signify amusement and continued to knit without dropping a stitch. Charlotte watched the smooth rhythm of the needles, but she was not thinking of them.

"Sir Roland," she said, "has a problem also, although it is different from mine. His sister is quite old enough to decide things for herself—and, anyway, he would never force her into matrimony, unless she is willing—I mean, unless it is her choice. I really cannot like to bother him with my worries, when he has ones of his own. It is something of a shock to me to find that Sydney is of an age for romantic involvement. That Cleone! So pretty, so—so predatory, and Sydney cannot *see* it."

Aunt Emilie switched her knitting and started back across another row. She and Charlotte exchanged smiles.

"I suppose you are thinking that I act like an old mother hen," Charlotte continued. "Someone must guide Sydney, for he has had no experience of females except Cleone. Do you think Oxford will fill his mind? Sir Roland thinks he needs new places or something to give his mind a new direction."

She was not able to say more, for the duke came in at that point and threw himself into a chair.

"I say!" he exclaimed. "It is the oddest thing. I ate a large lunch in Hays, but already I am hungry again. Do you think travel does that?"

Aunt Emilie was smiling fondly, and Charlotte laughed. "That and fresh air," she said. "I feel the same way, which tells me that I must go up and change for dinner. Tell Auntie your first experience in buying a bonnet."

As she went out the door, she heard Sydney say, "There was only one in a window, but I could tell Mercy was very taken with it, so I said, 'Let's go in.' "

Eleven

The next morning there was rain, as had been threatened the previous day. Mostly, it was a disobliging drizzle, which Sydney viewed with disgust. He would not be able to take Cleone to look for trout in the brook, nor walk about the pond. But he threw on a cloak and trudged down the hill to make peace with her.

Charlotte watched him go, proud of his gentlemanly instincts, yet fretting that the weather would keep other beaux away and allow Cleone to direct all her wiles toward Sydney. She hoped Mercillia would be present, for that would at least keep Syd's attentions divided. Her father could not have guessed, when he brought the chaplain's family to Heritage, that the chubby little Beecham girl would grow to be a bewitching young lady who might spell all sorts of trouble for his son and heir. Nor had Papa lived to see this happen. But Charlotte had, and she was as anxious as any doting parent might be. The Beechams had been family for so long that even Charlotte thought they belonged at Heritage. Still, Sydney's whole future was at risk.

It did not occur to her that such worry was not the usual lot of sisters. Parents might suffer this same anguish, but it was *their* role to cope with problem offspring, not the place of an unwed girl who was only twenty-four.

Fortunately Sydney had not realized that he, a duke, need take no orders from a sister. Nor was she yet aware that she need not be responsible for every breath he drew. The older he grew, the less her opinions would carry weight. It was inevitable that Sydney should soon discover that a duke need answer to no one.

At the present time, however, such was his amiable nature, that he did not think to defy Charlotte's opinions . . . or recognize Cleone's efforts to bend him to her own wishes.

Halfway down the slope he met Sir Roland riding up it.

"Horrid drizzle," growled Sydney. "Even under trees there is no escape, for the drops come through."

"Why walk out in it?" asked Sir Roland reasonably.

"Well, you are out," said the duke.

"Yes," said Sir Roland, "but I am not grumbling."

Sydney was not an ill-humored fellow. In a milder tone he said, "The truth is, my reception at the Dower House may not be too cordial. Daresay you saw Cousin Maude and her daughter were cool when we returned from the Knob th'other day."

"In a pet," Sir Roland agreed. "All the more reason not to grovel . . . sure to make the chill last longer."

Sydney looked surprised. "You may be right."

"Do the pretty, but do not stay long," advised Sir Roland. He nudged his mount with a heel and continued toward the castle.

"He may be right," muttered the duke. Stiffening his spine, he walked briskly to the Dower House, where he was admitted by a young maidservant and told the ladies were in the parlor. She did not say that Mr. Todd and young Alexander Guinn were also present, but they were.

It was not in Mrs. Beecham to be cold to a duke. She welcomed him graciously, while Cleone smiled alluringly with just enough coolness to torment. He was glad to have a pleasant greeting from Mercy and the men.

"Hear you went on the Knob the other day," said Alexander, not realizing this was an unwelcome topic. "Lucky thing. The trail will be slick today."

"Yes," agreed Sydney, "and the view of no depth at all.

Cleone, we will have to wait for dry weather before we look for trout in the brook."

Mr. Todd said, "Never say there are *trout!"*

"It's a rumor," Sydney said. "I haven't seen any. In any case, if they are there, they will be hiding from the rain—"

" 'Fraid of getting wet!" guffawed Alexander.

Mercy clapped a hand to her mouth, but Cleone and her mama only looked bored, so Sydney said, "The first clear day we will walk over, won't we, Cleone?"

And of course she said, "Yes."

By degrees Cleone and her mama thawed a little. It was not their intention to offend the duke, only punish him a wee bit.

Mr. Todd pulled a chair near to his hostess and sat down to engage her in polite conversation, which left the young people to cluster at one end of the room. Mercy mostly listened to the trivial chatter and managed to maintain an air of interest in trout, crops ahead of schedule, "hordes" of children in the village asking to be run down by horses, and games of croquet. Nothing was said of riding today.

When some mention was made of archery, Sydney asked Mercillia if she had ever seen this ancient sport. To his surprise she said she had tried it.

"Only as a game. My papa said women were not meant to wield swords, or to come into close bodily contact with daggers and such things. But, given a bow of suitably light weight, and steadiness of draw, they might be formidable."

"Fight?" cried Cleone in scandalized accents.

"Well, I never did *that,"* Mercy said. "It can be a game, you know, with a straw target."

"There are bows in our armory," Sydney said. "I never thought of ladies drawing them. May be too brittle now, after long disuse. Ever try archery, Alexander?"

"No-o," the young gentleman replied. "I've seen contests of it at village festivals. Don't know how they can manage to aim the things up in the air and then hit a target set up yards away at the ground."

Mercy did not offer to explain, not liking to be a center of attention, while Cleone, who always wished to have attention, said, "Men like such lethal things. I have seen village men hitting each other and rolling in the dust. Ugh! Then everyone *cheers* and they go in the pub for *ale.*"

"It is only sport, you see," Sydney explained.

"Better than bad feelings bottled up," Mercy added. "Or so my papa says."

"I cannot like to see fights of any sort," Cleone declared.

"No-no. Not for delicate females," said Alexander quickly, making plain that she deserved better amusement. "What would you say to a pik-nik in our orchard? Mama is planning one for Miss Roland and her visitor."

Cleone clapped her hands, and Mercy, from whom attention was turned, fell silent.

"We will have to wait for the ground to dry out and trees to stop dripping. However, Father is a good weather prophet, and he says this drizzle is not going to last long."

"But will not the ground stay wet?" asked Cleone.

"Father says not," said Alexander. "The orchard slopes slightly and drains well. Sorry we don't have a pond or brook to offer."

As Cleone had a pond to see every day of her life, if she wanted, and as novelty was always enjoyable, she said gaily, "An orchard does sound nice—and it will be shady."

Alexander said, "Oh, see what I have done! Given away Mama's surprise. You must not tell her."

The duke spoke for all them, saying, "We will be clams. I hope Squire Guinn is right. Rain is a bore."

All eyes turned to the windows, upon which water was pattering gently and obscuring the view. They perfectly well knew that without rain crops would wither away, but at the moment *boredom* seemed much more depressive, and they were glad to have a novel party to anticipate.

"I hope this rain will end soon," sighed Cleone, who never concerned herself with crops.

Sydney said it should. "There are no black clouds. Notice how light it has grown. A good deal more so just since I have been here . . . or is it the company of pretty damsels that has made it seem that way?"

His sister would have been astonished at this gallantry. To Cleone, it was what she had come to expect from her beaux. Her mood began to improve, so much so that she began to laugh and tease her two gallants. When, after some minutes, Alexander noted that it was time he was expected at home and the rain seemed to be letting up, she told him goodbye blithely and turned her complete attention to the duke.

Mercy, noting she was neither needed nor wanted, withdrew to her aunt's side, where she was not particularly welcomed by that lady. Fortunately, Mr. Todd demonstrated his gentility by rising and offering his chair. However, as her aunt had no smile for her, Mercy said she had left a book unfinished and, if they would excuse her, she would go along to the library.

The chaplain was there, with his nose in a book, and he raised his eyes for a moment to see who had entered, but as his mind was still on the tome in his hands, and as Mercy curled into a deep chair and closed her eyes, he soon forgot her.

In the drawing room, the one person who might have given some thought to Mercillia was busy appeasing Cleone. He extracted her promise to ride with him when Mrs. Guinn gave her pik-nik; he would, he said, bring a curricle and his most showy pair, with a tiger up behind them to lend distinction, all of which Miss Cleone Beecham found to her satisfaction.

For a young duke, raised by an adoring sister under the benign eye of a maiden aunt, Sydney was remarkably unspoiled. His attitude toward everyone, from boot-boy to Sir Roland (the nearest friend of title), was considerate; his nature was very good, with the result that he was served willingly.

Cleone, on the other hand, was forgiven much because of

her beauty. Pets and pouts were tolerated, though they did not add to her consequence. Unbeknown to the girl's mother and Lady Charlotte, Cleone's campaign to capture the duke was watched by every servant of the castle and every villager of Fallford, though there was no talk about it.

Charlotte would be horrified if she guessed, for she supposed only Aunt Emilie, Sir Roland, and herself were aware of the danger.

Certainly Sydney was not.

Charlotte's chief worry was that her brother should recognize Cleone's aspiration and be flattered by it. However, for the present, Sydney, in his inexperience, supposed Cleone's coy manners were simply the way girls behaved.

But now Mercillia had come into his ken—intelligent, serene, self-effacing, without artifices—to confuse his understanding of the delicate gender.

Sometimes he did not understand what Cleone meant by her widening of eyes and tossing of head. They were certainly interesting—though he did not always know how to respond—and they held his attention. She had pretty *curves,* too, and a way of making him feel admired, which was irresistible.

With Alexander's going away, Sydney remembered Sir Roland's advice: "Do the pretty, but do not stay long." Well, he had done that, and enjoyed doing it. A profound respect for Sir Roland led him now to say, "You must be wondering if I have a home and a seat opposite my sister at meals. Look. The rain is giving me a chance to get up the hill without a wetting. Good day, Cousin Maude—Cleone—Mr. Todd."

The elder gentleman lurched to his feet.

"Walk out with me," the duke said, without thinking that his own word would be law, but it was. He still had not learned that the wishes of a duke—himself—must rule, though Mr. Todd said farewells to the ladies and accompanied him outdoors.

At the driveway they separated, one going to warm himself with a glass of wine before the small grate in his own parlor, and the other to report at the castle that Cleone was all graciousness and seemed ready to walk or drive with him whenever he might propose it.

This was not news to Charlotte. She said calmly, "I am glad you did not linger. Cook has luncheon almost ready. There is to be a fish soufflé."

He exclaimed, "Not trout!"

"No, of course not. The fishmonger brought salmon, and we must use it up while it is still fresh."

"Quite right," agreed Sydney. "I suppose we will have salmon in various forms for the next meal or two."

"Yes," she said. "A change from chicken."

"Keep us from cackling, I daresay," he approved.

Aunt Emilie was halfway down the stairs when the gong sounded for lunch. They waited for her at the door to their dining parlor and went in together to a pleasant repast of soufflé and mixed green salad.

"I did not see anyone from Sir Roland's manor at Beecham's place," Sydney said.

"No. The three of them were calling upon Auntie and me."

"I met Sir Roland on the driveway as I went down. He was alone then."

Charlotte explained that the others had come shortly afterwards. "Mr. Macnaghten brought Kate in his carriage. We had a pleasant visit. How was yours?"

Sydney hesitated. "Satisfactory. Alexander Guinn was there, but he did not linger, and Mercy went off somewhere."

"No one else?"

"Todd, chatting with Mrs. Beecham about nothing of any consequence, as far as I know. Cleone was cool at first—blaming me for *her* not riding—but warmed up before I left. Are all females easily offended?"

"Of course not."

"Well, we are back on good terms. The first good day we are to walk to the brook. Mrs. Guinn is planning a pik-nik, and I contracted to take Cleone in my curricle. I'll have m'tiger wear his red coat. She will like that, don't you suppose?"

Charlotte supposed Cleone would like any vehicle if Sydney drove it and she rode in splendor beside him. His sister saw that she must make some plan for transporting herself.

It was several days before an invitation came from Mrs. Guinn. By then the rain had definitely blown away and the soil was drying. Along with the sunshine came Mr. Macnaghten to offer a ride in his carriage.

"March says Sydney will be sure to escort Miss Beecham, and her parents will come in the chaplain's gig. You must let me call for you," he said.

"But I am out of your way," she said, feeling an imposition, but appreciating the offer.

"Now, don't deny me the pleasure," he insisted. "Tell you what—I will come for you first, and we can have a chat on the way back to pick up Sir Roland and Miss March. That way she will have less time to muss her skirts! Ladies fret about things like that, don't they?"

Charlotte was amused. As if a few extra minutes in a carriage would matter to Kate! But she understood Macnaghten's effort to make her easy about taking him out of his way, so she said he was very thoughtful. Aunt Emilie, who was keeping her respectable by sitting with them, nodded approval.

"If Lady Emilie is invited also, why, I will just sit with my coachman when we pick up the Marches," he added, but Charlotte explained that her aunt seldom ventured out.

Though Mr. Macnaghten may have thought it was odd for an alert-seeming lady to go nowhere and never say anything, he did not indicate this. He simply wished to be of service to Lady Charlotte, it seemed.

What a pleasant gentleman he was!

Charlotte accepted his offer, thinking this way she would have a few minutes to be private with him and find how his suit progressed.

Naturally, he did not discuss personal affairs in Aunt Emilie's presence. If he had been accepted, Charlotte thought he might have reported *that.* Since he had not done so, she could only assume Kate still kept him dangling. But his spirits were good. He must hold some hope. And as Charlotte liked him very much, she would continue to hope for his winning Kate.

When Mr. Macnaghten had gone, Charlotte said warmly, "That is a charming man, Auntie. Do you not think so? If Kate March does not mean to accept him, surely she would have sent him away. It is all a mystery. I wonder what Sir Roland has been able to discover about him. If it were anything bad, surely he would have sent him off post haste."

Then she thought—though she did not say this aloud—that Kate could not be set against him or *she* would have sent him away! Trying to see into people's minds was like reading a novel where pages were missing.

Charlotte was careful not to indicate to her aunt that a few moments (walking the carriage horses) would allow time for private communication between Macnaghten and herself. If this was a clever plan on his part, he must have manipulated both Kate and her brother also.

She did not even consider that the gentleman had any other reason for desiring a private talk with herself. He had made his interest in Kate March quite plain from the first.

So Kate was older than Macnaghten? He did not seem to care a whit for that. Nor did he appear to have any concern for what Kate's dowry might be. That Charlotte's own might be greater seemed of no interest to this gentleman. If he had been making up to herself, she would have doubted his sincerity for sure!

She sighed.

Aunt Emilie paused in her ever-present needlework, but being reassured by what she saw in her niece's face, resumed her knitting.

"People," said Lady Charlotte, "are sometimes difficult to understand."

Twelve

As soon as the duke awoke, he realized that the spell of damp weather had ended and Cleone would be expecting a stroll.

"Morning, Hoad," he said cheerfully to his valet. "Just the day for a long walk."

Thus clued to his master's plans, Hoad laid out black Wellington boots and buff kerseymere trousers which tied under the instep. There was a brown coat, a figured claret waistcoat, white shirt with modest collar points, and a creamy cravat.

Young gentlemen of the neighborhood copied Sydney's styles, though he was unaware of this and gave little thought to it. It was Hoad, therefore, who set the fashions in Fallford.

When Charlotte joined her brother at the breakfast table, she knew at once that he was dressed to squire Cleone somewhere, and, sure enough, he said blithely, "I promised Cleone a walk to the brook on the first dry day. This is a perfect one, isn't it? Astonishing how a few wet days can make one forget how great the balm of sunshine!"

"On people as well as crops," she added.

"Lord, yes. We will go through the village to save climbing up a slope and down again. Will you come with us?"

Charlotte thought that if she was invited, no tête-à-tête was planned, so she declined, citing vague duties, and when a clock chimed ten, she went to the door to watch him start down the slope. The whole length of this was visible except the last part, where trees at the Dower House hid the gate to the village. He was halfway down when Sir Roland appeared on his favorite hack; the two exchanged greetings as they passed, but neither halted, so Charlotte waited at the open door for Sir Roland to come up to her.

"Good morning," he called as he reached the circle of gravel before her. "I am coming in to wait while you put on riding clothes, since it is too fine a day for you to stay shut up in a stone pile!" He jumped down, flipped his reins around a convenient post, and came forward, smiling.

"You must put on your riding dress immediately, Lady Charlotte," he said. "This is no day to be indoors. Macnaghten is taking Kate to Hays in his carriage to buy something-or-other that she seems to need—probably a headache powder, or some such thing. Who knows? Perhaps they only want to enjoy the air. Will you believe this? She is taking her maid along as chaperone, so poor Macnaghten will have no chance to propose again!"

Charlotte was laughing. "Then you are not needed to act the chaperone? By all means we must have a ride! Come in and have a sherry or an ale or something, while I change my dress."

Sir Roland said he wanted nothing except to get her into the fresh air, so she flew upstairs while he went into the library to glance at newspapers.

She was quick, and they soon set out on horseback, at first idly roaming meadows.

"I have several bits of news for you," Sir Roland said. "This is a chance to talk privately."

Charlotte said she had suspected that.

"For one thing," he continued, "I have had two answers from Oxford suggesting times for me to bring Sydney for an interview, yet how can I do this with Macnaghten still dangling? We would have to be gone several days. Why is Kate so—so uncooperative? Why can she not make up her mind?"

"I do not know," she answered.

"Can you explain her thinking?"

Lady Charlotte shook her head. "She has not even mentioned the situation to me."

"So what do I do about leaving the area?"

She thought a moment. "Why not take Mr. Macnaghten with you?"

"With me?"

"Yes. He took Sydney away to races for several days. Kate might even miss him."

"I hadn't thought of that. Very good! We will see. Let us canter here."

"Here" was an idle meadow, so they breezed around it, horses enjoying the exercise as much as riders. Then they left the field for a shaded area.

"Another thing on my mind," Sir Roland said, "is this business of Sydney and Cleone. Is it still worrying you?"

"Yes," said Charlotte, losing the glow brought by their romp in the meadow. "It is a difficult matter. I hesitate to speak to Cousin John—or Maude—and cause bad feelings in the family. I wish I thought Cleone had *some* strengths of character, but I fear there are only ones of self-will."

"No doubt about that!"

Charlotte was silent for a moment. "One way or another, life is certainly going to change."

"Yes, but you must not look upon Sydney's going to Oxford as a bad thing. It will help doubly by getting him away from the minx and enriching his education and experience."

"Sydney is with her—Cleone—now. Something about a walk to look for trout in our brook."

The brook in question tumbled gently off Audley land, and ran along a gully for a short distance before bending to cross beneath the road at Fallford's northern end. There was a pretty pool at the bend, and just upstream of this a footbridge connected the Hays road with Audley woodlands. It was a sweet spot, though whether any trout swam there was a matter of some doubt.

Troublesome Cleone had spent a restless night. The bright

morning that she rose to greet meant the duke would surely be coming for her, and she hoped to make the most of this time with him, before he could get away to Oxford.

Mama had said she must be clever. So . . .

Upon rising, she chose a reticule, old and worn, but kept because it had bright purple beads on it that she had thought might be useful sometime—like today. Inside she tucked a handkerchief, for a lady always carried one. Then she scrabbled through her jewelry box, at last selecting a silver pin which was shaped like a full-blown rose and adding it to the reticule.

These arrangements made, she took from her wardrobe a simple muslin frock—last year's, but a becoming shade of blue. With luck, her mama would not notice and wonder at such a choice when Sydney was coming.

Then she went down to breakfast and distracted Mrs. Beecham by asking about Mrs. Guinn's pik-nik.

"Yes, we are invited," Mrs. Beecham said. "Yes, we will go." She might spurn the Guinns when planning her own parties, but was not above going where the duke had been invited. "After all, the duke has asked to take you in his curricle." Her voice was resonant with satisfaction.

When they had finished their meal, Cleone reminded her mother that Sydney was to walk with her today. "I will start on, Mama. Tell him I will meet him at the footbridge."

"Shouldn't you wait until he comes, dear?" asked Mrs. Beecham.

"I want to walk slowly," Cleone explained. "He has long legs and will catch up with me."

"Oh, yes," agreed her mama. "Much better not to trot so fast as to become overheated."

Thereupon, little Miss Beecham tripped out the door, through the castle gate, and into the village street, with a shabby reticule (unnoticed by her mama) attached at her waist, and a villager hat hung from her arm.

There were curtsies and bows, and pulling of forelocks

enough to please her as she made her way toward the brook. Once past the carriage bridge and pool, she turned onto the footbridge and looked into the water. The pool, she could see, had a bottom of flat rock, and was only ten or so inches deep. Perfect for her purposes.

She detached the reticule from her waist, watching for Sydney's approach. There were several trees here, but she was able to see him before he saw her. With a little cry of distress she tossed her reticule into the water and was hanging upon the handrail when he joined her.

"Oh, Sydney," she cried. "I have dropped my reticule!"

"Into the pool? Yes, I see it. Has it purple beads?"

"Yes. Oh, how careless of me! I was leaning over the rail to hunt for trout." She looked up at him piteously.

The duke said confidently, "I will fish it out. Will water ruin it?"

"Well, I do not *think* so," she replied with pretty distress. "I hope not, for it is my fav—"

To ignore this appeal was not possible for the duke, who murmured, "Let me see . . ." and strode across the footbridge to Audley land, where he began untying his trouser straps from beneath his boots and then hopping on first one foot and then the other to yank off footwear.

Cleone followed slowly from the bridge, murmuring inspiring things like, "Oh, Sydney, you are wrinkling your fine trousers!" and "How clever of you!" and "I am such a trouble to you!"

"Nonsense," he retorted, vigorously rolling up his trouser legs, which were sure to give Hoad palpitations when he saw the result. Then he also ruthlessly shoved up his right sleeve, waded into the brook, and began to look for the reticule that needed to be rescued.

Although clearly visible from the elevation of the bridge, the reticule was not easily detected now, for here were just enough small ripples to reflect changing lights. Even the purple beads did not wink at him.

"Oh, Sydney! You are splashing your clothes. You must come out," she pleaded charmingly. "I feel so guilty."

He grinned and replied that the water felt delightful. "Don't know why I haven't waded more often." Thereupon, he began to churn about, as a village child might have done.

Cleone started to laugh and clap her hands at such antics.

"It is not fair," she complained. "Boys have such fun. Is the water cold?"

"Cool," he said, moving around easily on the smooth rock bottom, loose stones having been long ago carried away for fence material or chimneys. "I cannot see your reticule." His own splashing had made this more difficult.

Cleone, who cared nothing for the lost purse, cried, "It is not *fair!*" and then "Look the other way!"

When obeyed, she promptly stripped off her shoes and stockings, and catching up her skirt, stepped into the water.

"Oo-o-o!" she cried, which of course made Sydney turn his head to see the entrancing sight of laughing eyes, bunched skirts, and dimpled knees.

Just about anyone from the village, Dower House, or castle would have been shocked had they seen such abandon in a gently reared maiden. Fortunately, no one came along the Hays road at that time.

But on the hill above, where a bridle path branched to Audley Knob, Lady Charlotte and Sir Roland had halted, debating which way to go. Charlotte, with an idle glance through a gap in the leaves, saw the game below and gasped.

Sir Roland, turning his eyes the same way, muttered, "Good God!" He grabbed Charlotte's rein to keep her from plunging down the trail. "Let me handle this," he said sternly. "You will only make a mull. Go home. And guard your tongue. I'll return Sydney to you, and the chit to her father. High time he was ruling that house!"

Charlotte nodded mutely and turned back, while Sir Roland moved down the slope, the laughter of the young people and the slush of the water in the pool hiding the sounds of his approach. They neither saw nor heard him until he was upon them.

Sydney gaped, and the little temptress dropped her skirts to eddy about her in the water.

"Come out at once!" commanded Sir Roland, dismounting.

"Wading. We were only wading," Sydney said, as he sloshed to the bank, red with mortification, for he knew such childish activity would reflect upon the dignity of a duke, though it had all begun in the simple—reasonable—rescue of Cleone's reticule.

Cleone, somewhat tangled in wet skirts, hurried onto the bank, where she stood dripping.

"Thank God, you were not seen," said Sir Roland. "You are not children any longer, though such behavior could not be more childish."

"It was the reticule," Sydney explained. "Cleone dropped it from the bridge, and I was trying to fetch it for her."

Sir Roland said, "I see." And he *did.* "Why was this young woman in the water also?"

She looked sulky and replied nothing.

Sir Roland then ordered the duke to put on his shoes and start walking. "You will have to go home by the hill path, so as not to be seen," he said sternly, adding, as the duke endeavored to roll down his trouser legs and wipe his feet upon them so as to be able to get on his boots, "I will allow five minutes for a head start, in order that you and Cleone not be seen together in such a disgraceful state. We must all go by the path, not to be noticed by villagers."

Cleone had begun to wring out sections of her skirts, so that they no longer dripped, only hung wrinkled and darkened by wetness. Sir Roland said nothing to her, making plain that he understood her part in this debacle.

When Sydney had disappeared into the trees upon the hill, Sir Roland hoisted Cleone to a sideways perch on his saddle and handed up her slippers and stockings. Her hat lay forgotten where she had cast it.

Fortunately, no one from the village passed by, and when Sir Roland judged enough time had elapsed for Sydney's sufficient lead, he began to walk up hill with a firm hand below the horse's bit.

They did not see Sydney until they emerged from the woodland. He was some way ahead, approaching the castle, and did not look back. Sir Roland marched resolutely to the Dower House with a damsel who wore a pouty expression. He sent her upstairs to make herself presentable, and, himself, knocked upon the chaplain's study door.

Mr. Beecham was surprised to see him and half rose, only to be waved back to his chair.

"It has been my disagreeable—but fortunate—lot to come upon your daughter and His Grace *romping* in the brook."

The chaplain fell back with a gasp.

"Only romping, I am thankful to say," continued Sir Roland. "Sydney says that she had dropped her reticule into the water and he was trying to find it. Whether he saw it fall, or Cleone told him so, I do not know. At least it explains why he had shed his shoes and gone into the pool. What Cleone was doing in the water, holding her skirts above her knees, I leave you to discover."

"Merciful heaven!" moaned the chaplain, clapping a hand to his forehead.

Relenting a bit, Sir Roland added, "I do not hold Sydney at fault. He has had no experience with feminine—er, wiles, and in this case things went no farther than I have told you. No one saw them, except . . . no one came near the pool except me."

The chaplain said, "Thank God for that."

"Yes."

"What can have possessed my daughter? I have been in the habit of thinking her a little lady!"

"So she has seemed," agreed Sir Roland. "But I fear her mother aspires to a match with the duke and has encouraged that idea."

Mr. Beecham moaned faintly. "Little friends—from childhood."

"Yes, but not children now," said Sir Roland forcefully. "You must understand that Cleone can expect no match with the Duke of Audley." He was feeling somewhat tyrannical, but thought it was important to make matters plain before Mrs. Beecham got hold of her husband.

The poor gentleman, a faithful servant of the Church, shook his head distressfully. "Poor Maude! She had hoped Cleone to do better than she did with me. Yes, I can understand her dreams for our child." He sighed. "But what can I do now? Must I resign?"

"Not that, I think," the irate visitor said, relenting somewhat, for the problem was not Mr. Beecham's fault, except in allowing his wife to rule his household and indulge in improper ambitions which he had not suspected.

The chaplain sighed again. "Cleone is such a pretty little thing. I daresay she did not realize—"

But Sir Roland would not let this pass. "She realized, all right. Didn't I hear that your wife comes from the area of Bath? Is there no kin to whom you can send the girl for a while? Or a Bath Seminary, perhaps? That would be even better, for she would soon find she is *not* a princess and other young ladies have ambitions, too."

Mr. Beecham shook his head mournfully. "I have not the funds for that, and of relatives—there are none left."

Sir Roland buffeted him on the shoulder. "Well, do not despair. There will be some solution. I'll have a word with Lady Charlotte."

Cleone's papa looked even more distressed. "Must she know?"

"Yes, she must, and she will be most grieved. But it need go no farther than the six of us—the three here, Sydney, Lady Charlotte, and myself. I must tell you: I absolve the duke of any plot. It is up to you to discover what your daughter's part may have been."

The troubled father clicked his tongue regretfully. "So pretty—so full of spirits—and I am uncertain what to do."

"Begin by speaking plainly: No More Tricks. Punishment is up to you." Then he added, "Modest behavior is a young woman's greatest attraction."

He bowed, snapped his heels together, and exited rather pleased at having spoken sharply to a need he had long noticed. Mounting up, he rode directly for the castle.

Thirteen

For a second time that morning Sir Roland approached Heritage Castle and left his horse at a post, telling the servant on duty to let it wait for him.

"Where is Lady Charlotte?" he asked as he stripped off his gloves.

"In the private parlor with Lady Emilie, sir."

"Eh? Ask her to come to the library for a few moments, please. You needn't worry about my horse. I won't be here long," Sir Roland said and walked to the designated room as if he lived at Heritage, which in a way he almost had done, the two families having been in and out of each other's homes for decades.

Charlotte came with a flurry of skirts. She left the door open to preserve proprieties. "I have not seen Syd," she said breathlessly, "but I heard him enter and go up to his room. What you did about that pair I do not know, but I *thank you.*"

He pressed her hands together and led her to a chair.

"All started out innocently—at least on Sydney's part. How it would have ended if we had not come along, there is no saying. If seen, they would have been the gossip of Fallford, which may have been Cleone's aim."

Charlotte let out a pent breath. "I had not supposed she could be so wicked."

"Not quite that. Spoiled. Ambitious. Trying to manipulate—"

At that point Sydney entered, closing the door behind him.

"Charlotte," he said in a rush of words, "did I alarm you? It all started out so harmlessly, a sort of rescue mission. Cleone had dropped her reticule—"

"Did you see her do that?" interrupted Sir Roland.

"No, but she pointed it out—beyond her reach, beyond mine. She was very upset, and it seemed only kind to fetch it for her. I promise you I had no notion *she* would prance into the water!"

"Yes, yes," agreed Sir Roland, examining his cuff. "But think—if you had been seen by anyone in Fallford—even one of the children—*such* a story as would have gone around the neighborhood."

The young duke cast a desperate look at his sister. "Would it have been so very bad?"

Sir Roland answered for her baldly, "Yes."

"But it was only a p-prank."

"Would have been more than that, by the time it traveled from person to person."

"What happened to the reticule?" asked Charlotte.

"Good lord!" said Sydney. "I had forgotten that! It was a favorite, Cleone said. I suppose I must go back for it."

"No!" said Charlotte and Sir Roland in one voice, and Sir Roland added that he would send someone to fetch it, if village children had not already discovered it and fished it out.

"Don't say fish," the duke begged. "Trout started all this." He smiled a little crooked smile which was endearing.

It was clear he spoke truthfully, and Charlotte, always willing to be believe the best of him, said, "What a coil! At least it is ended now, thanks to our friend." With return of her self-possession, same her graciousness. "Will you join us for luncheon, Sir Roland? Oh, dear—" her eyes began to dance "—I do believe we are having salmon again!"

"Do us a favor, Sir Roland," Sydney urged, beginning to recover, "We have already had salmon once."

Sir Roland drew out his watch and consulted it. "By the time I can reach home they will have given up on me. Perhaps you will see if your luncheon will stretch for four . . ." He gave Charlotte a particular look, and she understood she was to absent herself.

Charlotte left the room, and Sir Roland seized the moment to speak man-to-man with the young duke. "I acquit you of wrongdoing," he said. "It was all a prank. Or you thought it a prank, but to involve a young lady is—er, dangerous. Might be expected to protect her good name, don't you know? In fact, sometimes ambitious young ladies *promote* scandals—"

"Oh, surely not Cleone!"

"We will never know for sure, will we? As you go into society you may find any number of females eager to throw themselves in your path."

"Good God!" exclaimed Sydney.

"Yes. A duke, you know." Sir Roland did not add "young, personable, and rich."

Lady Charlotte returned to say that the servants had finished the salmon and she could offer their friend some very good ham. From the depths of anxiety about her brother, she soared to euphoria, so great was her relief.

The lunch gong sounded, and they joined Lady Emilie for the meal. Sir Roland entertained them then with a proposal to leave on the morrow for Oxford, if Macnaghten agreed.

Sydney thought the company of two gentlemen could only be finer than that of one. Cleone appeared to go out of his mind, and he spoke happily of the trip, which led his sister to suppose that Cleone as yet had no real hold on his heart.

"Can you be back in time for Mrs. Guinn's luncheon party in the orchard?" asked Charlotte.

Sir Roland said he thought they could, if they got away at first light the next day. "Macnaghten is off with Katherine, but they should be back in a matter of hours. If he does not go with us, we will have to make another plan, but—"

"Mr. Macnaghten is in a mood to be accommodating," Charlotte pointed out.

"Yes. Good fellow," said Sydney, not considering the fine

points of Kate's being chaperoned in her own home. "But I just thought: Guinns' pik-nik! I had offered to drive Cleone. How can I bow out of that?"

Charlotte looked to Sir Roland, who said calmly, "You will be expected to drive her, if you have offered. The last thing we want is any obvious change of habits. Taking a tiger?"

"Yes. In a red coat to dazzle her."

"That will do admirably. Avoid private talks, eh?"

"Yes. I will."

"Then it is settled," said Sir Roland. "When Kate and Macnaghten return from Hays, I will send word if we can leave for Oxford in the morning. Five days should be enough. Barring broken wheels or such, we will return in good time for Mrs. Guinn's hospitality."

After the meal, Charlotte and Sydney accompanied him to the door, Aunt Emilie watching from the hall with an approving nod. Sir Roland's horse waited patiently where he had been tied "for a few moments" more than an hour previously. Sir Roland mounted.

"I will take this good fellow around for a drink before going home," he said, heading for the castle's stable yard. They did not see him again that day, for he left by the castle's main entrance at the turnpike, along which his own manor was located.

"How will I placate Hoad for the state of my clothes?" Sydney asked his sister, when Aunt Emilie had left them alone and the servant at the door had retired to his bench in the cloak room. Charlotte retorted that she was sure he had told Hoad plumpers before this.

Now that Sir Roland had gone, the emotions of the past two hours came rolling back on her like a tide. If only Sydney could be installed at Oxford immediately, instead of several weeks later!

Kate March and Mr. Macnaghten stopped briefly that afternoon on their way home from Hays. They accepted cups of tea, and conversation was easy and casual. Charlotte thought it best to leave the Oxford trip for Sir Roland to propose. Evidently he did this promptly, for before the dinner hour a note had come for Sydney, saying Mr. Macnaghten would join their expedition and the duke was to be ready at half after seven.

In line with her new attitude toward her brother, Charlotte did not rise early to see him off, but left the responsibility of being ready to him. In fact, she did not even wake, so sure was she that he was in good hands.

When she did arise to meet Aunt Emilie in the breakfast parlor, it was somehow strange to find no place set for her brother.

"I think I will make a call upon Mrs. Guinn," she said. "Perhaps I will go even farther along the turnpike and visit other acquaintances whom I seldom see. If Sydney is going to be miles off at Oxford University, we are sure to be lonely. You and I will rattle like dice in Heritage Castle, Aunt Emilie." Her aunt nodded, and she continued, "We must invite visitors. I have really neglected neighbors, haven't I?"

Lady Emilie did not respond to this random talk any more than she usually did. In any case, she could never be persuaded to find fault with Charlotte.

"I think, perhaps, that I will take Mercillia along to call upon the squire's wife today. She must find the Dower House oppressive. Besides, it will be more comfortable if she is acquainted with the Guinn daughters before going for the outdoor party in their orchard. Imagine! Lunching in an orchard! And Mrs. Guinn with a very pretty dining salon to use!"

So saying, she dashed off a note to Mrs. Beecham, requesting Mercy to be ready to join her carriage at ten.

At the Dower House the note was delivered to Mrs. Beecham, who then had a servant take it upstairs to her niece, not deigning to carry the message herself. Mercy was overjoyed. The atmosphere at the Dower House had been gloomy, though Mercy did not know the reason. She welcomed a chance to get away for a few hours and had even taken down the box with Mlle. Galatoire's beautiful bonnet, having some idea of wearing it, when a petulant Cleone entered.

"Mama says you have been invited to drive with Lady—*what is that?"*

"My best bonnet," Mercy answered. "I had thought to wear it today, but believe I will save it for a more important time."

"It is beautiful!" said Cleone, taking it from her hands. "May I try it on?"

Mercy had no wish to see Cleone in her special bonnet, but could not say no, when Cleone was already putting it on her head and posing before the mirror.

"Oo-oo! It is perfectly lovely, and would look so well with my blue-sprigged green muslin. May I borrow it?"

Upset by the sight of her precious bonnet upon the head of one she thought quite remarkably beautiful, Mercy for once mulishly cried, "No! No indeed. You have many pretty bonnets and dresses. I wish to wear this myself."

"Don't be a pig. See how it becomes me!" said Cleone, too determined on her own wants to be tactful or to wheedle.

Being well aware that if Cleone knew Sydney had helped her to choose the *chapeau* she would be even more insistent, Mercy said, with an idea of placating her, "Not until I have worn it first." She seized the bonnet from her cousin's head and stowed it back in its box.

Cleone, pouting, said, "Why must you be so selfish?" and flounced out of the room, leaving Mercy to wonder if she *was* selfish and to suffer pangs of self-doubt.

It was a subdued young lady who finished dressing and went down to wait for Lady Charlotte's carriage which, fortunately, came soon.

Charlotte, who was female herself, and not so ancient, soon realized something was wrong, but tactfully asked no questions, and by the time they were a mile upon the turnpike Mercillia was responding in her obliging way to comments about this stretch of road.

"You are really my excuse for this trip," said Charlotte,

smiling. "I have been neglectful of friends beyond Fallford, and plan to pretend that I want them to meet you—which of course I do—but I also hope this will make them forget my failings."

Mercy, who thought her ladyship was quite without flaws, almost as much so as her dearest mama, said happily, "I thank you. My papa says that there are none so agreeable as English gentry."

"Well, some have odd quirks," responded Lady Charlotte with a twinkle, "but—yes—we can enjoy them."

At Squire Guinn's manor they were welcomed cordially by Mrs. Guinn and her daughters, who were aged fifteen and sixteen and who promptly took Mercy off to their bedchambers to see the kittens that each cherished.

After a brief and pleasant visit here, the callers continued to the home of Mr. and Mrs. Blakely. There were no young daughters at this place, for Mrs. Blakely had no children and was, herself, only recently a bride. They took coffee here, as their hostess seemed so eager to serve it in dainty cups with small napkins that had her new initials.

Then they went on to Howerton Manor where there was a daughter, Mariam, rather sober but very sweet, and a sixteen-year-old son who joined the ladies with friendly manners and no indication of boredom.

Although Mrs. Howerton and her children urged the visitors to stay for an informal luncheon, Lady Charlotte declined and took Mercy away after saying she hoped Miss Howerton and her brother would visit Miss Pope at the Dower House. Evidently each family received a pleasant impression of the other, for Mariam and young Geoffrey promised to return the call some day soon thereafter.

"Thank you, dear Lady Charlotte," said Mercy fervently, before stepping down again at her temporary home. "Papa was right. I have met such kind people today, and there are also the Marches, and Mr. Todd, and Mr. Macnaghten and—of course—everyone at the castle." She was blushing when she finished, which Lady Charlotte thought added to her charm.

I am quite curious to meet the parents of this dear creature, thought her ladyship, but the idea went right out of her head, for upon reaching the castle she found Kate March about to turn away in a gig, with a groom beside her.

"You cannot leave now!" declared Charlotte, beckoning her servant from the castle doorway and transferring her reins to him so that she could step down. "That is Jonas you have with you, isn't it? Jonas, help your mistress down. You can take the gig around to the stable and then come up to the castle for a meal with the duke's people. No objection, Kate! I fully intend to keep you for luncheon with me. We must make the most of our freedom."

"As if the duke hampers your style—or Roland mine, for that matter," protested Kate. Nevertheless, she, too, relinquished her vehicle, and followed Charlotte into the castle.

There were, of course, several strata of Society between a duke's daughter and a baronet's, but neither of the ladies gave this any thought, for a close association had existed between the families for several generations. Charlotte did not hold herself aloof. She had never taken her place in London Society or scaled the heights of the *ton.* It was true that a difference of nearly ten years had prevented them from becoming intimate; also, Katherine had been north for several years of Charlotte's maturity. Still, Charlotte was inclined to extend to Sir Roland's sister the trust and appreciation she felt for him.

She led Katherine indoors and bade her take off her hat. "We will not be formal about this visit," she said. Then, having sent a message to her housekeeper that they would entertain a guest at lunch, she settled Kate in the family parlor. Aunt Emilie was not there, but could be expected when the lunch gong sounded, which it soon did, so neither young woman advanced any intimate topic.

"Do you think our men will return in time for Mrs. Guinn's orchard party?" Charlotte asked.

"Roland seemed to think there would be no problem," Kate replied. "This route is one he travels often. He expects to go at top speed for longer hours than you or I would find comfortable. As for changing horses, can you imagine anyone's trying to ring in nags on that threesome?"

"No, I cannot," said Charlotte. She was wondering how to ease her guest into a discussion of Mr. Macnaghten when the door opened and Lady Emilie Held joined them.

This did not add to the conversation, for Lady Emilie merely smiled upon Kate in a kindly manner, and sat down about six or seven feet away.

Kate returned the smile, and told her hostess that Roland kept horses of his own at Birmingham. "After that they must use job horses. They will not only travel fast, but long hours which would exhaust us."

"At least they only go to Oxford. Sometimes I believe the reason I have never been to London is that I cannot face such a tedious journey. If I were allowed to ride my Prince," Charlotte said, "I might last for the distance."

Kate shook her head. "Your own good sense will keep you from doing that. Why, Roland would frown on such a thing." As Charlotte started to speak, her visitor added hastily, "Oh, I know it isn't his place to say what you may or may not do, but I am sure he would raise all sorts of *reasons* to deter you, until you came to the *reasonable* conclusion yourself."

This made Charlotte gurgle with amusement. "I think you are trying to avoid using the words not let. This is all very strange when *you* are not inclined to seek his advice in your own situation!"

Katherine flushed, and Charlotte wished she could call back her last sentence. But perhaps—just perhaps—it needed saying, and Kate needed to hear.

Aunt Emilie cleared her throat and held out a bit of embroidery for Katherine March to see.

It was Charlotte's turn to blush, though only slightly, and that was because she admitted to herself that Kate's private affairs were not her business. But she admired Macnaghten so much and knew Sir Roland did also; she felt it might be a kindness to give Kate a wee push.

Fortunately, the butler put the awkwardness behind them by entering to announce luncheon.

Fourteen

It had never occurred to Charlotte Held to wonder at the lack of formality in her ducal residence. She had been reared mostly by a single parent who cared nothing for formality or lavish occasions involving numerous guests to be housed and entertained. His land was his chief interest, and, of course, his children. At his death, Charlotte, as eldest family member remaining, took charge, continuing in her papa's style. The influence of Chaplain Beecham was not greatly felt, except when he pointed out mildly that Charlotte must have a resident chaperone. The young lord's aunt, Lady Emilie Held, was then persuaded to give up her snug rooms at Tonbridge Wells and come home to Heritage Castle.

Did Aunt Emilie mind relinquishing her independence? If so, she gave no indication, but returned to her girlhood suite in the castle and managed to continue a quiet and unobtrusive existence much like the one she had led in Tonbridge Wells. The children, Charlotte and Sydney, tolerated her presence and even became appreciative of her unruffled calm. It never entered their heads to think her peculiar, only self-effacing.

Although Charlotte did not realize it, by her mild manner Auntie Emilie was teaching her womanly qualities of gentleness and grooming and poise. Called upon to direct and command a huge staff, Charlotte might have become sharp and domineering, had it not been for the serene and feminine example of this aunt.

The two young people brushed along together with a sort

of filial relationship, Charlotte as a mother, and Sydney as a son. Charlotte's fond nature kept her from being dictatorial, while his amiability prevented rebellion on his part. They thought nothing odd about the small family, and neither did anyone else. Servants were loyal, legal advisors assiduous, neighboring friends supportive. Sir Roland, who had been a close friend of the previous duke, was always ready to guide by both example and advice.

There had been another relative, an uncle, between the late duke and Lady Emilie, but he had been sent off long years ago in some sort of disgrace and had not been heard from in twenty years—unless some of the duke's men of business were still sending an allowance to Australia or Brazil or some such place. Sydney and Charlotte had never known him and never thought of him. If Lady Emilie did so, she did not mention him.

Of cousins there were remote ones, living in Kent, and one very distant gentleman said to be an intimate of the Prince. The connection was so slight as to be of no concern to anyone in Fallford Village of Shropshire.

But now the serenity of Heritage Castle was threatened by a pretty little witch at the Dower House, so Sydney must be sent away to be exposed to other dangers at Oxford. It seemed to Charlotte that her peaceful life was coming to an end, and while Sydney's life might be expanded, her own would be shrunk.

Eventually, she admitted to herself, Sydney would bring a wife to Heritage, and her own reign would end. She could not look forward with any pleasure to travel or life elsewhere. What? Not be able to mount Prince and canter about the fields and woodlands of the manor? Tonbridge Wells would not satisfy her! . . . Perhaps dear Auntie would be willing to settle with her somewhere else, such as London, or even Paris.

In the meantime, there were a million details of Heritage to keep her busy. And in Mrs. Blakely, the new bride in the neighborhood, she might find a congenial friend.

After Kate's visit, Charlotte sat down to write a cordial note to Mrs. Blakely, inviting her for luncheon two days later. Then she went up to her chamber and astonished her maid by dragging out her dresses for a critical survey.

In this she had no role model, for no one of her acquaintance was known to be fashionable, though Cousin Maude took special pains to garb her daughter attractively. Use Cleone as a model she would *not!* The modiste in Hays would be sending a new gown any day now, and perhaps Mrs. Blakely would have all the latest fashions in her trousseau. Sad to think, she herself was older than that young matron . . . but not so very much. That her own restrained style had impressed the bride did not occur to her. There were always fashion journals to be consulted; she must order several.

The bride's visit passed off very well. Mrs. Blakely arrived in a smart new curricle, with a groom in livery driving her, and a pink sunshade to protect her complexion. Charlotte, who gave no heed to the sun's rays, was not impressed by that, but did admire the young lady's poise when received in a duke's castle. The two eyed each other and were pleased by what they saw. Both, being in command of a handsome residence, fell readily into domestic talk, and if Mrs. Blakely was puzzled by Lady Emilie's silence, she did not show it.

Mrs. Blakely could be counted an asset to the neighborhood.

Mr. Blakely was scarcely any better known to Charlotte than was his bride. His choice of wife being so good, he himself rose in Charlotte's opinion. And Sir Roland, whose advice to extend her scope had brought about an interest in things beyond Heritage, must be thanked anew.

Had Mrs. Blakely met Miss March? Yes, Miss March had kindly paid her a call, which Charlotte with some chagrin noted had come before her own. Lady Charlotte also learned that Mr. Blakely, with wonderful consideration, had brought his Intended and her mama to visit his house before their marriage, so that they could see what her new home was to be.

"He is so truly thoughtful," the bride said happily, and Charlotte felt a twinge of envy.

Someday Sydney would be bringing a dewy girl to supplant his sister. She must be prepared for this, she told herself sternly.

After luncheon, Lady Charlotte took her guest on a tour of the castle, showing the magnificence of the state rooms and the comfort of the ones preferred for use by the family. Mrs. Blakely admired all with no indication of envy. She was truly a very sweet young lady, such as Charlotte hoped Sydney would eventually choose as his duchess, a far cry from the ambitious Cleone Beecham.

With Cleone in her mind's eye, Charlotte compared the two. Cleone was more beautiful, less appealing, more exciting, less pliable, more self-centered, less interested in others, more demanding, less appreciative. When she added up the assets, Mrs. Blakely easily won out, but would Sydney have reached the same conclusion? Would a very young gentleman see what his sister recognized in any girl?

"I am sorry my brother is not here to meet you and welcome you to Shropshire," Charlotte said to her guest. "He is visiting Oxford with some thought of enrolling there."

"Oh, he must!" exclaimed Mrs. Blakely. "My husband was there for a time—at Trinity College. I have heard many tales of high jinks and a *leetle* learning."

"Pray do not tell Sydney that!" said Charlotte. "We hope he will study prodigiously."

Mrs. Blakely laughed merrily. "I do not think my husband let books interfere with his education, but he is certainly serious about important matters now."

This Charlotte found a little unnerving. "I am relying on the influence of our friend, Sir Roland, to settle Sydney in the proper college with suitably severe tutors."

"When you know my husband better," replied the bride, "you will see college did not ruin him. He is everything delightful."

Charlotte said, "I already know him, though not well. Your recommendation is reassuring." She hoped Sydney would not follow a similar path, even if it led to his being "delightful." Sydney's nature was already good; what she desired was his maturing.

Mrs. Blakely was clearly an amiable creature, perhaps having a biased view of her husband by reason of her being so newly wed. Charlotte was prepared to like her. Indeed, she did like her, and was willing to include her in the small social circle of Fallford. "You and Mr. Blakely must dine with us before Sydney leaves to take up residence at Oxford. Have you met my cousins, the Beechams? Mrs. Beecham's niece, Miss Pope, who is visiting, was with me when you and I met. She would welcome a friend, and having lived for a time at Oxford, may share some memories with your husband."

Mrs. Blakely clasped her hands together with pleasure. "Yes, such a dear creature. Oh, there is no end to the delights of my new home!"

Charlotte wondered if she would feel the same when she had encountered Cleone.

"Mrs. Guinn has invited us to a luncheon," Mrs. Blakely added happily.

"In the orchard? Have you accepted? Mercillia and the Beechams will be going."

"Yes, Mr. Blakely and I are happy to be included."

"Good. Sir Roland and his sister will be there. And their visitor, Mr. Macnaghten, also. I do not know whom else Mrs. Guinn may have invited. We must hope it does not rain."

"It must not! That would be dismal. I look forward to seeing Miss Pope again."

"You and she will prove congenial, I am sure," said Charlotte. She did not suggest that Cleone Beecham would prove a friend also, for Cleone—who might be improved by a wholesome friendship—was interested only in men, and one in particular.

Sometimes Charlotte's better self wondered if she misjudged the chaplain's daughter out of concern for Sydney's happiness, but then she remembered blatant flirting, and posturing, and bouts of ill humor. It would take a man who wanted only an ornament for a wife to tolerate a nature such as this. In a way it was sad, for she did not think riches and the envy of other women would make Cleone contented in the long run. Perhaps the girl would be saved from herself by falling in love with some man, rich or poor, who would make her forget herself.

However, such thoughts did not swerve Charlotte from her instinct to protect her brother.

Mrs. Blakely had not been on her way home more than an hour when Mrs. Beecham paid a call upon a not very welcoming Lady Charlotte Held, who forced herself to make some effort to receive her graciously. Mrs. Beecham could not know (and could not ask) if Charlotte was aware of what had happened at the brook.

"Such balmy weather," the visitor said as graciously as possible, weather being a safe topic. "I declare it was pleasant to walk up the hill from the Dower House."

"I hardly think of that *slope* as a hill," returned her ladyship contrarily, "but, yes, it is delightful weather that we are having. I hope the men are enjoying the same and not slogging through mud. Oxford, where they have gone, you know, is quite beautiful, though also dreary—like anywhere else—when it rains."

"Yes," agreed Mrs. Beecham in an effort of goodwill. "My husband was not so fortunate as to study there, but he has spoken of visiting libraries at the university. They are rich—encompassing, he says. He would like to delve into them, he tells me. I do not understand such a passion for dry old books, but perhaps it is because he is so scholarly."

Mr. Beecham's absorption was well known in the village, although Charlotte had often wondered if it was partly a protective shield. She said pacifically, "A serious student."

There was a pause, and then the visitor raised the topic of

Mrs. Guinn's unusual orchard party. "I have told the girls that they must wear broad brims to shield their complexions."

Although Mr. Macnaghten had offered Charlotte a place in his carriage, she wondered how the family from the Dower House would be transported, since Mr. Beecham had only a gig, so she was obliged to ask, "Have you a way of reaching there?"

"Oh, yes," returned Mrs. Beecham triumphantly, *"Sydney* is driving Cleone, and Mrs. Guinn is sending Alexander to fetch Mercillia, so my husband and I will go comfortably in our gig. We care nothing for fashion, you know."

This was only fifty percent true, but Charlotte allowed it to pass, glad that she need not offer the ducal carriage. She made some effort to appear her normal self, so that the visitor would not guess she knew Cleone's connivery. It would relieve her feelings immensely to accuse Cleone of trying to maneuver Sydney into matrimony before he was fully grown, a fate he had miraculously escaped through the intervention of Sir Roland, but to raise the subject might have the very effect that she wished to avoid.

The two, boy and girl, were only a year apart in age, and during their childhood had romped together in the castle's halls and attics. With the Beechams' move to the Dower House the relationship became more formal, a matter of calls at proper times of day; and when Cleone had let down her hems and piled up her hair for evening parties, there was a subtle change, a new awareness, between them. It might have come to nothing had Maude's daughter not coveted an exalted position for herself. No chaplain's or vicar's wife did Cleone intend to be! Sydney, a year older but less worldly, had no suspicion of her schemes, thinking only how beguiling his playfellow had recently become.

Though full of guile Cleone might be, she was still very young and not as clever as she supposed. The "dropped" reticule failed of its purpose. Undismayed, she teased and ogled Sydney and Alexander Guinn and other uneasy youths of the neighborhood while casting about for substitute plots to ensnare the duke. For the present, eagle eyes of parents and cousins were upon her. She would have to try something else. No trick this time. Just a way to outshine in allure all the other girls who might attend Mrs. Guinn's orchard lunch . . .

Charlotte did not underestimate her.

After Cousin Maude, Charlotte had only one other caller before the men returned from Oxford.

The chaplain came on reluctant feet to apologize for his daughter's unladylike behavior. He was quite truthful in saying that he could not understand how she could lend herself to such a romp. The aspect of a devious plot he still did not comprehend, for in everything he was accustomed to be led by his wife—if not by his Maker. Plots were beyond his ken. Even apologizing was difficult, as it involved something he could not and never would understand.

When he blamed himself for his child's shortcomings, Lady Charlotte was compelled to interrupt, saying, "My dear Cousin, enough! Whatever misbehavior took place, it was not *yours.*"

He did not take offense to her speaking so assuredly.

"Sir Roland suggested perhaps a Bath Seminary for Cleone," he said, "and I begin to think it might be the answer, but I feel sure it would be beyond my resources—oh, please do not think this is a wretched *hint!* There must be another way of dealing with the problem. I am meditating on it earnestly."

Lady Charlotte, who had an idea that poor Cousin John was not only meditating, but also agonizing and blaming himself for others' absurd ambitions, and confessing all sorts of *sins* that were not his own. She commanded him forcefully to place blame where it belonged and not usurp it.

To this he responded meekly, "You are so right, my dear. Such a good head on your shoulders. Your father would be proud. Something, alas!, that cannot be said for the supposed patriarch of my house."

"There you go!" cried Charlotte. "Assuming more blame! Are you afraid to fault your wife?" She could scarcely believe she was speaking so critically to a clergyman more than twice her age and a cousin to boot, but she refused to fall into the slough of which she accused him, "Oh, *do* see that the thoughts and actions of others are not yours!"

John Beecham stared at her. "You think they are not?"

"I *know* so," she declared.

"Your papa would be proud of you," he repeated. "And you will have reason to be proud of Sydney, I think."

When he had gone, she sagged upon the nearest chair and pressed a hand to her forehead to see if her head had swollen. Since it only felt knobby as usual, she sprang up and raced for the stairs to burst into her aunt's chamber and fling herself at Lady Emilie's knees.

"Oh, Auntie," she cried. "I have been beastly to Cousin John—commanding him to be what he is not. How do domineering women find passive men? Am I domineering? What a horrid thing to be!"

To her surprise, Lady Emilie began to chuckle as if she had made a joke.

Fifteen

Charlotte was in her chamber just past lunch time of the fourth day since Sir Roland's carriage had set out, and she did not hear it wheel up before the family entrance of the castle. When commotion arose in the lower hall as the duke's servants hurried to receive His Grace, and the duke's voice asked, "Where is m'sister?" she came running downstairs.

"Sydney! You are home already!"

"Aye," he replied, seeming to her bigger than life. "Such speed as we traveled! Sir Roland goes fast when he goes anywhere! Even Macnaghten was surprised—said Sir Roland had hitched racers for most of the journey."

Charlotte hugged him joyfully. "Come in the parlor, dearest, and tell me *all*."

To her he looked taller than when he had gone away, more assured, alert, mature.

By this time Aunt Emilie had descended and had her cap knocked crooked by an elephantine embrace.

Then they went into the favorite parlor, leaving several servants and Sydney's Hoad to wrestle for one portmanteau. All three sat down, though Charlotte perched forward on her chair.

"Now tell me!" she commanded.

Sydney said, "Of course I will. But where shall I begin? Oh, yes, Macnaghten claimed Sir Roland was using racers, but he would not do that. Had his own best teams for the first two and last two laps, and seemed able to command excellent teams when we had to hire changes."

"That is all very well," interrupted Charlotte, "but what I want to hear is about Oxford."

"Ancient," he said. "Everything seemed ancient."

"But did you like it?"

"Oh, I found all most splendid. So much is ages old. Well, even centuries. Of course at Heritage Castle we are accustomed to antiquity, but it was still exciting to see where men have studied over several centuries—All Souls nearly four hundred years old, Balliol five hundred, Pembroke only two hundred or so, but refounded on Broadgates. Sam Johnson studied *there,* though he didn't have funds, they say, for as long as he would have liked. Every college seems to claim sundry greats. I did not need Sir Roland to tell me how fortunate I am to have Heritage to supply any fees I must pay."

"It is not the cost, dearest, but the desire you may have for education that matters," Charlotte interposed. "One hears so much of student riots—drinking, gambling, and other excesses. You can experience such things without enrolling at a college!"

"Yes, Sir Roland says the same. He told me roundly that I must expect to study if I am to please you."

"Oh, yes," declared Charlotte, "I am willing to be the ogre who drives you, if one is necessary."

Sydney sprang from his chair to give her a hug. "Such a beautiful ogre! Well, I agreed to work hard. Sir Roland says you have sacrificed a great deal for me—I never realized this and am quite determined to make you proud."

"I am already that," she returned fondly.

"Well, prouder. I'll do my best, dearest."

"Good," she said. "Now sit down again. You have not told me what college you have chosen."

"Well, not the Divinity School. I have no leaning in that direction. And not Wadham College, though it is quite beautiful with restful proportions. Wadham is little altered in two hundred years, they say. I think, Charlotte, it will have to be Papa's college, Merton."

She encouraged him, saying, "Fine. But why?"

"Somehow it seemed right to follow Papa, though nothing is signed and sealed yet. Sir Roland studied there also, but you must not think he tried to influence me. Indeed, he almost leaned backwards not to do so. Perhaps the bagwig with whom we had an interview was most persuasive. Oh, not intentionally. It was his kind and unhurried manner, yes, and his seeming interested in a former student's son."

"Was he there when Papa was?" she asked.

Sydney said, "Not as a professor. He was a student himself then. Seemed to remember Papa as one who did his work dependably without being committed to a scholarly future."

"Thinking more about Heritage, I daresay."

Sydney agreed. "Papa kept reading things here. I remember his trying to show me books on farming, but I was too young to be interested. Did he urge books on you?"

"Yes," she said. "Classics mostly."

"And I suppose you stuck them back on the shelves like I did?"

"You are wrong. I read them."

"Did you? I should have known. Sir Roland says you are very well-read for a lady."

Charlotte made a moue, and Sydney hastened to add, "He meant a compliment for you. Said I would have some work to do to catch up with you."

"Well, I am five years older," she reminded. Looking at him thoughtfully, she had the feeling that he had suddenly become adult. That would be in the natural course of things, but habit had kept him about twelve or thirteen in her mind's eye. It was her own attitude, her constant mothering, that had held him back. Nineteen! No wonder Cleone had caught his fancy . . . too convenient by far!

Besides her being near at hand, Cleone was an enticing bundle of femininity and wiles. *She* would certainly not add to his book-learning.

"Why did you groan?" Sydney demanded suddenly.

"Did I? I suppose I was thinking how busy the future will be. Did you actually enroll while you were at Oxford?"

"No. Papers will be coming. In the meantime, Sir Roland says, I must start to survey our own library. He is making a list of things for me to read before the term starts." He made a fearful face. "Seems a shame to waste a glorious summer reading dry tomes, when all outdoors says 'Come!' "

"If Sir Roland recommends certain books," she replied, "you can be sure they will not be dry. I rather expect the tutor we had living here must have introduced you to some fine ones already."

"Oglevie was a decent chap," Sydney admitted, "and I learned a few things from him. Harrow was a help, too. Better face it . . . I may not be a scholar."

"That is all right. But not a profligate, I hope!"

"No, no. Word of a Held."

His word being dependable, he was presently saying, "I promised to drive Cleone to Mrs. Guinn's luncheon. It is tomorrow, isn't it? Should I send a note to confirm the hour, or show myself down there so they can see I have reached home and intend to keep the engagement?"

Charlotte, with her new cautious attitude, said, "Whichever you find easiest. The luncheon is called for one o'clock. You can drive the distance in twenty minutes."

"Oh, easily," he agreed. "The Beechams are accustomed to my calling often, and I have been gone several days. Perhaps I had best call today." He consulted a bronze clock upon the mantel. "Three should be a good hour." He grinned at his sister. "Hoad will be wanting to get his hands on me to smarten me up. I will go up to him, if you and Auntie do not mind. Have I talked so much? It's past two already!"

He blew them kisses and went into the hall. It sounded as though he were taking the steps two at a time.

Charlotte lifted her shoulders. "Still part boy, part man. The *boy* is nothing to cause worry . . ."

She sighed, moved to close the hall door, and then went

over to the grate to stare down at the small fire which did little except to convey an essence of hearth and home, Outdoors the sun was warm upon the sloping driveway to the Beechams' dwelling. Before long, she heard Sydney's boots upon the stair, more sedate steps now, going along the hallway to the outer door.

What Sir Roland may have said to him in the space of several days she did not know, but having utmost faith in the dependability and unflappable nature of that gentleman, she was able to remain calm and hope for the best. Cleone could not be evaded forever, either by her or by the good-natured duke.

As usual, Auntie Emilie said nothing, so Charlotte spoke to her. "The last thing I want is for Sydney to rush into marriage at the age of nineteen, but marriage to the right sort of girl might be protection against a wrong one."

From a west window she watched Sydney walk at a steady pace down to the Dower House.

She was so very glad to have Auntie to bear her company while her brother was in the tiger's lair. Auntie might say nothing, yet by her presence would be a comfort. Even though Sydney seemed to have his feet on the ground, Charlotte could not feel easy about the lures of the Dower House.

Fifty minutes later, when the duke returned, he was composed, inclined to be quiet, as if he had lost his bright spirits. Had something happened?

"Any tea?" he asked.

"A bit early," Charlotte replied, "but why not? I would like some myself." The bellpull was near the hall door. Instead of pulling it, she stuck her head into the hall and said to the footman on duty, "Tea, please, Farris."

"Certainly, m'lady," Farris responded, as if there was nothing he would rather do than carry orders to the kitchen. Indeed, Lady Charlotte suspected that he would not be adverse to exchanging words with a certain bonny kitchen maid.

As he sped down the hall, Charlotte returned to her aunt's

side, saying, "Sydney is not the only one who fancies himself a beau. Farris has his eye on our little kitchen maid."

To her surprise, Sydney chuckled. "Are you trying to play mother now to a servant girl?"

His sister replied with nearly a snap, "Why, yes. Since you have suddenly become a *man,* I must look elsewhere for my chicks."

He frowned. "Well, now, Mother Hen, I am only four days older than when you last saw me. Never mind me. If you must mother someone, think of little Mercy."

Charlotte looked at him sharply, forgetting the local Tease. "Do not say that dear girl is being mistreated!"

"Oh, no. Not that. Just ignored." He hesitated. "Mercy was the only lady at the Dower House to show any curiosity about my journey and the possibility of my enrolling at a college."

"Surely they were glad to see you!"

"Yes, I think so. However, the Beecham ladies showed no interest in Oxford or my plan of study. Why was that?"

Before she could answer, he had continued: "Mercy said it was a splendid idea to choose my father's college. She asked if I had engaged rooms for next Fall—"

"Oh," interrupted Charlotte, "have you done so?"

"No. Sir Roland will tell you about that. Mercy wanted to know if I had seen the Bodleian Library. She asked if we had stayed at a small hostelry near the corner of the High and Turl, where her family had lived during their time at Oxford, and—do you know!—I believe it may be the very inn to which Sir Roland took us! Right in the middle of things, which placed us most conveniently."

"What did Mr. Macnaghten have to say about your future school?"

"Not a great deal. He is a Cambridge man, you remember, and too polite to make comparisons. Always good-natured about sights and meals and accommodations. As a matter of fact, I expect I would have liked Cambridge equally well, but it does make sense for me to follow Father."

"He would be pleased," Charlotte said in approval.

Sydney went on to tell of things he enjoyed seeing. "There were no crowds of students at this time of year. We ventured everywhere—into quadrangles and buildings—and examined bridges over the Thames and the Cherwell." As he spoke he became more and more enthusiastic, forgetting the dampening response he had encountered at the Dower House.

Aunt Emilie and his sister seemed to understand.

Charlotte deemed it wisest not to ask if his appointment with Cleone on the morrow was still in force; she had thought it was sure that Cleone would hold him to it.

They were all relieved when tea arrived—soothing to the palate and state of mind. Scarcely had each drunk a cup and asked for more, than Sir Roland rode up to Heritage and brought ripples of warm air into the parlor. He reported that Mr. Macnaghten had taken Kate to call upon Mrs. Howerton. Charlotte set aside her cup to pour a fresh one for him.

He said, "Thank you, my girl. I do not know why the sight of tea so readily begins to soothe one. Yes, I will be glad to have a cup. No sugar. Oh, I see you remember."

He took the cup, sipped cautiously, and finding his tongue not scalded, settled in an armchair to enjoy the familiar beverage. "Sydney talking your ears off?"

Lady Charlotte said, "Not really. It looks as though you are going to be obliged to explain why he must rent rooms at Oxford."

Sir Roland eased back in his chair, looking slightly sleepy. "Only think. He will have some consequence to display. Who will believe he is a duke, unless he lives in some style? At the minimum he must have at least two rooms for himself and a niche for Hoad."

"Do you really think that?" asked Charlotte, brows knit.

"I more than think it," he said. "I know it. Surely you must admit some elegance is expected of a duke."

Charlotte looked skeptical. "A duke of only *nineteen years?*

Might other young men think he is getting above himself—I mean, trying to impress in a smarmy way."

Puzzled, the duke looked from one to the other.

"I would not do such a thing," he insisted.

"Certainly not," agreed Sir Roland. "A pair of rooms, a gentleman's gentleman, a tilbury for travel, a pair, and groom—those will be only modest assets. With less, all would suppose you not up to snuff. With more, you would be labeled an upstart. Everyone walks about Oxford; no saddle horse is needed or expected. If there is an occasion for a mount, one can be hired. Put Hoad in charge, Sydney. He will know what is proper."

"Hoad is no older than I. What can he know?"

"Everything that older servants will have taught him."

Sydney turned to Charlotte. "What do you think, Sister?"

"What do I actually *know?"* she countered. "Sir Roland is more experienced than you or I, Sydney. We are fortunate that he has been like a father to us."

Sir Roland gave a short bark of laughter. "Not that, I beg! Remember my single state. My—er—dignity."

She wrinkled her nose at him. "I think you are teasing us. Syd, Sir Roland has proved himself our friend many times over. Let us agree to whatever he suggests. Was your valet with you at Merton College, dear sir? He *was?* Perhaps he would be an—an advisor to Hoad."

Aunt Emilie had dropped her sewing to her lap, so interested was she in the discussion. Pink rose in her cheeks when she noticed their attention to herself.

"Lady Emilie is always a model of propriety," Charlotte said. "I will never be the equal of her."

"I think," said Sir Roland, "we all wish Lady Charlotte to remain exactly as she is."

Momentarily, Charlotte was silenced, warmed by their neighbor's implied praise. Always her brother and aunt dealt kindly with her; she loved them dearly. She was blessed in the company of Auntie Emilie, but for an outsider, a mere neighbor to be concerned for her and Sydney was both unexpected and heartwarming. When had she known Sir Roland to be anything but kind, even when advising against her first inclination? For someone who was only a neighbor to be constantly attentive and helpful was an added blessing. Had Papa sometime before his death commended them to Sir Roland's care?

Sydney and Sir Roland, she discovered, had gone off into a discussion of what Sydney should be hastily reading. Presently they rose from their seats and went along the hall to the library.

She heard Sir Roland say, "Didn't your father have an inventory of his books? Surely he must have."

"I think so," Sydney answered. "I am ashamed to say that I cannot remember—if I ever knew."

Barely audible to the ladies was Sir Roland's voice saying, "New times are coming, my lad!"

The ladies in the parlor exchanged knowing looks.

With no father for the last nine years to hold as a model of what a gentleman should be, Charlotte had unconsciously compared all males, young or old, to Sir Roland. She knew her papa had respected him. With her own eyes she could see he was always smartly garbed; as for his manners—they were truly those of a man of breeding. She wondered why he had never married. If there had been a matter of disappointment in love, surely she would have heard that. True, he was sometimes absent on travels for weeks on end, but never was there a rumor of ladybirds and the sort of thing of which gossip was made!

She and Sydney were fortunate to have such an advisor.

When she added dear Aunt Emilie, kind neighbors, faithful servants, and, yes, solid Cousin John Beecham to her list of blessings, she felt thankful indeed. She had hardly noticed the passing of years—but now, suddenly, her focus of interest was to leave Heritage and go out into the world.

What would she do with herself?

Sixteen

The sun cooperated with Mrs. Guinn by rising brightly in a summer sky with only a few delightful puffy white clouds in view. If Squire Guinn thought a pik-nik in his orchard was nonsensical, he indulged his wife obligingly by having a suitable area mowed and raked; some of his field men were appointed to carry out tables, blankets, and cushions, and to string ropes for securing horses.

Pik-niks had been heard of, although never before experienced by gentry in Fallford. Sometimes children carried baskets of lunch into the countryside, and field-workers might squat to munch a midday meal where they worked. Now a *party* in such circumstances was thought both amusing and innovative.

Mrs. Beecham was not sure she approved. "Showing off," she muttered, though of course she did not want her daughter to be left out. So she warned the girls again to wear broad-brimmed hats and went upstairs in good time to choose and don her own ensemble.

Since Alexander came early for Mercy as planned, Cleone was unhampered and unobserved in preparing to dazzle the duke. She meant this to be a special time with His Grace.

Mercy had gone, and Mrs. Beecham was still in her chamber when Sydney arrived. Before he could step down from his curricle, or even hand over the reins to his tiger, Cleone skipped from her home, blue-sprigged green skirts billowing, and a picture bonnet with blue and green gossamer streamers framing her beautiful, smiling face.

The tiger, proud of his scarlet jacket, scrambled down to assist her to a seat beside his master. For a moment Sydney said nothing.

"What a glorious day!" she cried happily. When he did not immediately answer, she added, "Just meant for us."

He turned his team and drove into the village street.

"You are looking charming," he said carefully. "New bonnet?"

"Yes," said Cleone, peeking at him sideways. "I hope you like it."

"Oh, I do," returned Sydney gruffly. He cleared his throat and added tonelessly, "Where did you get it?"

Cleone tittered. "Silly! It is a bonnet you have seen a hundred times. I trimmed it anew myself." She waited for the duke's praise, which was slow in coming as he negotiated an entrance to the turnpike.

"I see," said the duke, who was seeing more than she had intended.

"It is meant as a surprise for you."

Sydney said, "It is that, all right."

"Mama," she explained, "thought I should wear a bonnet with a broad brim to protect my complexion, but this goes so well with my dress, do you not think?"

What Sydney thought he did not readily say. Presently, he asked lightly, "Mamas usually know best, do they not?"

She giggled happily. "But I was thinking of *you,* Syd. I wanted to be worthy of a duke's smart curricle—and his company, of course." It did not bother her that Sydney's tiger, balanced behind them, was hearing every word.

"You will outshine all the ladies," he said flatly, which was what she wanted to hear, so she did not notice the tone.

She began to prattle and cast little alluring side glances at her escort, who continued to stare fixedly at his horses' ears.

Presently, Sydney, who had scarcely heard what she was

saying, asked in a colorless voice if Mercy had obeyed her aunt and worn a broad-brimmed bonnet.

"Of course she did," said Cleone scornfully. "She always minds Mama slavishly. I, for one, care nothing about sunlight. It is more important to look one's best for one's escort, isn't it, Your Grace?" The respect of his title was intended to flatter, though she had always called him "Sydney" since they romped as children. "Alexander Guinn came for Mercy—not a very exciting escort—not much more than a boy," she said dismissively, implying that Sydney Held, Duke of Audley, was far superior to a squire's stripling.

Sydney made a sound somewhat like *oof* and flicked his horses to a sharper speed. The charmer beside him clapped a hand to her bonnet exclaiming, "What fun to fly!"

At the rear the tiger tightened his grip. He did not relish flying from a small perch. What had made his master race recklessly with a delectable filly like Miss Beecham aboard?

Sydney did slow for the turn into Squire Guinn's driveway. They arrived at the orchard with Miss Beecham flushed and somewhat windblown and quite enchanting to every male eye.

It was obviously going to be a large party, for several young beaux gathered to welcome Cleone and assist her from the curricle. Another carriage was drawing up behind them, so Sydney stepped down and handed his reins to his tiger, who prepared to move the vehicle to another part of the orchard. After a quick glance to see that his passenger was fully occupied, the duke went to speak punctiliously to his hosts, and then, after casting an eye across the gathering, made his way to Mercillia.

She was looking neat as wax in gown and bonnet that he had seen her wear another time, but there was a hurt expression in her eyes and angry red upon her cheekbones.

"Your new bonnet," he stated.

Mercy whispered, "Yes."

Tucking her hand upon his arm, he said, "Let us walk down this row of trees."

Struggling to gain control of her feelings, Mercy went with him willingly, the high color beginning to fade.

"I do not suppose you gave her permission?" he asked.

"No. In fact, I was quite rude in refusing to let Cleone wear it," she admitted.

"When have I ever seen you be rude?"

"I was very abrupt," she amended.

"Well, Charlotte will take you to buy another. Have Mlle. Galatoire create something new. I do not suppose you will want to wear this one?"

"No," said Mercy. "No one would believe it is really mine." It seemed her conscience must be bothering her, for she hurried to say, "My aunt was kind to take me in without forewarning of Mama's and Papa's leaving England suddenly. I should remember to be appreciative of her kindness. Perhaps it was wrong to—to impel Cleone to take my hat. Should I have told her she might wear it?"

Sydney made an ignoble noise. "Ach! Did she ask your permission?"

"Yes, and I am afraid that I said 'no' most ungraciously."

"Strange," murmured Sydney. "Cleone told me that I was a silly not to recognize an old bonnet that she had trimmed anew herself."

"Old! Trimmed anew!" cried Mercy.

"Well, you may be sure that I recognized Mlle. Galatoire's handiwork."

"But what did you *say?"*

Sydney pursed his lips. "What could I reply? She would never forgive me if I exposed her trick with m'tiger listening."

"Oh, very true," Mercy agreed. "I suppose I shall have to be forgiving—my mama would expect it of me—but it will be very uncomfortable."

Sydney, who had had some scales removed from his eyes, was not quite ready to see the whole of Cleone's self-interest.

He ventured to say that Cleone had been so much admired and probably had not thought the matter through. "Very likely she did not consider the disappointment to you. Charlotte and I will take you again to Mademoiselle."

"Perhaps it will not matter. My parents may come for me soon," Mercy said.

"From Greece? They surely cannot explore ruins and travel back to England so swiftly. We must commission Mlle. Galatoire to design something more splendid for you. You may want to order a new frock from Charlotte's modiste, one that will outshine Cleone's."

By this time Mercillia, though believing it was impossible to equal her cousin, much less outshine her, had lost her angry color and calmed considerably. She was grateful for the duke's kindness.

"I am keeping you from the other guests," she said. "We must return to the group."

"There is no hurry," he replied. "See, others are strolling through the trees."

"Yes, but I must not monopolize the chief guest. Oh, there is Mrs. Blakely with a gentleman I do not know."

"That's Blakely. Let us join them."

They strolled back to encounter the newlywed couple who received them warmly, and introductions were made. Mr. Blakely was known to the duke, though at least ten years older; they had little in common but met congenially since the young ladies seemed happy to renew an acquaintance.

Mr. Blakely was tall and slim, with a face rather too thin to be called handsome, but the fond expression on it, when he looked at his bride, was quite endearing to those who saw it. Mrs. Blakely was all smiles and sparkles; one of such amiable nature must always be welcome in the neighborhood.

The foursome drifted back to where food was being set out upon the tables, and presently took plates of delectables and sat together on a blanket.

Lady Charlotte did not at first notice this, for the crowd

was milling about, choosing food and finding seats, but when she did so, she thought, *How kind of Sydney,* and then, *But what of Cleone?*

Cleone was with another group, all young gentlemen, all laughing and talking as they ate. There was no sign that Cleone even noticed Sydney's defection, and Lady Charlotte, having never seen the bonnet that Mercy had bought, remained unaware of angry currents.

"Mercy cannot know many here," Sir Roland said as he sat beside her. "Notice how Sydney is being kind to her."

"Yes," she replied. "We know he has a kind heart. I am continually thankful for that. The other girl is Mr. Blakely's bride, whom Mercy and I met recently. She seems a sociable creature. Have you met her?"

"Not yet, but I will make a point to do so."

Mrs. Guinn and her younger son, Peter, came to join them.

"Have you everything you need?" she asked. "The servants will pass trays. You must not miss anything, but do save a bit of appetite for a new *gâteau* that my cook has been saying prayers over!" She was comfortable and happy in the company of Charlotte and Sir Roland; she preferred to avoid Mrs. Beecham's sharp tongue and had invited her only out of courtesy to the local clergyman. Mrs. Guinn was the daughter of a barrister at Birmingham; she was not bookish or smart, but ladylike in speech and behavior and generally regarded as an excellent housewife and mother. She sensed Mrs. Beecham's scorn (though who was *she* after all?) and peeped to see if the chaplain and his wife were comfortably situated. Cleone, she noticed, was the center of a group of beaux.

"Oh dear!" said Mrs. Guinn. "Cleone has all the single men, and Mariam Howerton has only the company of her brother! Peter, do you think you—"

"Certainly, Mama," he replied, demonstrating the excellence of his upbringing by standing immediately and taking his plate so as to eat with the young Howertons, whose parents were ignoring them, being deep in talk with another county family.

Looking to where Mercillia and Syd were talking as they ate, Charlotte thought, *Perhaps Sydney sees he is needed more by Mercy, who does not know many here.* It was like him to be kind to the girl. Mrs. Blakely and her husband were joining in a spirited conversation with them. Mrs. Blakely, Charlotte thought, was eager for friends in the neighborhood. Too bad Mercy was not staying.

Sir Roland's eyes met hers. "That is a congenial group," he said. "You can see Sydney will be acquiring quite a circle when he has been a while at college."

"Oh, is he to go there this Fall?" asked Mrs. Guinn. "My husband is making sounds of sending Alexander somewhere, although his tutor is still with us."

"Will he not be staying for Peter?" said Charlotte.

"Yes, but I cannot say how long. Peter is wheedling about a career in the army, which, of course, I cannot view with any peace of mind." She sighed. "Thank heaven he is young yet. If we put off a difficult decision, maybe we will never have to make it."

It was a philosophy that made Lady Charlotte and Sir Roland smile.

When the large and luscious *gâteau* made its appearance, it was escorted by two maids in ruffled aprons and was greeted by an admiring crowd who rose from their blankets and pillows to cluster about the table where the Guinns' butler took it upon himself to slice this piece of art and expose a layer of ground apricots in rum. The maids held plates to be served and passed them out to guests.

If the persons present had never previously graced a pik-nik, they formed an exaggerated impression of such entertainments. No one was stung by a bee or annoyed by a gnat, and sitting on blankets kept ants away. No apples fell on heads. The air was balmy.

Mr. and Mrs. Beecham were among the first to leave, perhaps to maintain the chaplain's ecclesiastical dignity . . . or perhaps he wished a nap. His wife had had the pleasure of seeing Cleone surrounded by beaux, and though the duke was not one of them, numbers counted for something. At least Sydney came forward now to take away Cleone's empty plate and help her to her feet. Neither had anything to say to the other, but Mrs. Beecham did not notice this, as her husband was leading her away to their gig. When she looked back she caught a glimpse of Sydney's helping Cleone to step into his curricle. There was only one other vehicle between them as they rolled down Squire Guinn's drive.

"I hope you did not feel I was neglecting you," Alexander said to Mercy, replacing the duke at her side. "I saw Sydney was lunching with you, and I did not like to force myself upon him—a duke, you know."

Mercillia, ever attentive to feelings, said soothingly, "We more or less drifted together with Mr. and Mrs. Blakely, and it seemed natural to sit with them."

Alexander said in a relieved voice, "I see. You won't mind waiting a bit before we leave? Mama will want me to speed guests on their way."

She waited comfortably with Lady Charlotte until a number of guests had gone and then watched Alexander hand that kind lady into a carriage with Sir Roland, Miss March, and Mr. Macnaghten. In the last carriage, a tilbury, she went off with Alexander, having had a pleasant time because of Sydney's attention to her, despite Cleone's duplicity.

What she would say to Cleone she could not decide, and in the end—that day at least—she was obliged to say nothing, for Cleone was not visible when they reached the Dower House.

Mercy's beautiful bonnet lay abandoned upon Mercy's bed.

The girl looked at it sadly. As Sydney had so readily understood, she would never wear the bonnet herself, and to burn it up would be difficult, attracting unwelcome attention. To give the bonnet to Cleone's *maid* did not occur to her, as that would be diabolical and her mind did not work that way. So she placed it amidst its tissues in the box provided by

Mlle. Galatoire and stuck it in the top of her wardrobe, where it might be conveniently forgotten when she returned to her parents.

In an odd way, Cleone's wearing her bonnet was a compliment to Mercy's taste. To forestall any other thefts, Mercy thought it might be well to lock her door, which turned out to be impossible, as Mrs. Beecham had taken away the key on the theory that young ladies should have no secrets so important as to lock them up. Chaplain Beecham would never enter a lady guest's room, and there were no young brothers to worry about. Only a larcenous daughter.

At the castle, the duke was uncertain whether to tell his sister about Cleone's trick. He had seen the bonnet in Mercy's hands originally. He saw it on Cleone's golden locks today. There was no way to escape the hurtful truth of Cleone's having taken it. His loyalty—his infatuation with pert Miss Beecham—was severely strained, and he concluded that perhaps Charlotte need not know. It was possible, just barely possible, that Cleone would find a way to make amends.

He might have spared himself debate. The first thing his sister said to him when they had both reached home was, "Explain!"

"So you guessed something was wrong?" he replied, shrugging his shoulders.

She said, "So far I do not think Cousin Maude has guessed anything, but I smell a mystery. Tell me at once!"

He sighed and flung himself in a chair. "It is not pretty. The bonnet you saw upon Cleone's head was Mercy's treasured *chapeau,* taken without her permission."

Lady Charlotte was too cautious to pounce upon this treachery. "And you think Mercy is—er, disappointed?"

"Crushed," said her brother flatly.

"You mean that Mercy will never want to wear it now?"

"Would you?" he asked.

"No, I would not. Oh, dear! I daresay Cleone never gave a thought to Mercy's feelings."

Sydney said, not very hopefully, "Perhaps Cleone was overcome with the beauty of the hat—it went very well with her frock—and she just didn't realize Mercy would be hurt."

This was too much for his sister. She burst out, "When did that girl ever think of someone else?"

Sydney blanched. "She didn't mean to harm—"

"Did not *care,*" asserted Charlotte. Then the stricken expression on his face made her add more pacifically, "She has not had much experience with competition, of course. In Fallford she has been Number One—hasn't had to consider other girls."

"That's right," he said eagerly, "no competition in Fallford. Bound to be a little—spoiled."

Lady Charlotte made a slight gesture with her hands. "You said it, not I."

"When she thinks it over," he persisted, "I am sure she will realize—make amends somehow. Surely her mama will explain—"

"That her cousin should be glad to lend her bonnet?"

Sydney, being unable to condemn his old playmate completely, said, "She didn't *steal* it. She can give it back with an apology."

"Cleone? Apologize? Even so, do you think Mercy will wear it now that her cousin has put her mark upon it? Not likely! I will have to take her to Mlle. Galatoire for another—"

"That is just what I told Mercy!" he exclaimed.

"Making promises for me?"

"No, no. That is, not exactly. I said *we* would take her to Mlle. Galatoire again."

She smiled suddenly. "That is exact enough for me. Yes, we must see that she has a splendid new bonnet. Very likely Mrs. Blakely would like to go with us."

Sydney said, "Oh, jolly! I will give you ladies a fine meal at The Grenadier."

Seventeen

"Where," asked Mrs. Beecham of her daughter when she had her alone, "did you get that bonnet?"

"Oh," Cleone replied lightly, "I borrowed it from Mercy. I have already returned it."

"Her mother has excellent taste. Borrowed it, did you? Perhaps Mercillia will give it to you. It certainly blended well with your gown."

Cleone said vaguely, "I do not know if I really like it all that much. I did not receive many compliments."

"Well, if you decide you want it, just give Mercillia a little hint," said her mother. "After all, we are keeping her, free, for an undetermined time. She is a meek creature and must have seen it looked better on you than it would have done on her."

Having thus been indirectly assured that purloining her cousin's bonnet was quite all right, Cleone dismissed the whole matter from her mind. What she did not so easily overlook was Sydney's neglect of herself. She hoped her mama had not noticed.

But her mama *had.* "How did you let Mercy monopolize the duke? That was a serious mistake, let me tell you," Mrs. Beecham said with a gimlet look at her daughter.

"Well, Mama," she replied smoothly, "there were so many gentlemen around me as soon as I stepped down from the curricle—there just was not *room.* I did not think it was wise to let Sydney suppose he was that important."

Mrs. Beecham thought about that. "Perhaps you are right," she allowed. "Must keep him a bit unsure. Yes, make him more eager to attach you."

When Sydney did not call the next day, both ladies wondered if a mistake had been made after all. Instead of Sydney, a note arrived from Lady Charlotte, requesting Mercillia to drive with her and Mrs. Blakely to Hays the following day. They now knew something was wrong. They were very cool to their houseguest, but somewhat relieved the next day when the carriage had stopped for Mercy, to find the duke was not with it.

They saw the carriage turn left, obviously going to fetch Mrs. Blakely, and although the Beecham ladies watched for it to come back through the village and head for Hays, there was still no sign of Sydney when it did so. They hoped he was coming to call at the Dower House, but he did not.

Sydney, planning a surprise for his sister's guests, had left early by horseback and was waiting at The Grenadier when the ladies reached it. Instead of a groom or the host of the inn, the duke himself was at the carriage door to hand them down gallantly.

The younger ladies were gratifyingly glad to see him, though his sister exclaimed, "Syd! What are you doing here already? We intend to do some serious shopping."

"Oh," he replied breezily. "I have my top boots to collect. Perhaps you will take them back in the carriage for me? I won't interfere with your tour of the shops, but you must let me have the pleasure of giving you lunch."

Shaken by this further evidence of her brother's rapid maturing, Charlotte managed to agree to their meeting him at one o'clock for a meal which he would choose. Then he bowed and went into the inn, calling for the host, and Charlotte led the girls from the inn yard without saying another word.

Her guests were alive to the sights of Hays.

"This is a delightful town," Mrs. Blakely said. "There is so much in Shropshire for me to see and admire!"

With an attitude like that, the bride would find a warm welcome, Charlotte thought. She glanced at Mercy and found her smiling; that one was quieter, yet pleasantly compliant. The three of them were destined to be congenial. Charlotte was eldest, of course, though not a married lady and not sophisticated, even though mature beyond her years—beyond what the other two would ever be. Charlotte admired Mercillia for her sweet lack of guile and Sue Blakely for her enthusiasm and gaiety. She realized she had been missing the delights of girlhood friendship.

Since Mlle. Galatoire was the target of the day, they went first to her. She and Mercy greeted each other like friends of long standing, with a outpouring of French.

"It is so good," declared Mademoiselle, "to hear my language spoken—*c'est vrai!*—so well." While she and Mercy discussed another style of bonnet, Lady Charlotte and Sue Blakely prowled, looking at hats and trimmings on shelves, and even peeping into the back room where Mademoiselle worked her magic.

"My husband is so generous to me," Mrs. Blakely whispered earnestly to Charlotte. "Beautiful new hangings in my boudoir and the smart curricle in which I came to your house with a servant driving—until my husband has taught me how to do so myself—and pin money such as Papa never gave me! Why, I can wish for nothing. It is delightful to find there are good shops in Hays, although I need nothing now."

Charlotte said, "You are fortunate."

"Yes, I know," returned Mrs. Blakely. "Papa was not so generous to Mama, though I think he might afford—" She broke off, turning pink.

"Mr. Blakely must like to show his love for you," Charlotte said with a smile.

Sue Blakely flushed more deeply and said, "Oh, yes!"

Lady Charlotte had never been in need of any material

thing, but she thought, wistfully, that it might be wonderful to receive an outpouring of love. She said, "Then you do not wish to purchase anything today?"

"Oh, no," Mrs. Blakely answered. "I need nothing."

Meanwhile, Mercillia had examined several pretty bonnets in the shop and had almost settled upon one, because she was anxious not to disappoint Mlle. Galatoire, but the Frenchwoman said, *"Non! Non!* These will not do. We must try something different." She rustled into her workroom and returned with a partially finished bonnet of yellow straw. "This brim should be of a size to suit your face—and the color so complementary to your lovely brown hair."

She set the bonnet upon Mercy's head and the other ladies gathered around to view the result.

"Voilà!" exclaimed Mademoiselle.

Her customers sighed, "Ah!"

The lining of the poke was silk of a curious greenish yellow which added a tawny glow to Mercy's gray eyes and set off the creaminess of her complexion.

Mlle. Galatoire said, "I have not trimmed the crown as yet, you see, but I think—some cream and yellow flowers of silk—yes, and a touch of green—and some delicate loops of very narrow brown ribbon . . ."

The viewers sighed again, and Mercillia said happily, "I have a yellow dress—not new, but a favorite."

"Voilà!" pronounced Mademoiselle triumphantly a second time. "I shall complete the bonnet soon, and it shall travel to you on the mail coach. It will not take long. Two days, perhaps."

"Do you promise two days?" demanded Mrs. Blakely.

"Certainement."

"Then," said Mrs. Blakely, "I shall plan a garden party. We shall include the gentlemen so they can admire Miss Pope also."

Mercillia, somewhat overwhelmed, made small sounds of deprecation, but Lady Charlotte, recognizing both her friends needed reassuring—Mrs. Blakely for usurping leadership and Mercy for unaccustomed attention to herself—quickly said a garden party would be perfect for this tirne of year. "I shall have to review my wardrobe to see what can compete!"

"A new bonnet?" inserted Mademoiselle skillfully.

"You are forgetting the one you made for me two months ago. I shall wear that . . . but Miss Pope will eclipse me." She arched her brows and pretended a sigh.

Mercy looked guilty until she decided Lady Charlotte must be making a joke, for she thought no one could eclipse her ladyship. Then she said, "A battle of bonnets!" and the others tittered.

From Mlle. Galatoire's they went to a bookshop where Lady Charlotte wished to purchase fashion magazines. That done, she and Mercillia had accomplished their bits of shopping, but they took Sue Blakely to visit other vendors, so she would know where to find linens and lotions and gloves and slippers, when she might have need of them.

"The selection is very good," Sue said. It was plain that she was prepared to approve of everything connected with the county of her new home.

This attitude so obviously found favor with Lady Charlotte that Mercy was compelled to say, "Mama and Papa *told* me I would enjoy Shropshire, and I do!"

Sydney was waiting for them in a private parlor, and not one of the ladies gave a thought to the remarkable honor of being the guest of a duke, so easy was his manner and so comely his appearance. He had a very light wine ready for them, a local wine, not to be despised and not too heady. It made the meal festive.

"Sit here, Charlotte," he said, seating her. Then he placed the girls on either side, and took a chair facing his sister, so as to divide his attention courteously between the three of them.

Charlotte wondered when and how he had learned to handle ladies so smoothly. Then she realized he was talking with

Mercy, and as Sue Blakely was claiming her own attention with a question about doctors in the area, she turned to Sue and answered that Hays had two doctors and there was great rivalry between them. She mentioned two names.

"My mama will be glad to hear this. In the excitement of viewing my future home—my new home—she quite forgot to ask about this, so I must write her about two doctors in Hays. I am extremely healthy, you must know, but Mama worried about my going to another county where there might be no physician nearby."

"There is no one in Fallford," Charlotte said, adding with a wry smile, "We do have an excellent veterinarian."

Sue giggled and said, "Well, I will not tell Mama about *him.*"

"Both the Hays doctors will come to Fallford if needed. Mr. Hoyt is most respected. So is Mr. Murry, for that matter, and *he* will gallop on horseback if the need is urgent."

Meanwhile, with some interest, Sydney was asking if the usurped bonnet had been replaced.

"Oh, yes," returned Mercillia happily. "Mlle. Galatoire had several from which I could choose. Then she said *'non'* and brought out one half-finished, and we agreed I should buy that."

"Tell me about it," Sydney said. Having been a party to the original choice, he seemed to think his approval was needed for the replacement.

Mercy said, "No, indeed. You must be surprised."

"Not fair! Why, I feel this new bonnet must be half mine."

She shook her head. "That is nonsensical. If you claim half you should be obliged to wear it half the time, and I would be deprived of half a bonnet."

"Very true," said Sydney, being serious about such nonsense. "At least tell me the color."

Mrs. Blakely, who had caught this word, broke off her conversation with Lady Charlotte to exclaim, "Oh, Mercy has bought the sweetest hat, and I am to give a garden party so everyone may see it."

"Must I wait until then?" asked Sydney, assuming a put-upon tone which appeared to delight Mrs. Blakely, who replied:

"Indeed you must."

"Just tell me the color!"

The ladies exchanged looks.

"Well, then, yellow," said Mercy.

"Ah," said Sydney, as if the color of a bonnet was immensely important. "Of course. Yellow. So it will not be necessary for the sun to shine."

"Indeed it must!" asserted the bride. "I insist upon sunshine for my garden party."

Mercy, who was practical, thought it high-handed to expect the sun to shine on command. She said, "Suppose it rains?"

"Oh, it cannot. My husband will order a beautiful day."

Her hearers thought such confidence in a husband was so impressive as to be some sort of tribute to Mr. Blakely. For all his living nearby, Charlotte scarcely knew the man—just how-do-you-do in passing and a few words exchanged at Mrs. Guinn's party in the orchard—but she was willing to assume that Sue Blakely was in a position to know her husband best. She was not so naive as to suppose all husbands were devoted to their wives. Her own mama was so long gone that she could not judge her father's attitude, but as for Cousin John, certainly Cousin Maude domineered *him.*

Luncheon was concluded with a custard heaped with rich, fresh whipped cream. Then they went out for a final walk about Hays's town square, Sydney leading off with Mercillia, telling her something of the town's ancient history, and leaving his sister and Mrs. Blakely to straggle behind to look at stonework and dooryard gardens such as caught their notice.

"Which came first, Heritage Castle or this town?" Mercy asked.

Sydney said he was ashamed to admit he did not know.

"The castle came before Fallford, a ferocious ancestor of mine having seized the land in some sort of skirmish. About Hays I am not so sure. Parts of it look ancient—"

"Like the Norman tower of the church?"

"Yes. The rector might know more. I remember Papa's saying he is an antiquarian—in his own age as well as in his knowledge. Are you going to say I should know these things?"

She began hastily, "I would not presume—"

"Well, you should. I should know everything about this area, as well as the English history that Oxford will teach me."

In her gentle way she defended him, saying, "You cannot be expected to know *everything* about—"

"Sir Roland says I must, if I am to take a seat in Lords one day."

She had not thought of anything so awesome as that, and it silenced her.

"But I do know about this horse trough, having watered my horses here often enough," he said blithely. "Nothing is more practical than to know where to find water for one's cattle." He indicated a stone basin at one side of the town square. "This is fed by an ancient stone sluice from a spring up the hill. Roman work, I daresay. Never fails."

Suitably impressed, Mercy said, "My papa will want to see this when he comes."

"Does he have an interest in Romans?" the duke asked.

"Anything ancient. Why, this must have been here hundreds of years, if Romans constructed it."

"Great engineers," Sydney affirmed.

"Yes, that is what my papa says. I have visited Italy, but only the northern part. I would like to see Rome."

"Jolly fine, they say. Aqueducts would put this simple pipe to shame, though the principle is the same. Makes one look at little Hays with some respect."

Mercy raised the subject of Hadrian's Wall. "We spent one summer near the border, and I remember Papa's tramping day after day to look at the remains of what Hadrian built early in the second century."

"To keep the Picts in their place, I daresay," said Sydney.

"Papa said it was to mark the northern boundary of Roman Britain."

"Ah! What you say sounds reasonable." That little Mercy should be telling him such things made him even more eager for college. "I must hope to learn more at Oxford."

"Oh, yes! I do envy you."

He gave a look at Mercy's upturned face. "I believe you do, little one," he said. Having a sister who was knowledgeable in the ways of landholding (learned from her father), he was not surprised that Mercy should have absorbed certain information from hers.

"How did your father learn about so many ancient things?" he asked.

She said, "He is so full of curiosity, you see."

"And has he made you memorize everything he discovers?"

"Oh, no. Papa has not forced anything on me. He has an air—an aura, you might say—that makes one want to *listen.* The poor dear would like to have a son to tramp ruins and scratch in dirt with him."

"So he instructs you?"

"Yes, but I like learning. Mama goes with him everywhere and makes sketches of what he thinks important. Then she paints things that she finds especially beautiful."

Anyone hearing would have thought the Popes an unusual family. They certainly did not sound like any family Sydney knew. That his own family, with a young woman in command of a very grand ducal estate, was somewhat remarkable, did not occur to him. His disposition was easy; he seldom found fault with anyone, certainly not a sister who cherished him and guarded his interests at all times. He was beginning to realize that Charlotte did not view Cleone as he did—a dazzling little beauty who kept him dancing her tune by assorted wiles and lures.

Mercillia, on the other hand, was much more restful, and when she talked with him separately was astonishingly knowledgeable in interesting subjects. He was beginning to expect other stimulating persons at Oxford; a university, he concluded, would be more than books.

The same thought was in Charlotte's mind, though with a difference. More than books, yes, but *what?* Not gambling and other excesses, she hoped. Keeping an ear for Sue Blakely's conversation, she watched Sydney talk happily with Mercy and wondered if he could see the difference between her and Cleone. Between Sue and the Guinn girls and Mariam Howerton and the flirtatious Cleone Beecham. Without being aware, Charlotte sighed.

"Are we tiring you?" Mrs. Blakely asked quickly.

"Not at all," Charlotte replied. "I was thinking how much I shall miss my brother when he goes off to Oxford. The castle will seem dull for Auntie and me. Just think! Auntie talks very little, as I expect you have noticed. How somber meals will be!"

"Never fear," said Sue promptly. "I shall invite my brother for a visit and he will stir things up."

If this unknown young man was anything like his vivacious sister, he would be a welcome addition to Fallford. Charlotte was conscious of curiosity to know how old he might be . . . and whether he was at all dashing . . . and single.

"Perhaps your brother will have other obligations and interests," she suggested carefully.

"Oh, Giles is always willing to meet new people. I have looked up to him for ages."

An *elder* brother, Charlotte concluded.

Eighteen

"You were an excellent host," Lady Charlotte told her brother when they had both returned to Heritage Castle by their separate ways.

"I enjoyed your company," he replied. "Always yours, of course, but also that of the new members of our neighborhood. How did your shopping go?"

"I bought only these," she said, indicating several journals spread about her on the settee where she was sitting.

Sydney pushed some fashion magazines aside and sat beside her. "Those two—those girls," he said, "are very pleasant company. One cannot be gloomy in Mrs. Blakely's company—or Mercy's. The more I think about Mercy, the more I am sure that she hesitates to put herself forward in company, but one-to-one she has intelligent things to say."

"Well reared," Charlotte opined. She was wise enough to stop there and not mention Cleone Beecham.

"I think," he said ruefully, "that her education has been better than mine. Now, don't blame yourself! I only mean her education has been on other lines. For all I know, she may not be able to multiply thirty-seven by fifteen, but her papa and mama have certainly schooled her in the things that interest *them*—history, antiquities, and such."

Charlotte smiled at him. "You are not accustomed to hearing young ladies discuss things like that."

"No," agreed Sydney. "All I hear is flirtatious talk."

Again Charlotte did not pick up his choice of word. "One

meets each person on his own ground. At Oxford you will meet all sorts of people with all sorts of ideas, some of which may be quite bad. Whom you believe and whom you admire must depend upon their principles—upon the common sense of what they say."

"You are afraid I will be led astray," he accused.

"Well, yes and no."

"Do not worry, Charlotte. Father was not around when I reached an age to make critical judgments, but you and Sir Roland have been here to keep me pointed right. Mercillia says I am fortunate."

"Mercy does!"

"Yes. And it is true. I shall try to be worthy of you."

Then he went off to scan Heritage's library for books that might tell something about the history of Hays and the surrounding countryside, leaving his sister to mull over their conversation and long to tell Sir Roland about it.

Sir Roland did come calling after dinner that night, but Sydney monopolized him with questions; besides, Auntie Emilie was omnipresent, so Charlotte had no chance of private words with him.

"How is it that you left Katherine and Macnaghten alone?" she asked.

"They have gone for cards with the Guinns," he replied. Before he left, he said to Charlotte, "If the morning is fair, as it seems likely to be, let us have a ride."

There was nothing that Charlotte would like better than to unburden herself about the new serious aspect of Sydney and to ask if it was sure that Sydney would be accepted at Oxford. What course of study he would choose was as yet unknown. If he was to go, she needed Sir Roland's opinion about his best program.

"Will you ride with us, Sydney?" Sir Roland asked.

"I would enjoy a morning canter," answered Sydney, "but I promised Cleone a walk around the pond. Then there are some books I want to search for amongst Father's."

"Oh?"

"Ones about the history of Shropshire, and Hays especially. Mercillia was asking about Roman ruins."

Sir Roland cocked an eyebrow. "Was she? I might have something, if you do not find what you want here." To Charlotte then: "Will nine suit? While the air is freshest? Bring a groom, if you want to venture far."

Lady Charlotte replied that she was ready for a long ride "to shake the fidgets out" and would bring Andy.

Auntie Emilie was nodding her approval, but no one noticed.

Their neighbor's departure took some of the vigor from the room, so the Helds soon decided it was bedtime and went up the stairs together to separate in the upper hall with fond "good night" and "sleep well" and "pleasant dreams."

Charlotte thought, as she had done hundreds of times, that they were fortunate to have Sir Roland for a friend. She was able to snuggle into bed and, for once, not worry about the machinations of Cleone Beecham and her ambitious mama, even though Sydney planned to take Cleone for a walk. Already Sir Roland seemed to have taken subtle charge of Sydney, and she knew she could depend upon the wisdom of this neighbor and friend.

Sydney had not appeared at the breakfast table when she went down the next morning. There was no reason for him to eat as early as she and Aunt Emilie did. Like others of his age, his energetic actions were interspersed with sprawling abandon on a bed, and meanwhile Cleone would have her "beauty sleep." Ten or eleven would be time enough for him to call at the Dower House.

At Sir Roland's manor, the owner, who was no slouch, had his breakfast early and issued routine orders to his staff. As he had anticipated, the day was fair. He finished a hearty meal and rode off to Heritage Castle. Kate would probably rest until noon. Charlotte he expected to be ready for him, which she was.

Andy was waiting with Prince and another horse, and Charlotte came outside as soon as the footfalls of Sir Roland's horse were heard. He did not dismount, for Andy tossed her to her saddle.

"Let us go eastward," she suggested with a nod of greeting. "There are some fields I have not looked over for a time."

He agreed readily, so they set off at a trot with Andy following a discreet distance behind.

"Did you sleep well?" Sir Roland asked.

"Very," she said. "It is wonderful the way you deal with my brother. We are both old enough now to realize why our papa looked upon you with such favor."

"Well, thank you. But have you stopped to consider that *he* was an example to *me?"*

"No," she replied in some surprise, "that had not occurred to us. He died while Sydney was still a child, and although I was fifteen, I did not think beyond my brother's needs. He was bereft and I—"

"Thought only of meeting those needs?"

"Yes."

"Well, my dear Charlotte, it is time for you to think about your own needs."

She glanced back and saw Andy was far enough behind not to hear the conversation. "Actually, I have none."

"Nonsense! A beautiful young woman should spread her wings."

"Wings? I have hoofs!" she exclaimed, sending Prince into a canter.

Sir Roland was only a couple of strides behind her, and Andy spurred also with a grin, not intending to race with his mistress, but keeping a watchful and admiring eye upon her equestrian form. He was pleased to be chosen over Pucket to escort her and knew she could match anyone in handling a horse.

They crossed a field, sailed easily over a hedge, and drew up at the far side of a second field.

"How could I do that in London?" she demanded, hardly even breathless.

"Well, you could not," Sir Roland admitted, "though you could swoop over ballroom floors with great effect."

"Are you pushing me to London again?"

He grinned. "My dear girl, I would not 'push' you anywhere. Only consider the jaded beaux who would welcome a new diamond to brighten the London scene. What about *their* pleasure?"

She frowned at him. "You know I care nothing for the opinion of dandies. How superficial Society sounds!"

"Sydney will be going there before long," he reminded. "You must be in a position to guide him—recognize social leaders as apart from climbers—depress pretensions of the wrong sort. You will have to go with him. How much better to be acquainted ahead of that time! If you mean to be useful, you must establish yourself first."

Charlotte said she had not thought of that.

"I will make a prediction," Sir Roland continued. "If you go to London when Sydney goes to Oxford, by the time he is ready for Town you will have acquired a husband and an elegant London residence of your own."

"I had not even thought of the problems of opening Audley House," she admitted, ignoring his suggestion of her own establishment, but turning slightly pink. "Here comes Andy. Let us move on."

Sir Roland said no more about her future. "There are cattle in the next field. Shall we turn off to the right?"

They did as he suggested, rising slowly, until the castle lay below them, and Fallford lower still.

"Look south," he said. "There is a glimpse of my chimneys."

"Oh, I do love our lands," she replied. And then a moment later: "What in London can compare?"

"Perhaps nothing. But sooner or later Sydney will go there.

A duke, you know, must take his place in Society. I am not talking about sowing wild oats."

"Papa cared nothing for London."

"Yet he went there from time to time."

"Yes. And you are right—Sydney must take his proper place. I have been so anxious about his choosing Cleone as a very improper duchess that I have thought of little else."

"She is quite beautiful—"

"And knows it."

"You are forgetting one important thing," Sir Roland said. "Sydney is going to measure any enticing female against *you*."

"Me!"

"Yes," said Sir Roland with a warm smile. "A homegrown, close to hand, highly competent lady."

Charlotte frowned at him. "You helped to raise me."

He was silent for a moment, then said carefully, "If so, you are a credit to me."

"Please!" said Lady Charlotte. "Let us speak only of Sydney." She cast a glance at him. He was looking—quizzical?

"Very well. My last word about Sydney—this morning—is that he is beginning to see Cleone's true colors. But whatever her colors, his chief thought now is for Oxford. You need not worry about his going to London for a while. Race you across this field!"

He did not let her win.

Indeed, she could not, Prince being no match for his powerful horse. Andy straggled behind as they flew toward a distant hedge.

Eventually they reached the southern border of Heritage land and halted to see if any traffic was moving along the turnpike. A fourgon passed, and presently two dusty riders. They moved lazily through a sheltering grove of larch trees to reach the stone gateway of the castle's state entrance, and from there, upon the formal driveway a mile or so to the stone pile of the castle.

"It is not beautiful, is it?" Lady Charlotte murmured. "But somehow *pleasing.*"

"Well, Palladio might not think so, but we can enjoy its noble proportions," he replied. "Succeeding additions have added bits of—er—flavor, and the aspect is one of strength."

"You are being polite," she accused. "Your home is truly a thing of beauty."

"But with less antiquity."

They had halted to view the castle, and now moved ahead.

"I cannot feel Cleone is worthy of Heritage," she said pessimistically.

"No, but don't surrender to her yet. She is a very young girl with dreams of grandeur. Did you not have daydreams when you were seventeen or eighteen?"

She said seriously, "No, not that sort."

"You were busy raising your brother, which is not, *not* the usual occupation of a maiden. I have never known a young women with less self-interest!"

She shot a sideways glance at him, and he seemed serious.

"Who is to reign as Duchess of Audley is very much in *my* interest! I could not continue to live here and watch that little minx make Sydney's life horrid."

They were halfway up the driveway, from which point there was a splendid view of the castle.

"Would you want me to have a serious talk with Syd?" Sir Roland asked.

"Could you?"

"I suppose so, but I do not recommend it. Might put an idea in his head, which may not be there now."

Charlotte gave him a little, contrite smile. "I knew you would set me straight in my thinking. Sydney calls me Mother Hen, and that is what I am! Hen-witted!"

Sir Roland laughed heartily, making Andy, several yards back, wonder what could be so jolly.

They continued around the castle to the stable yard, where Pucket come out to assist Lady Charlotte to the ground.

"Will you come in for coffee or tea?" she asked Sir Roland, but he said it was time he went on duty at home as a chaperone of his sister.

"We both have odd duties, have we not?" she asked.

Sir Roland ducked his head in agreement, touched his crop to his cap, and cantered back toward the main gate of Heritage.

When he entered his home by a rear door, two servants told him that he had a visitor waiting, and upon his reaching the front hall, his butler was just carrying in a tray of coffee to the library.

"It's His Grace, sir," said the butler, endeavoring to open the door and keep his tray level at the same time.

Sir Roland turned the knob, standing back for the servant to precede him.

Sydney had been at a window. "I heard a horse, but did not look out in time to see you pass."

Sensing from Sydney's solemn demeanor that the visit was important, Sir Roland said, "Well, here I am, and Vonner has brought coffee for you. I will have a cup, too, Vonner."

The servant had set down his tray. He went to the door to speak "cup" to another outside, then returned to pour out a serving for the duke. Sir Roland's cup came almost immediately, and Vonner poured for him also. Then he went quietly away, shutting the door to leave them in privacy. Like his master, he had read a certain seriousness in the duke.

Sydney stirred his cup, took a sip, and then set it aside.

"With all this business of going off on my own to Oxford," he began slowly, "I had fallen into the way of thinking I could manage quite well on my own."

Sir Roland said, "Yes?"

"Well, already I discover I cannot cope as well as 1 thought."

His host studied the duke's serious face. "Cleone?" he asked.

"Yes. No," said Sydney. "At least, not what you are thinking. She may be in a pet with me. I have displeased her more than once over the years, you see. I have always more or less let things blow over. She comes around eventually. The thing is, this time she is being rather—uh, unpleasant to that little Mercillia, who doesn't know how to retaliate and would not do so if she did."

"Where is Mrs. Beecham in all this?" demanded Sir Roland.

"Almost as bad—as unfeeling as Cleone. I do not understand what is going on at the Dower House. *Mercy* does not complain, but things are pretty chilly there."

"What does Charlotte say?"

Sydney colored slightly. "I have not asked her, because—because she does not have the best opinion of Cleone, and I do not want to stir up family fights."

"When did you and Charlotte ever fight?" queried the older man.

"Never had need to," the young duke said with a half-smile. "It is Charlotte and Cousin Maude that might come to blows, and that could be messy." His coffee was cooling, but he sipped a bit. His face was troubled, a nice face as always. Amiable. Sir Roland liked the clearness of Sydney's brown eyes and the steadiness when they met his own.

"Generally," said Sir Roland, "I would advise never to interfere in females' squabbles, but I take it you feel Mercy is being hurt."

Sydney said, releasing a breath, "That's it. And her being alone in the world, so to speak."

"You will have to tell me more," Sir Roland said patiently.

The duke set aside his coffee cup again and leaned forward earnestly. "Cleone does not ride, you know. I went down to take her for a stroll around our pond, the day being so mild and pleasant, but she said the breeze disturbed her hair and stirred up dust—or pollen—or some such thing to annoy females. You know how they want things to be Just So. Anyway, a lizard, a tiny creature, ran across the path, and she said suppose it ran across her shoe and soiled it. In the past I didn't hear nonsense like that from my old playfellow!"

"So then?" encouraged Sir Roland.

"Nothing must do, but we must return to the Dower House. Mercillia was there when we went into the drawing room. She came forward to speak in a friendly manner, and Cleone said, in what I am afraid was a very cutting manner, 'Don't hover.' "

" 'Hover'?" repeated Sir Roland.

"Yes. It was hurtfully said. Oh, over the years I have seen Cleone be cross a time or two, but there was no reason to turn on her cousin like that!"

"What did Mercy do?"

"Do? She backed away, of course, but I could see she was hurt, and what could I do? Not quarrel with Cleone in front of her."

"No, of course not," agreed Sir Roland. "I need to know what Charlotte thinks of this."

Sydney said it was very strange. "She is avoiding the subject of Cleone . . . I wonder if you had something to do with that?"

Regarding him steadily, Sir Roland said, "I might have or I might not. It is not always easy to tell for sure if a woman takes advice."

Sydney ran fingers through his hair. "Like to give it, though! I daresay Charlotte has some idea that I am under the cat's paw, but I am *not*."

Sir Roland said he was glad to hear that. He took a swallow of coffee. "The thing is, Charlotte *cares* about you and doesn't think you have compared Cleone to other young ladies. Have you done so?"

"What young ladies? Those silly Guinn girls? Nice enough, but not a serious thought between them!"

Sir Roland dismissed the Guinns: "Still too young. They will look more promising in a couple of years."

"Not to me!"

"No, to someone else. I suggest you forget about local girls and concentrate on your books, Sydney. After a time on your own at college, everything, girls included, will look different to you."

"Well, I hope so," said Sydney fervently, "but this does not solve the problem of Cleone's coldness to Mercy."

Sir Roland's eyes narrowed slightly as he examined the face of the young duke. "You have seen that words can wound."

"Yes!"

"But not slay. Mercillia, by not retaliating, has grown in character, hasn't she?"

Sydney said "Yes!" again with a different emphasis. "Will Cleone learn something, too?"

"Possibly. Though maybe not what we think she should. In any case, it is not up to you to teach her. Your own character, your own attitudes are what you will be held responsible to maintain."

"I see. Yes, sir. Thank you for setting me straight. Charlotte thinks I should pattern myself after you."

"Good God!" exclaimed Sir Roland, thunderstruck. "Has she said *that?*"

"Well, not in those words exactly," answered the duke. "Just that we are fortunate to have you to keep us steady."

"Makes me *unsteady* to hear that," the baronet declared.

Sydney grinned suddenly, "Then I need not be ashamed to be unsteady also. In the meantime I can—"

"Take the elder Miss Guinn for a drive," inserted Sir Roland. "Then take Mercillia. Then, perhaps, Cleone."

"I see. Play no favorites?"

"Exactly."

"But what if Cleone keeps wounding Mercy, sir?"

"Then leave Cleone off your list. Who is the duke around here? Leave her off if she can't be civil to her cousin."

Sydney said, "Yes, sir!" and went away in more cheerful spirits.

To himself, Sir Roland said, "Egad! Will Charlotte part my hair with a milking stool? It is difficult to play at being a father!"

Nineteen

While Mrs. Blakely was waiting for a warm sun to dry her paths and lawns so that she might invite guests to a garden party, her husband had an idea to please himself. He was quite willing for Sue to plan what she chose for neighboring ladies, but he had the notion that the gentlemen might like some activity, especially if it would attract the ladies' admiration.

"What would you say, my love, if I have a target set up for some pistol shooting? Oh, not on top of your ladies, but within their view."

Mrs. Blakely, being still in bridal euphoria, said, "Oh, yes—if you do not think the noise will make the ladies nervous?"

"We won't be so close as that. You plan to set your tables in the open area of the herb garden, do you not? If the ladies are sitting there, they will have a view of the west lawn, which is where I can place targets."

"We will hear the claps, I fear," Sue objected.

"Yes, but the breeze will be blowing away from you across the openness of the lawn and will carry off much of the noise. Good shots will very likely bring cheers, and that would be a pleasant sound. It will be interesting to see who is best among us."

Giving reluctant agreement, Sue asked what weapons he would use.

"Well, one does not compare pistols to guns. Perhaps we can have a contest with each. I have my father's dueling pistols which, as far as I know, he never fired, but they have been kept well oiled for action."

Sue looked dismayed. "Dueling pistols! Have you never used them?"

Her husband chuckled. "Never, my love. That is one sort of match I will never win."

"A duel? Oh, say you never will be party to one," she begged earnestly.

"Never," he promised, stealing a kiss, to the interest of a passing gardener. "But you know I hunt from time to time, so I may do better with a gun."

And such was her confidence in him that she assumed he would win any rifle match, though she had never watched him shoot a rifle—or even hold one.

The lawns dried, a date was selected, and invitations dispatched. It would not be so large a group as Mrs. Guinn's had been, no more than could be seated comfortably at several tables in the herb garden—Lady Charlotte, of course, and the duke, Sir Roland, Miss March, Mr. Macnaghten (who seemed to have taken root in Fallford), Squire and Mrs. Guinn with their sons and daughters, three from Howerton Manor (the son being thought too young). That made sixteen, counting the hosts. Sue wished to invite her new friend, Mercillia, and realized to do so she must include Chaplain and Mrs. Beecham and that very *trying* Cleone. She also thought of Mr. Todd but, as her numbers were an even twenty, dismissed him from her calculations, his being no more than what she might call a recognizable face. She wished her brother might visit in time to join the group, but she had had no word from him since writing to suggest that he come to meet "darling Lady Held."

In the neighborhood of Fallford, summer life went on naturally with workers in the fields and orchards. Landholders rode about to see that all was as they desired. Although the duke went on rounds with his bailiff, he had time to take Miss Guinn for a tour of the lanes, with his scarlet-coated tiger puffed with pride behind them. Sydney did not find Miss

Guinn very conversable, so when he had exhausted his own patter of this-and-that, he stopped at Fallford's small hostelry to have lemonade brought out for his guest. This was more successful than conversation, for Miss Guinn was delighted to have a crowd of villagers see her with His Grace; nervousness had made her throat dry, so she sipped lemonade happily. When Cleone Beecham passed down the village street and saw her, Miss Guinn's cup overflowed with joy.

The next day Sydney called early at the Dower House. Miss Beecham had not yet descended, but her mama and Mercillia were just finishing breakfast. He was able to invite Mercillia for a drive, which annoyed her aunt, as was seen by her grudging permission, and to whisk Mercy away before Cleone had even discovered he was in the house.

"When shall I see the new chapeau?" asked Sydney, tooling his curricle northward past the village green.

"At Mrs. Blakely's garden party and not before," replied Mercillia, considerably more at ease with him than she had been a few weeks earlier.

"Well, that plain straw will do for today," he said with a side glance at her. "I expect you to dazzle Mrs. Blakely's guests. It should be soon, if this sun lasts. Now, we will soon see the trout pool."

They rolled across the carriage bridge.

"See. Here is the footbridge."

He drove onto the verge and stopped the team; his tiger jumped down to take charge of the horses, and Sydney assisted Mercy from the curricle. The footbridge and pool held no shame for him, for he had not willfully misbehaved there. In fact, he was not even thinking of purple-beaded reticules when he led Mercy onto the footbridge. She knew nothing of his close escape from scandal.

"Oh, what a charming spot," exclaimed Mercillia. "Do not tell me this is a Roman bridge." Her eyes were dancing.

"Silly girl!" said the duke. "You know it is not. An earlier footbridge here was rotting and my father replaced it a dozen years ago."

Soon they were calling each other Mercy and Sydney without being aware of having abandoned formality. The duke had no exalted ideas of himself, and both of them were very young.

"If there is a Roman well at Hays, I thought this might be a Roman bridge." Her eyes were twinkling, so he knew she teased. "After all, Caesar built a wooden bridge across the Rhine."

"Did he? By Jove!"

"Roped together, my papa says. I have not seen the spot."

"Amazing girl—the things you know!" Sydney said admiringly. "I have the feeling that I belong at the village school, not Oxford."

"But, Sydney, of what *value* is knowing what Caesar built? You will study all sorts of important things at Oxford. Oh, I *envy* you!"

"Then come along."

She frowned slightly, which only made her face more interesting. "You know women don't—cannot. So unfair—though I daresay not many would want to do so."

"Well, while you are at Fallford, you are welcome to borrow whatever books you may want from my library." As he said this, he suddenly realized he had said *my* library when forever he had thought of it as *Heritage's* library. "Let us go up now and have a glance at it."

If Cleone, watching from a window crossly, thought Mercy's drive was short, she soon saw the curricle was not stopping at the Dower House, but continuing up the slope to the castle.

Sydney's tiger was instructed to wait with the curricle, while he led his guest indoors, calling for Lady Charlotte who appeared on the landing of the stairs.

"Oh, Mercy," said her ladyship. "Good morning."

Mercy sketched a curtsy.

"Pay no attention to us," advised Sydney. "We are going to look over the library for Roman ruins."

"Ruins in *there?"* laughed Charlotte.

"No, no," said Sydney. "In books, goose. Come along, Mercy. We will see what we can dig up."

"Use no shovels in our library, please," admonished Lady Charlotte, amused at their interests. Seeing Sydney lead Mercillia to the library and leave the door wide open, she returned to her chamber, confident that the footman in the lower hall would be chaperone enough.

"Wherever can we begin?" wondered Mercy, turning in the middle of the room to scan walls of books. "This is a huge collection."

"I have not found Papa's catalog—if indeed he had one," Sydney admitted. "Sir Roland said there should be one. Perhaps we should look for that first."

Mercy said she could not like to pry into drawers. "Let us each take a section of shelves and see if it holds a particular category."

"Very well," said the duke, glad of her willingness to help. "I have already discovered that the section to the right of the door is mostly very old ledgers of farm business. The one next to it may be just as boring, so I will take that, if you will start to the left of the door. But beware of dust. I should not like you to dirty your pretty frock."

Mercy said gamely, "I do not see a sign of dust. Lady Charlotte would never allow such a thing."

"Probably not," he agreed. "But reach no higher than your head. I'll use the ladder for upper books."

Since not all the spines were labeled, it was necessary to pull some volumes partway out to look for a title, and even then some had only medallions on the front and must be lifted from their niches to be opened.

"These are in very good condition," she said.

"Someone comes from London every year or two to keep

them from moldering away," he said. "Charlotte can tell you. Oil the covers—things like that."

She said, "If that much care is taken, there is sure to be an inventory."

"I need to learn so much," he muttered. "Without Charlotte, Heritage could have crumbled away, for all the notice I've paid."

"Well, you are beginning to learn a great deal. I daresay you already know the condition of every fence and ha-ha."

He halted with a volume in his hand. "Made a survey of the cottages with Lewis, our bailiff, recently, as a matter of fact."

"That is a good beginning . . . look at this, Sydney. Maps of Shropshire, I think."

He strolled across to see the book she held. "Ah! May be useful."

With heads together they examined the book superficially, then exchanged glances of accord. Her gray eyes held a sweet and friendly expression; his were brown and warm.

"Put it on the table, so we can look at it more closely later," he said.

"Suppose, I put it crosswise above its neighbors," she suggested. "Then we can easily notice it again and also will know where to return it when we have finished with it."

"Oh, very good!" approved the duke. He released his hold upon one half the book and returned to his bank of volumes, all of which seemed to be looking at him with serene gray eyes.

When Charlotte entered an hour later, they had moved farther apart, and each had set volumes horizontally. Mercy had marked most, for she had a positive thirst for knowledge, and Sydney had three.

"This looks like an odd game," Charlotte commented.

"No, no," said her brother. "A way of marking books that may be useful to us."

"If you plan to read all these, we will be out of touch for weeks," Charlotte teased.

He replied that they had not nearly finished. "You do not mind if I leave certain volumes oddly placed?"

"No, indeed. It is your library, after all. But you must eat occasionally. Lunch is soon to be served. Mercy, I have sent a note down to tell Cousin Maude that we are keeping you. Will you come upstairs and wash the dust from your hands?"

Mercillia cast a quick look at her palms. "They are not so soiled, for the books have been well dusted," she said, "but of course I must go to your table perfectly clean."

Charlotte took her to her own room for a quick wash, after which they joined Aunt Emilie at the head of the stairs to come down together.

"I am famished!" Sydney greeted them. "Who would have thought sorting books would promote such an appetite?"

"It is not books, but being young and male that causes it," his sister replied, leading them to the dining parlor.

During the meal they discussed Mrs. Blakely's garden party.

"Weather could not be better," the duke said between bites.

"Yes," agreed Charlotte, "the lawns will be dry enough now not to spoil ladies' slippers or hems. I was never entertained at Mr. Blakely's before, since he had no mother or sister to receive me. I will be interested to see how he has maintained his property. Mrs. Blakely seems to think all is perfection, and I daresay he brought all to prime condition before bringing home a bride. They seem quite devoted, do you not think?"

"Yes, I do," replied her brother immediately. "She is a jolly sort. Makes one think well of matrimony."

Lady Charlotte smiled at Sydney's adjective and exchanged an amused look with Mercillia. "Marriage is not simply a matter of jollity. Amiable give-and-take counts for much, I think." Who was she to make pronouncements like that? What experience had she had? She only spoke of what seemed important to herself.

Even so, Auntie Emilie, who had never been married, was nodding in agreement.

"It is what I have noticed about my parents—a oneness," Mercy said, and then blushed violently and ducked her head over her plate.

Charlotte thought it an odd sort of oneness that let Mr. and Mrs. Pope go off for months to Greece and leave their daughter to the not-so-tender care of Maude Beecham, yet she *did* see unusual poise and maturity in this young girl.

With not much enthusiasm Sydney pointed out that it would be necessary to make some plans for transportation. "Suppose I send down our carriage tomorrow for Cousin Maude, Cousin John, and the girls. You can go with me in my curricle to the Blakelys' entertainment, Charlotte."

His sister opened her mouth to say he would prefer to squire a young lady (someone less than twenty-four). Only in the nick of time did she remember this would mean his making a choice between Cleone and Mercillia.

"I would be charmed! Mercy is not the only one with a new garment! My dress has come from Hays, and you must be suitably impressed by my wearing it in your company."

"I shall be honored," declared the duke, bowing his head so grandly as to almost sweep crumbs from his plate.

Mercy laughed and clapped her hands.

"Oh, Syd is being most ducal!" Charlotte declared.

"But not enough so to be granted a description of Mercy's new *chapeau!*"

Mercy bit her lip and shook her head violently.

"Well," said the duke decisively, "Charlotte and I shall not drive off from our gate before Mercy has come out of the Dower House for us to see her in Mlle. Galatoire's newest creation. Face facts, my girl!"

It was not until they were leaving the dining room that anyone remembered Sydney's tiger, who had been left for hours before the family entrance to tend the sleek curricle and its well-bred pair.

"Yipes!" cried his lordship, smiting his forehead. "I completely forgot my horses!" He strode down the hall to the outer door. "Gone!" he ejaculated.

The servant on duty at the door said placidly, "Gone around to the stable an hour ago, Your Grace. Tiger said he thought the horses needed water."

Despite his mortification, Sydney laughed ruefully and said it was a good thing to have a tiger with practical sense.

"Do not send for the curricle again, Sydney. I can easily walk down the slope, and the weather is pleasant," Mercy said.

"I will escort you," he replied firmly. "Besides, I need to tell Cousin Maude they are to have the carriage for Mrs. Blakely's garden party."

So Mercillia fetched her bonnet, reticule, and light, unused shawl from the library where she had left them, and they set out, Charlotte watching from the doorway.

"Did I work you to death?" asked the duke.

"No indeed," she assured him. "I can help you anytime. They must tire of seeing me at the Dower House."

"Well, we don't!" he declared stoutly.

Both Cleone and her mother were in the drawing room when Sydney and Mercillia reached their destination. Neither had any glad words to say, although Mrs. Beecham went forward.

"Good afternoon, Cousin Sydney. Cleone, here is Sydney to see you."

Cleone offered a frosty smile to the duke and ignored her female cousin, saying, "Will you not sit down, Syd."

"Not this afternoon, thank you. I have been working in my library and am not fit for proper calls." He turned to Mrs. Beecham. "I only came, Cousin, to say that I am sending my carriage for you, Cousin John, and the girls—to take you to Mrs. Blakely's garden party."

"But your sister—" she began.

"Oh, I have promised her a ride in my curricle," he said

quickly. "The weather outlook is good for several days, I believe."

He glanced about for Mercy, but she was already halfway up the stairs. "Charlotte is waiting . . . Good afternoon," he said vaguely, bowed, and went out. Either Beecham lady he could have dealt with satisfactorily alone, but two at once? Best to go quickly.

The conscience of neither Beecham lady would allow them to upbraid Mercy for usurping Cleone's place and time with the Duke of Audley, and the chaplain, coming from his study in time to hear Sydney's farewell and to sense his ladies' mood from their disgruntled expressions, said with unusual sharpness, "You are not gracious to your niece, madam wife."

Mrs. Beecham opened her mouth to protest, but he continued: "Your sister has entrusted her only child to you. She is a dear girl, and though only a connection of mine, must be made welcome in *my* home." Having shocked them by strong words, he retired to his books, leaving his wife and daughter speechless.

Mrs. Beecham was first to find her tongue.

"Sydney is only asserting his independence," she said. "Mercy is no match for you, Cleone, or of any consequence."

"Cousin Charlotte seems to have made a pet of her," Cleone complained with a sulky look.

"No, no. She is only trying to distract him from serious thoughts. Hasn't he taken that insipid Guinn girl for a drive? You may be sure his sister proposed that."

"She has taken Sue Blakely under her wing, too."

"That is just my point. She is trying to make him attentive to all the young ladies in the area, so as not to single out *one*. But none can match you for looks, and I daresay—if you put your mind to it—you can attract Sydney more by being *sweeter* and more open and *admiring* than any other. Bees go for honey, you know!"

Cleone did know. Her temper was hot and quick, but her

mother made sense. "Why did Mercy have to come here just now?" she grumbled.

The cold war ended, and what Mercillia made of this there was none to say; *she* remained as gentle as she had been reared. So it might be said that Mercy won without fighting, though Cleone studied to improve her own lures. Perhaps a taste of jealousy might revive the duke's attention . . .

So the climate warmed at the Dower House. Mercillia was quick to notice this, and she concluded that her cousin had only been in a grouchy mood and had recovered. The swing of moods was not something Mercy understood, but she knew they happened. Her own faithful maid had fits of being glum, yet reacted to the changed atmosphere in the next few days by smiling unusually much.

The next day must be perfect.

And it was.

After lunch and a rest upon her bed, Mercillia went happily down in her new *chapeau* to await the coming of the duke's carriage. Her dress, though not new, had been exquisitely fashioned by a French dressmaker and was wonderfully suitable for her, being of light yellow with hand-embroidered scallops about the hem and the cuffs of sheer, matching sleeves. She looked delectable and very feminine, which, indeed, she *was*.

Cleone was not impressed, for her style was considerably more sophisticated. She wore a light frock of cornflower blue that enhanced her eyes marvelously. It billowed out behind her so as to make other ladies' gowns look positively limp. To maintain this picture, it was necessary for her to walk about a great deal, but numerous gentlemen were eager to offer arms for the support of her slim, artistic hand. She was very gay and gracious to them.

Though she made no more of him than of the others, the Duke of Audley was one to stroll about with her, until he was called to take his turn at the pistol competition. He handed her over to Mr. Guinn, which was quite a comedown for such a diamond, but Cleone was as gracious to him as to her bachelor beaux.

When Mr. Guinn asked if she would like to take tea, she said oh, yes, she *would,* and allowed him to lead her to the herb garden, where she chose a chair that turned her back most casually to Sydney's performance.

Lady Charlotte, Mercillia, Sue Blakely, and Katherine March stood together to watch Sydney shoot. He did not even hit the tree upon which the target was set.

The ladies groaned, but Sue added that her husband prophesied the same result for himself. "They will do better with rifles," she quoted her husband as saying. "That contest will come later."

While the contest continued, Sydney came to join the four interested ladies, and where he went Cleone managed to follow.

"Mercillia has a pistol," she told them, sweetly awed.

"What!" exclaimed His Grace.

"Yes," admitted Mercy, realizing that Cleone had snooped in her belongings. "Papa thought I might need it for protection."

Sydney asked, wondering, "Do you know how to shoot it?"

"Oh, yes," said Mercy. "Papa taught me himself."

"Then Mercy must represent the ladies in this match!" Cleone declared gaily with sparkling eyes.

Though other ladies looked rather shocked, some of the men, hearing, urged a demonstration, and Mercillia found herself being propelled willy-nilly to the firing line.

Mr. Blakely regarded her doubtfully, and reluctantly handed her a loaded dueling pistol.

"It is somewhat heavier than mine," she murmured. "More difficult to hold steady." Would her parents have objected to this display? She thought to refuse might make a more uncomfortable scene than to shoot. She turned her right side toward the target, raised the gun, and fired.

"Good God!" cried Mr. Blakely.

Mercy had missed the target, but struck the tree one half an inch below it.

Cleone was forgotten as all the men surged around Mercillia to congratulate her, and ladies streamed out of the herb garden to see what was causing the excitement.

"Closer to the target than I was!" the duke jubilantly told anyone who would listen. "A great deal closer! With her own pistol she would have beat us all."

Twenty

Seeing that Mercillia was exceedingly embarrassed, Lady Charlotte said firmly that she must sit and have some soothing tea. She nudged her brother, and he said, "Oh, yes!" and led Mercy to the herb garden, where she sank into a chair and a maidservant supplied her with a hot cup. Other ladies found seats around her, as Sydney returned to the competition.

Mrs. Beecham, one might imagine, was not pleased with her niece, but for once kept a lock on her tongue, as other maids distracted the ladies with trays of watercress sandwiches, fruit, and dainty assorted cakes.

Mercy's high color began to fade, and when, eventually, conversation turned to other things than pistols, she was able to relax and enjoy Mrs. Blakely's hospitality. With her hostess on one side of her and Lady Charlotte on the other, she could not feel rejected—or even guilty. It was better, she found, not to meet her aunt's eyes.

Across the lawn Mr. Blakely organized the gentlemen into a rifle competition, moving them a greater distance from the target. As he had told his wife, he shot better using this weapon. All the men did so, with Mr. Macnaghten, the unknown, winning the laurels. After some gathering around the target for jawing and spouting, they, too, were ready to go for refreshments amid the ladies.

With twenty to talk there was a great deal of noise. No one heard or noticed a high-perch phaeton coming up the driveway to halt before Mr. Blakely's front door. The driver, a tall young man, with hair so blond as to be almost white, stepped down, shrugged off his drab driving cloak, tossed it and his hat to his servant, and commanded Blakely's servant, who had come out to meet him, to "do something" with his rig.

He heard the sounds of merriment and spied figures beyond the house, so strode buoyantly across the lawn, calling, "Am I welcome?"

"Giles!" cried Mrs. Blakely, swooping to him with joy. "You are just in time to meet my delightful neighbors."

Her husband was close behind her to welcome his brother-in-law warmly, as who would not, when the gentleman was so comely, with becoming side-whiskers and bright blue eyes, and so obviously an extrovert, as fine as fivepence.

Cleone was sure to view him with favor, just as surely as his eyes settled on *her.* Being presented to his sister's guests, he managed adroitly to fetch up beside Miss Beecham for an exchange of light repartee.

Mrs. Blakely's party, which had been going very well, became a resounding success.

"Oh, Giles does liven things up, doesn't he?" she whispered to her husband.

He pressed her elbow to him and turned a smile down toward her, which would have revealed to anyone who might be watching that Mr. Blakely was as enchanted by his wife as she by him. It was an exceptionally warm relationship for the times.

When refreshments had been eaten, and everything said that could be said, guests began to wilt, though Giles Dunlop brimmed with good spirits, not the least exhausted by a five-hour drive to Fallford.

Vehicles were summoned, passengers loaded.

"Ask the little blond beauty to stay for dinner," said Mr. Dunlop into his sister's ear.

"What! It was Lady Held that I invited you to meet," she whispered, turning slightly aside so others would not hear.

"Yes, but it's the blonde with the signaling eyes that I aim to know better."

"Not for you, dearest Giles, can I do that," she responded briefly, before bidding goodbye to Mr. and Mrs. Howerton. When momentarily free, she added, "It would be very poor form to single Cleone out from the group. You will have to pay a call on her mother and the chaplain."

"Chaplain!"

"Cleone's papa is the duke's chaplain."

Giles said no more until the last guest had gone. Then he resumed the conversation as if there had been no break. "Very well. I shall go to call. But where, exactly?"

"The Dower House of the castle. You will find Mercillia there, too. She is on a long visit while her parents are in Greece."

Giles remained cheerful, but raised his brows. "So I call on all four? Not precisely exciting. Daresay I shall have to invite the saucy temptress for a ride in my phaeton."

"Yes," said Mr. Blakely, who had reserved comment until now, "and take your servant along, or Mr. Beecham will not permit her to go outside the fence. We don't allow scandals in this neighborhood. There are eyes everywhere."

"Oh, dearest," said Sue anxiously, "Giles means no harm. Flirting is second nature for him. He would not deliberately—"

Her brother said, "Certainly not! I might, you know, be serious about such a little charmer."

Mr. Blakely said flatly, "Not when you realize her dowry could be next to nothing."

Sue looked astonished to hear her husband speak so bluntly. Could her brother be a *rake?* Surely not, when she knew him to be the sweetest brother in the world.

He smiled at her. "Then perhaps I should pay more attention to Lady Charlotte, eh? Handsome woman."

"Giles!" Sue cried indignantly. "I hope you are teasing! Lady Charlotte is my friend. I will not have you make her the least uncomfortable."

Her husband inserted: "Giles will not do that. Lady Charlotte is too clever to be taken in by a Bond Street Beau."

"Bond Street B—! I say! That is libelous," Giles protested, and fell into great guffaws.

Mr. Blakely took him off to his study for a convivial cigar, while Mrs. Blakely scampered to her boudoir to apply calming cologne to her forehead and wrists. Her husband seemed to think a mild warning would keep his brother-in-law from causing titillating gossip in the neighborhood, but she could not be sure. She hoped to live in peace here for ever and ever.

None of the three—Mr. or Mrs. Blakely or Giles Dunlop—had the least idea that eighteen persons of Fallford environs were thinking of them. Gentlemen, having enjoyed the shooting match, generally were resolving to practice their skills so that no young girl could ever again outshoot them. Their wives and daughters—excluding Mercillia Pope—were wondering how to achieve an ensemble comparable to Cleone's cornflower blue.

Lady Charlotte, too, was an exception, for she rejoiced that Cleone, perhaps, had a new gentleman to distract her from pursuit of her brother. No mere Mr. Dunlop could compare with a duke in a worldly sense, yet this Mr. Dunlop had engaging ways to turn the head of an inexperienced girl.

No doubt Mr. Dunlop enjoyed turning heads.

On the day after Sue's garden party he was off on a tour of the neighborhood with beaming face and exquisitely knotted cravat, first taking morning coffee with a gratified Mrs. Howerton and Mariam. Then down the road to Mrs. Guinn and her excited daughters, where conversation would have faltered if the squire had not come in to jolly things a bit. Then on to Sir Roland's manor, where the master and guest from Carlisle had ridden off somewhere, leaving only Miss March to receive him. As she was too old to be an interesting flirt and not old enough to be a helpful dowager, and as a granite-faced maid attended her, he did not linger here.

Then it was up the main drive of Heritage to pay a call of

courtesy upon Lady Charlotte Held who was gracious, though somehow intimidating. But for accident of being born female, she might have been a duke. He had the uncomfortable feeling that she viewed him as a fribble. She was in riding garb and obviously intended to trot somewhere. So, after a few casual sentences, he was happy to follow her directions down the back driveway to the Dower House, where he fetched up just in time to be invited by Mrs. Beecham to share a cold collation. The chaplain and Mercillia joined them, but both were rather quiet. This meant that conversation fell upon the visitor, Maude Beecham, and her enticing daughter, which was quite satisfactory to the three of them.

He was not a duke, nor even a knight or baronet, but he was young, handsome, conversational, pleasantly self-assured, experienced in charming females. At this house he was a huge success. In the meantime, Giles's servant had found his way to the Dower House kitchen, where he gave Mr. Beecham's maids a flutter by a fair copy of his master's style.

Mercillia's companion, who had been charged by Mr. Pope to guard his daughter from triflers, was not to be cozened, but this particular servant was of no interest to Mr. Dunlop's man. Much too old for him!

When, in the drawing room, Mr. Dunlop asked courteously if Miss Cleone could drive out with him to show him the neighborhood, Mrs. Beecham cooed, "Yes—delightful." Before her spouse could reach a conclusion about this stranger who was well connected if a little brash, Cleone had run upstairs to fetch a bonnet and shawl, and Mr. Dunlop's phaeton was ordered to the front door.

Chaplain Beecham, as parent and clergyman, regarded Giles Dunlop with doubt. He sensed no evil in the young man, but neither did he see virtue. Unlike his wife he did not expect Cleone to attach the duke; merely, he hoped for a gentleman of sense and substance who might exercise some control over her. Raising a daughter, a very beautiful and headstrong daughter, was not easy for him. All too often he left decisions to his wife, who would usurp command in any case.

"If you are wide-awake, you can learn the secret of charm from your cousin," Mrs. Beecham informed her niece complacently.

But Cleone was the one to learn something.

Cleone had not ridden in a high-perch phaeton before, and she hoped Sydney would see her. Those two, Cleone and Giles, might both be said to have met their match. They drove about Fallford happily exchanging frivolities. Neither was serious, each highly entertained, until Mr. Dunlop made the mistake (if it was a mistake) of saying, "I understand your cousin is quite handy with a pistol. Scored better than some of the men."

Cleone pursed her lips in disapproval. "Everyone insisted that she shoot. I was mortified at her putting herself *forward,"* she declared.

"But how did they know she could handle a weapon?"

"She—she was said to own a pistol."

"Who said so?"

Cleone did not answer.

"I see," he said, to her chagrin, making it plain by his tone that he understood perfectly why Cleone's face had become red and her eyes furious.

At the next broad place in the road, Mr. Dunlop turned his team and returned to the Dower House, where he instructed his groom to assist Miss Beecham to the ground.

Twenty-one

Meanwhile, at the castle, Charlotte was of two minds about Giles Dunlop. As the brother of Sue Blakely, whom she was coming to like very much, he must be acceptable to her. No one could fault his dress, speech, or demeanor, but . . . she rather suspected he was something of a rattle. She must ask Sue if there was another brother, an older one, his father's heir, with whom this Mr. Dunlop might be trying to be competitive.

Anyone who could distract Cleone from the duke, Lady Charlotte would prefer to think a very good sort.

After Mr. Dunlop went away, Charlotte mounted Prince and rode leisurely through fresh meadows, thinking in a sober manner about the problem of Cleone and Syd. Sir Roland had told her to keep hands off, so she was endeavoring to obey, but it was not easy. If Cousin John was hesitant to command, she had had long years of doing so. Where would Heritage be if she had not? She hoped that it was not vanity that drove her! Every day for nine years there had been decisions to be made; Auntie Emilie was of no use with those, though her presence was a comfort. And Sydney—he was a carefree child, just now growing up. Growing up? Suddenly quite grown . . . and a bit alarming.

Mr. Dunlop might distract Cleone for a time, yet ultimately he would go away, and the problem of Cleone would not. The only help Mr. Dunlop might be was in exposing Cleone's fickle nature.

Sir Roland kept telling her that she needed a life of her own. Well, Syd and Heritage had been the focus of her life, and unhappy was the thought that she must find something else.

When she returned to the castle, that charming visitor, Macnaghten, was having a consultation with Pucket in the stable yard while boys were watering three horses.

"Hulloo, hulloo!" he said blithely. "We have come for a call—Kate and Roland and I. Would have been disappointed to miss you."

She smiled her gladness at seeing him, for he could lift her spirits as nothing else would. His perpetual good humor was irresistible.

"But where are the others?" she asked, accepting his help to dismount.

"Where would my Kate go but to the garden?" he countered.

"Why did I ask?" said Charlotte, stripping off her gloves and jamming them in a pocket of her riding skirt. "Let us find them. The three of you are just what I need to cheer my spirits."

"Oh, are they in a slump?"

"Not now. I hope you are prepared to walk, for the gardens of Heritage are numerous. Have you any idea which way they may have gone?"

"Not the least," said Macnaghten blithely.

She said, "I daresay it will be where things are in bloom, so we can eliminate vegetables. Turn in here. Hello? Marches?"

There was no answer, so they strolled randomly. Sometimes there was a vista to another section of the gardens, sometimes views across low plantings, but no Marches were seen. They ceased to call, drifting into comfortable conversation.

"Do you think I am a fool to wait for Katherine to fall upon my neck?" Macnaghten asked with a trace of wistfulness.

"No," Charlotte said, smiling encouragement to him. "I cannot see how Kate can resist your devotion."

He said ruefully, "I wish she could be as easy to convince as you."

Charlotte laughed and shook her head as Macnaghten reached out to touch the side of her throat.

"Look, you were losing a hairpin," he said, catching it and handing it to her.

She took the pin, saying faintly, "Thank you," for over his shoulder she saw Sir Roland and Kate staring at her from the entrance to another garden.

In a second they turned away and vanished.

"What is it?" asked Macnaghten, puzzled.

"Kate," Charlotte said. "I fear she misunderstood your gesture."

He cried, "Good God! Forgive me if I run."

But he lost his way in the maze of gardens, and by the time he reached the stable their horses were gone.

Distressed that such a simple courtesy could be so misinterpreted, Charlotte jammed the pin into her hair and went slowly to the stables, barely in time to glimpse Macnaghten galloping from the yard.

She stood a moment motionless, debating what to do.

"Were you looking for Mr. Macnaghten, my Lady?" asked Pucket. "He followed the others. Miss March was leading toward the main gate like a wind."

"Never mind, Pucket," she murmured, turning toward a rear entrance of the castle.

Inside, someone said, "His Grace is in the library with Miss Pope," but she scarcely noticed, moving in a gray fog to the family wing. At the library door, which was standing open, she hesitated a moment, staring blankly at Mercillia. Sydney was not in view, though his voice could be heard muttering something. Without speaking Charlotte turned away.

"Oh," gasped Mercy, "something is terribly wrong." A tear

welled from each eye and rolled down a cheek. "I should not be here! She does not want me here!"

Sydney dropped a book with a thump and came quickly to her side, unconsciously taking one hand.

"Of course you are welcome here," he said soothingly. "You are always welcome. Charlotte is exceedingly fond of you. I have heard her say so a dozen times." He put an arm around her and drew her against his shoulder.

Mercillia dashed the tears away with the hand that was not captive. "You did not see her face. So o-odd, as if she did not see me at all. Oh, what can be the matter?"

Sydney was hearing a description of a sister he had never seen before in all his nineteen years. "Sit here, in this quiet corner, while I try to get to the bottom of this," he said, leading her to a chair. "I will close the door so you will not be disturbed." In his whole life he had never seen his sister in a an "odd" mood—or Aunt Emilie either, for that matter.

Outside her door he tapped lightly, and a colorless voice said, "Go away."

He hesitated. "Is something wrong? Can I help?"

After a pause, sounding a little more natural, Charlotte answered, "I will explain later, Syd. To be thought so—so—base—"

By whom? Charlotte could not be base. No one could think so! Puzzled, he returned to the lower floor, where the library door stood open again. Mercy had fled.

Next morning Charlotte did descend for breakfast, but a sort of gloom lay on the house. Syd had begun to think women were fascinating creatures; now he concluded there was no understanding them—Mercy flying off—and Charlotte indulging in vapors, as she never did.

After a few more moments of thought, he went out to the stables, called for his horse, and galloped off to Sir Roland's manor, where he found the owner at home, but not particularly glad to see him.

"Well, what is it, Syd?" Sir Roland asked with barely concealed impatience.

The duke brushed hair from his eyes. "I don't *know*—all so odd—Charlotte in a strange *closed* mood and Mercy for no reason at all thinking she's to blame—not welcome or something. Charlotte came in looking strange—stricken—and here's Mercy thinking she must be to blame, and running home to the Dower House, where no one will be any comfort to her at all!"

Sir Roland had no clue to Mercy's state of mind, but he did know what was wrong with Charlotte, or supposed he did. He made some effort to pull his thoughts together.

"Sit down, Sydney. Why are you in a pelter? Women are creatures of emotions. Have to blow up sometimes."

"Charlotte never does," Sydney said flatly.

"Maybe it's time. Look here, I am more than twice your age and I have never figured them out."

"My sister," said Sydney staunchly, "is one great person. Something or someone has hurt her badly."

Sir Roland closed his eyes briefly. "My sister has spells sometimes. Can't always guess what sets them off." He said again, "Take a seat."

The duke flung himself down. "Mercy has the damnable idea that she's to blame for Charlotte's state. Doesn't feel welcome in that Beecham menage, and gets the idea she's not welcome anywhere. I begin to think I should offer for her so as to move her up to the castle."

"Offer for her!" exclaimed the baronet. "I thought you were mooning over Cleone!" His astonishment drove him to drop into a chair.

Sydney flushed scarlet. "Well, I was. But her fits of temper are getting closer. Unrestful, don't you know? No one gives a damn about Mercy down at that house—and she with her parents so far away! Mercy's a taking little creature—like a kitten, I mean."

"Kittens grow to cats," Sir Roland said to the ceiling.

"This one won't," asserted Sydney firmly. "Soft all through—like butter."

So fascinated was Sir Roland by this window into the young duke's mind that he almost forgot his own problems. "I tell you what," he suggested, "let us give Lady Charlotte a few days to get over whatever is making her cross—"

"Not cross, unhappy," Syd corrected.

"Unhappy. Then have a talk with her about Mercillia. She is going to think you are too young for matrimony. What would you do with her when you go to Oxford?"

"Take her along," said Sydney.

Sir Roland muttered, "Um, yes. Well, let's not rush into something as important as choosing a future duchess."

"But she is damned unhappy at the Dower House. Oh, she does not complain, but I can tell."

"Only yesterday you were enthralled with Cleone Beecham."

"It's been more days ago than that. Several."

"Well, so it's as much as a week. You cannot marry anyone at nineteen, unless Charlotte and that score of legal gents agree. Mr. Pope will have to come back to England to give his permission. If you say anything in the meantime, all hell will cut loose at the Dower House."

"Can we not install Mercy at the castle with Charlotte, Aunt Emilie, and me?"

"Not until Mr. Pope has agreed." Sir Roland had a good idea that Mr. Pope would be glad to snap up a duke, but he did not mention this.

"I can write to him, can't I?"

"*After* you have convinced Lady Charlotte that you are serious, but she—"

"Is in some kind of depression. Well, thank you, Sir Roland. We will have to do something about Charlotte. She respects you, I know, for she has said over and over that we could not get along without you."

The baronet looked slightly ashamed and mumbled that he did not *know* . . .

Twenty-two

As soon as the duke had trotted toward Fallford, Sir Roland mounted with a grim face and galloped toward the main gates of Heritage. He dismounted at the family entrance and was asking—requiring—to see Lady Charlotte before Sydney had greeted Mrs. Beecham in her own drawing room. On the hill, Sydney's servant on duty had no hesitation in delivering the baronet to the office where her ladyship sat staring at the blotter of her desk.

"She's gone again," he said abruptly. "Back to Carlisle, last night."

Charlotte did not ask why, for if Sir Roland had misjudged herself, it was reasonable to suppose that Kate had done the same.

"At her tearful request—" he could not resist the adjective, "I sent her and her woman in a carriage to Hays with my most trusted man who was to hire a post chaise for them."

Charlotte shook her head helplessly.

"Macnaghten has written you a note, which I was asked to deliver personally to you and see that you read it immediately. I did not like to do this, you may be sure, but he insisted."

She accepted the note and tore off the wafer sealing it, then read silently and quickly:

My lady,

From the bottom of my heart I thank you for encouraging me to hope. Kate has fled, but I saw at once, with joy in my heart, that she has not run *from* me but *toward* me and my home, even though she may not realize this. If I catch up with her before Manchester, which I certainly expect to do, I have a cousin who is a clergyman of some standing there whom I will persuade to see us properly housed until licensed and wed. Wish me well!

Macnaghten

Wordless, she handed the letter to Sir Roland, watching to see if he would apologize or make excuses. He did neither, saying only, "That is one load off my mind. Pray, be calm and patient when Sydney comes to you with his new plan." Then he bowed, and was gone, and Charlotte fled to the sanctuary of her chamber.

New plan? Sydney?

Her head had been aching, but with this word from Macnaghten she eased in spirit. Whatever Sir Roland and his sister had falsely held against her, must be wiped out. How could they have supposed she—or Macnaghten—could be so base as to dally and flirt behind their backs? The thought made her blood run hotly—Sir Roland, who had known her all her life!

But a sense of fairness made her admit to herself that from their angle of vision in the garden, Macnaghten's catching of her hairpin *might* have looked like a caress.

So she brushed her hair now until it was gleaming and put on a less shabby dress. Then she went down to Aunt Emilie in the family parlor, to wait for Sydney to come and tell whatever new scheme he had. A trip for her to Oxford to approve rooms for him? Perhaps they could include an extra room, so she could visit from time to time . . .

Sydney was a long time in coming. She hoped Cleone and her mama had not ensnared him. Surely there was some way of putting a stop to the schemes that she suspected they concocted.

She sighed as she thought back over the years of their relationship. The Beechams had come to Heritage nearly fifteen years before. Cousin John had had no gray in his hair as he did now; Cousin Maude was slimmer and her nose less pointed (or so it seemed). Cleone, at three, was a beguiling tot, who had already learned to pout, but who was quite adorable to see. She and Sydney had played happily in the nursery together.

The duchess, Charlotte's mother, had been alive then, which made a difference in the household, and from her death, when Charlotte was twelve, Nanny and Mrs. Figg, the housekeeper, reigned until she herself took over at fifteen.

Charlotte loved Heritage. She knew no other life. She did not resent the responsibilities that fell upon her at her father's death, but when the young duke walked in that noon for his lunch and announced that he had a mind to offer for Mercy Pope, Charlotte felt the world crashing around her.

Offer! Marriage! When she had only *begun* to think he was almost grown, though certainly not of age yet to succeed to his father's dignities and offices . . .

She could not believe her ears.

But as Sir Roland March would have said, Charlotte was a creature of strong character. She did not fly into a rage or succumb to vapors.

Heeding Sir Roland's advice and direction, she said, "What do you mean?"

"Offer to wed," he said. If truth were told, he would admit qualms at springing this upon his sister, but he had decided—especially at this last visit to the Dower House, when Cleone had sulked and Cousin Maude had been more *piercing* than usual—that Mercillia needed to be rescued.

"Her situation is so uncomfortable. Something will have to be done," he continued, adding in a rush, "not that she ever complains."

"She does not look unhappy," Charlotte mentioned cautiously. "Has she *said* so?"

"Of course not. Mercy doesn't carry tales. The way she is

always serene is one of the things I like. *You* are serene, Charlotte. It's what a lady ought to be."

Lady Charlotte smiled faintly, glad he could not guess that she was churning inside. "Well, that is certainly different from Cleone."

"Yes. Cleone has those teasing eyes, and one never knows when a volcano will erupt—it makes her interesting. But I am coming to think she would be exhausting around the clock!"

Charlotte did laugh then. Sir Roland's advice had been as wise as ever, and she was glad she had heeded it. The problem of Sydney's wanting to marry at age nineteen remained as serious as it had been a few minutes ago when he sprang it on her, but they were communicating easily and affectionately now. She thought she must continue to speak cautiously.

"You are quite right"—it was a good beginning to guarantee his listening—"Mercillia's situation is not a happy one, but she stays calm, which is always wise, and appears to make as few ripples as possible. She is secure in the knowledge that she will not be beaten—or starved—or set at demeaning chores."

"I should hope not!" he exclaimed.

"Cleone and Cousin Maude do not intend to be harsh. Their jealousy and frustration are simply popping out like a rash."

Sydney said with a wry grin that he had never heard a view such as this. "I daresay you are right, as I am accustomed to your being, but what do we do?"

"Make haste slowly. See Mercy as much as you want. Keep your manner friendly. Look for simple amusements. Make no overtures that would embarrass a gentle creature. After all, her parents may have promised her to someone else—"

"Oh, I hope not!"

"Well, it is unlikely. The better you come to know each other, the clearer will your wishes become. A duke, Sydney, cannot marry simply to amuse himself. You have to think of your heritage—I mean, your long family history as well as Heritage Castle."

Sydney gnawed his lower lip. "I see what you are meaning, but, Char, what about you? You are a handsome creature and could be setting the *ton* upside down."

"I am not sure that I want to do that," she replied.

After a pause, he asked, "Can we not have Mercy to visit us, where she will be treated kindly?"

"Dearest—no. Nothing would set the Beecham ladies more wild and subject Mercy to more hostile treatment. We will always make her welcome for meals and simple entertainments. Cleone must be invited, too, if we are not to have war on our hands. And we can invite other girls of the neighborhood to dilute the attention."

"How colorless it sounds!" he complained.

"Yes, but anything else might embarrass Mercy. You would not want that, would you?"

"No, no."

Charlotte moved near him to touch his shoulder. "There is one more thing, my dear. You must not forget that you are a duke. All the advisors and counselors that surround you—though you may not see them—will have something to say in the matter of when and whom you ultimately wed."

"Good God!" he blurted.

"Yes. Mr. Pope must be investigated."

"Worse and worse!"

She smiled, and her eyes twinkled reassuringly. "It will be discreet. The Popes will never know."

"You cannot think I will change my mind!"

"One can never be sure of *that.* If you are patient, at least you can be sure of being sure."

"Now you are talking in a circle!" he accused. "Have you any objection if I appeal to Sir Roland for good counsel?"

Charlotte was glad to be able to say that she had every confidence in Sir Roland's wise advice.

When he had gone away, she rang for sherry and sat down

hastily, limbs atremble. The interview had gone very well. Peacefully. But it had been a strain. She was thankful for Sir Roland's veiled warning about Sydney's new plan. And thankful, too, for a good relationship with her brother, which made sensible conversation possible.

Turmoil seemed to have followed Mercillia Pope to Fallford, although she could not blame that appealing girl, who was just the sort to make a comfortable wife for Sydney, a wife who could enter into his interests, earn respect from his hundreds of dependents, and *not* turn everything to chaos with demands and sulks. Oh, yes, Cleone Beecham, hung with diamonds, might add glamour to his dukedom, but she would also add tantrums to his homelife.

Nagged a bit by guilt, Charlotte wondered if she misjudged the chaplain's daughter. After all, she was quite young and had not learned to compete with other girls in mature fashion. What real competition was there in Fallford? Her parents should be exposing her to Bath, which her mother knew well from having lived near there, or Brighton, or one of the less expensive watering places.

It was not likely that Cleone would encounter another duke. There were few of those, and none so easily approached as was her papa's patron, but young men everywhere had eyes out for beautiful girls, and undeniably Cleone Beecham was one of those.

A house party, Charlotte thought. *I will plan a house party. Several young men and girls.* But the recent strain of Sir Roland's misjudgment and Syd's flights of fancy had made her too tired to think of ways to amuse eight or ten young people.

Or perhaps her exhaustion was only the result of too much sherry in the middle of the day. Recklessly she drank another glass and closed her eyes (just to rest) until the warning bell drove her upstairs.

Several days passed before a note came from Sir Roland to report that he was leaving to attend the marriage of his sister and Mr. Macnaghten. It was beginning to rain, so he would not stop at Heritage, but would call on his return to tell the details of the ceremony.

This was good news, and as neither Auntie Emilie nor Sydney knew of the near-rift between the Marches and Helds, all could rejoice in the event.

"I suppose Miss March—I mean, Mrs. Macnaghten—will really be tied to Carlisle, so we will not see her often," Sydney said. "Sir Roland is quite solitary, isn't he? I should not like that."

"If you mean he lives alone, that is true," Charlotte answered, "but if you mean withdrawn or not sociable, then it is not true at all. He sees everyone in Fallford almost daily, and others in the county at least half as often. I cannot like to hear you criticize him."

"I'm not criticizing," her brother said, aggrieved more at being misunderstood than at her chastisement. "He's a great gun. Should think he'd like to have a family of his own."

"Perhaps helping to raise us has discouraged him from wanting family life," she suggested.

"Rot!" objected Sydney. "I daresay he enjoyed it."

"Liked an infant duke trotting his pony across newly laid sod—or the duke's half-grown sister breaking a Sèvres vase in the formal parlor of his house?" she retorted.

Her brother grinned. "I had forgotten those things, but I tell you, Charlotte, his old nanny told me more than once that he got his own sitter-downer blistered for sliding on the stair rail."

"O-oh," she giggled. "Was Kate ever naughty?"

"She did not say so. Too serious to be naughty, I expect."

Charlotte said, "Somehow it suits Kate to be serious. As for Sir Roland, I would describe him as level-headed. You, Sydney Held, were a young scamp, though never wicked. Who but a scamp would think of being married at the age of nineteen?"

She should not have mentioned the word marry, for he immediately became serious.

"Sir Roland does not make fun of me," he said. "Girls marry at sixteen-seventeen-eighteen. Why can't I?"

"Because men need mature judgment so as to think for two—and maybe for three—or four."

"Fudge! Men may plow the fields, but their wives decide when they should change their shirts. How did we reach shirts? Anyway, we began by talking about Sir Roland's loneliness, if he *is* lonely. I am glad I have had you to keep me company. Wish there had been half a dozen of us!"

"For me to rear? Heaven forbid."

Sydney grabbed her about her waist and swung her in a circle. He had grown so strong.

"Enough, enough!" she cried. It was no boy who flung her about. Should she surrender, let him tie himself to Mercy? Heaven knew, she did not want the responsibility of finding a more suitable duchess. Any girl she chose might not appeal to Sydney at all.

The rain passed off, and Lady Charlotte invited Mercillia to drive out with her for calls to families along the Hays road, killing not one or two, but three birds with one stone, so to speak—getting Mercy away from the gloom of the Dower House, introducing her to more cordial young ladies, and (for herself) looking for respectable girls to include in parties at Heritage.

All in all, it was a success, with the sun shining warmly, and Mercy pretty in her yellow frock again, with her Galatoire bonnet. All the families that they visited were long known to Lady Charlotte, though she did not see them often, as they generally associated with each other and looked to Hays as their focus, rather than little Fallford. The girls and their mothers were well bred, not inclined to push themselves upon the ducal family.

Mercy was as usual, perfectly at ease everywhere, though not thrusting herself forward. Charlotte was aware of her own increasing curiosity to meet Mercy's parents and learn more of what must have been a unique upbringing. She could sense that the Popes had done something *right* in the rearing of their daughter, though—contradictorily—they had gone off so far as Greece, leaving her behind. Could Mr. Pope have sent Mercy to Fallford with some idea of attracting a noble suitor? If so, the Helds would never know. Surely Mercy did not.

Sir Roland was away the better part of a week, his sister having begged to go on to Carlisle to be married at her cousin's home, for she could not bear to exclude this fond cousin from the momentous event. Mr. Macnaghten was delighted, Sir Roland willing, and so it befell.

Sydney, as Charlotte to her relief discovered, did not cause waves of speculation and resentment in their area by devoting all his attention to Mercy. He made rounds with his bailiff, found his father's catalog of the library, and began a minor rearrangement of the shelves. Mercy helped with this, but there were no emotional scenes, only good-humored cooperation. He also spent time with Alexander and Peter Guinn, the three going twice to Mr. Blakely for instruction in better use of a pistol.

It was all very wholesome, except—

Mercy's eyes were always upon him and they glowed softly.

Oh, dear, oh, dear, thought Charlotte, *What can be done? He is sure to guess her sentiments.*

If Sydney did so, he remained calm, but his gentleness with Mercy Charlotte found alarming.

She was thankful when Sir Roland returned like a cool breeze from the north. All resentment seemed to be gone. He was himself again, their kind friend and advisor.

"Kate is very happy. I am glad for that," he said, "but now her stay so far away is permanent. Before, there were always visits here to look forward to, and my visits there to keep us in contact. Now, I must accept she is truly *gone.*"

"You both will continue to visit, will you not?"

"Yes, but her home is now with Macnaghten."

Charlotte said encouragingly, "Tell me about her cousin."

"Oh, a dear lady," he said. "So pleased to have Kate settled near her. I had met some of their friends in earlier visits; this time I met the whole of their acquaintance. Delightful people. They welcome Kate genuinely. I can only be glad for her."

"Nothing stays the same, does it?" she said wistfully.

He glanced across the room, where Auntie Emilie was showing a new needlework pattern to Mercillia, and Sydney was watching benignly. "I have something to tell you," he said softly. "Let us walk onto the lawn."

Twenty-three

They walked out on the lawn and did not at once begin to talk. Charlotte was conscious of a great relief that the misunderstanding between them had been washed away with the rain. She had looked to him so long as benevolent critic, guide, and friend, and now, with Sydney asserting himself, causing her to doubt her own views, she needed advice more than ever.

"You are not telling me your news," she prodded.

"It is not news," he said. "It is a conclusion I have reached, and I am pondering how to begin." He smiled down at her. "On my way back from Carlisle, it occurred to me that I would be passing not far from Hewell Hall, which is the residence of my father's close friend, Lord Penfold. He is well up in years, and I should have been to visit him before now. It was a perfect chance to call upon him, which is what I did. He welcomed me more warmly than I deserved, with no complaints for my not having come sooner."

"Could you enjoy a real conversation with him?" Charlotte asked, supposing the gentleman to be ancient.

"Certainly! He is thin and fragile and somewhat stiff in his joints, but his mind is excellent. When I remembered that he had married very young, I asked his opinion of youthful marriages. 'Depends upon the youth,' he said. 'I had no regrets.' And when I spoke of our Sydney and Mercillia Pope, he slapped his knee and exclaimed, 'That's my darling!' Will you believe this? Mercillia, it turns out, is the gentleman's godchild."

Charlotte's mouth rounded in astonishment.

"Yes," said Sir Roland triumphantly. "Sydney may never wed her, it may all blow over, but what Lord Penfold had to tell assures me you need not be afraid of her."

"Ah!" sighed Charlotte.

"Yes. Mr. Pope's father, now dead, was a gentleman of the first stare. Wealthy, too, from shipping interests. Mercy's papa was not his eldest son, but the family wealth was enough to establish our Mr. Pope very well. The girl's mother is—"

"Cousin Maude's half sister."

"Yes, granddaughter of a viscount. Quite charming. Stands to reason. She charmed Lord Penfold's friend, Pope Senior, and he gave the union his blessing."

"That," said Charlotte, "is what Mercy told me."

"Penfold seems to dote upon our Mercy and hopes to see her before she leaves Shropshire. Does this make you feel better?"

She nodded. "Yes, about the girl herself, but not about a very youthful marriage."

Sir Roland was smiling, yet he spoke decisively: "You are not thinking this through, my intelligent Lady Charlotte. You like Mercy more than a little, I believe. If you will cogitate a bit, if you will permit an engagement now, you will be able to cease your worry. Syd can safely go to Oxford—and anywhere else for that matter—and be fully committed as well as protected from his being embroiled with a wrong sort of female."

"Good heavens! I had not thought of that." She studied his face to see if he were teasing.

He looked perfectly serious, however. "In any case, there can be no engagement in the next two months or so, for Mr. Pope must be approached and who knows where to reach him?"

"Oh," she said, "my head is spinning."

"Nonsense. It never does."

"You do not know everything about me," she replied darkly.

Sir Roland chuckled. "I know you can get a mailing address from Mercy. I know I can send that to the duke's trustees and ask them to approach Mr. Pope."

"Letters back and forth will take so long."

"But I thought the one thing we do not want is *hurry.*"

Charlotte muttered he was talking rings around her.

By now Sir Roland was frankly laughing. "See here. Suppose the duke's trustees write Mr. Pope suggesting a *possibility*—send a courier, perhaps—and Pope tenders a quick answer. One does not dawdle with dukes. He may even come back to England to seal a splendid alliance for his daughter. In the meantime, if either Sydney or Mercy has a change of heart, no offer has been made or accepted and need not be withdrawn. A bit embarrassing perhaps, but not insulting. Whatever time it takes for me to get in touch with Sydney's trustees and for Mr. Pope to reach Fallford, will be enough time for the attachment to evaporate, if it is going to do so."

She shook her head ruefully. "What you say makes such good sense that I suspect there is something devious about it, but go ahead and write. I daresay you will do so, even if I don't give permission!"

"Now, Charlotte, you know I would not act behind your back."

"Oh, go ahead," she said. "Go ahead. Syd's *sister* will invite all the bonniest girls of Shropshire to a house party!"

He said, "Well, better invite young gentlemen also, if your diversion is to work."

"Of course. And you must come to ogle with the rest."

"One need not do that," he replied, "if one has already seen perfection."

Did he mean Mercillia, or could he be implying *herself?* Surely not, for she knew that Katherine was his standard. Fortunately for the conversation, though unfortunately for Lady Charlotte, Maude Beecham was in sight, nearing the carriage circle before the family wing of Heritage.

Quickly she said, "Oh, look. There is Cousin Maude, and

I will have to go back to receive her. You may congratulate yourself on having the last word."

He merely inclined his head slightly, and she turned away.

From relief Charlotte's emotions had shifted to curiosity, and then to astonishment, to doubt, uncertainty, embarrassment, and now to annoyance. Maude was carrying a basket, which made Charlotte wonder if it contained another pot of chives.

She and Sir Roland strolled to greet Mrs. Beecham at the castle entrance. Then he continued to the stables, and she led the chaplain's wife indoors.

There was no sign of the young people. Down the hall a door of the library stood open, suggesting they had gone there, which impelled Lady Charlotte to hurry her visitor into the family parlor and close the door.

Auntie Emilie, peacefully knitting, looked up and nodded a sort of welcome.

Mrs. Beecham had no time for her. She addressed Lady Charlotte in a voice that blended whine with wheedle. "It seems an age since we had a little visit from you, dear cousin."

"Surely, only a few days," Charlotte returned, being as dense as possible.

"Oh, it must have been longer than that," Maude said. "Why, your visits are the light of our days! But if you won't come to us, I must visit you! See. I have brought you a peace offering—well, a friendship offering. A wee pot of honey from my cook's brother's hive."

Since Charlotte knew that Mrs. Beecham's cook's brother was the same as her own cook's son, she was hard-pressed to maintain a sober face. She accepted the pot and placed it on the nearest table. Then she managed to say, "Thank you, Cousin. Sydney is fond of honey, and Auntie also, I think." She glanced at her aunt who nodded silently. "Sit down, Cousin."

Maude Beecham chose a chair, so Charlotte settled upon the nearest one, resolving to be gracious.

"Cleone was just saying 'We have not seen Cousin Charlotte recently, Mama,' so I thought I would trot up here to be sure that you are well."

"I am always well," replied Charlotte, though her face was a bit pale, which Mrs. Beecham did not notice, being intent on her own ambitions.

"I am glad to hear that." The visitor sighed, and when her hostess did not show any interest in her condition, she added, "I do wish I could say the same for my daughter. She is oddly depressed—I mean, it is odd for her not to be overflowing with good spirits. But she is unusually quiet—and—er—solemn. *Quite* wan, you see, not taking any interest in the young bucks who are constantly calling on her. I think"—coyly emphasized—"that she misses dear Sydney."

As Charlotte refused the bait, Mrs. Beecham continued, "She thinks—we *all* think there is no one so delightful as dear Sydney."

"Of course I am fond of his company myself," her ladyship said. "These are heady days for him, with visions of Oxford so soon to change his life."

"Ah! But will it be a *good* change?" Mrs. Beecham was prepared to pounce on any opening, so she said, "Will Oxford spoil him?"

"He is past the spoiling age," Charlotte pointed out.

"Perhaps other young men may make him forget the principles of his family—lead him *astray?*"

"If they do, it will be no concern of yours, Cousin Maude," snapped Sydney's sister immediately. Auntie dropped a stitch.

"But all his family—"

"I am his family," Charlotte retorted.

"You are closest, of course," agreed Maude in an effort to be pacific. "Surely you know we at the Dower House want the best for him."

Charlotte clamped her teeth so tightly that the irritating visitor had time to add, "Why, Cleone quite dotes on him. Indeed, I suspect her sentiments are more tender than that."

"She is a perfect ninny if she indulges in tender feelings for someone so far beyond her reach. I hope you do not encourage such aspirations."

"Only because her heart is set on him. I would not want to see her hurt."

"Neither do I want Sydney hurt by an uncaring wife."

"They make a splendid pair. Both so beautiful—" reminded the beauty's ambitious parent.

Charlotte said, "I prefer to think of my brother as manly. As for beauty, your daughter is beautiful in looks, Maude, but I see no sign of dignity in her."

"Oh, dignity," scoffed Mrs. Beecham. "I daresay Cleone would look dignified in a coronet."

"She would not wear a coronet twenty-four hours a day. There are other sorts of dignity required of a duchess."

Mrs. Beecham switched her approach. "But they are devoted!"

"Truly? Cleone *devoted?* Or aspiring to a title?"

"Cousins—so suitable!" persisted Mrs. Beecham, switching again.

"Yes. Distant ones," Charlotte pointed out. "A blood relationship is an obstacle rather than an asset. Oh, I agree that Cleone is of gentle birth, but her position in society depends upon a mere connection."

This, being a fact, could not be rebutted by an angry mother.

"There are also their unequal fortunes," Charlotte reminded.

"Fortunes!" cried Mrs. Beecham. "Who is to know, when all falls into the same pot?"

"All is already in one pot," replied Charlotte inexorably.

Her visitor sniffed and dabbed her nose. "But—but they have always been so fond of one another."

Doubting Cleone's affections counted as much as her ambitions, Charlotte replied, "Fond, yes. In love—I do not mean some romantic notion—but real devotion, no."

"What do you know about love?" demanded Mrs. Beecham, losing control. "You have never caught a beau!"

Yes, there was that. Charlotte was shocked to think her cousin would throw that in her face, and when she glanced at Auntie, she saw that meek lady was looking outraged. Being strong (as Sir Roland had always thought her), she replied steadily, "Love is more than catching someone. Love is *caring,* being kind, being generous, being selfless—not, *not* pouting, not demanding attention, not stealing another girl's new bonnet!" She had not meant to mention bonnets, had let her anger run away with her.

"What?" shrieked Cousin Maude. "Steal? Of course Cleone did not s-steal Mercillia's bonnet. She *borrowed* it! She said she borrowed it."

"Tells lies," said a voice from the other side of the room.

The two combative ladies stared in astonishment at Auntie Emilie, who nodded her head sharply and resumed knitting.

Mrs. Beecham began to sniff intermittently, pressing her handkerchief fiercely to her mouth as if to control its trembling.

Charlotte, who believed chastisement was due, wondered if Maude's display of grief was genuine; but her kind heart was beginning to trouble her, so she said in a gentler tone, "Things are not irreparably bad. The lie, the vanity, the snares laid for Sydney can be forgotten by all of us. What really matters is the expectation of self-gratification, the lack of concern for the feelings of others—a serious flaw."

The spectacle of Mrs. Beecham's face, blotched with what might be shame, and the obvious mortification that Mrs. Beecham seemed struggling to submerge, touched Charlotte's heart, so that she finished gently, "Sydney must not have a wife like that, you know."

"I suppose not," mumbled Mrs. Beecham into her handkerchief.

"The most serious part, Cousin"—Charlotte used the word to soothe the unhappy woman—"is Cleone's attitude toward others. She has caused pain for Mercy, which ought to worry you more than it appears to have done, shown her no kindness, exposed her to ridicule for shooting a pistol."

"That," said the troubled mother, "was Mercillia's fault for admitting she knew how to shoot!" Seizing upon this issue, she stiffened her spine and declared, "I was mortified, utterly mortified."

But Charlotte was growing hotter, too. "Then why were you not mortified by Cleone's luring Sydney into a prank that could have had serious repercussions?" she demanded.

Maude gasped." I thought you did not—"

"Know? Yes, I know, but I was willing to remain silent in order to keep peace in the family. Cousin John has borne enough pain about that. It is time for you and Cleone to understand she will *never* become Duchess of Audley."

"Never" was an intimidating word when said firmly by the daughter of a duke. Mrs. Beecham looked ready to try tears again, though she did not. "I suppose Mercillia has been complaining to you," she said bitterly.

"Did she complain about her beautiful bonnet?" demanded Lady Charlotte. "Mercy never complains, as you ought to know."

Mrs. Beecham did know, so she mumbled that everything had been serene before Mercy came. "I do not know why I let my sister impose on me," she muttered, as if manufacturing blame to assign to someone beside herself or her daughter. She dabbed her nose, collected her empty basket, and stood.

Charlotte had accompanied her halfway to the parlor door, when the door was opened from outside, and the duke appeared in the opening with Mercy at his side.

Mrs. Beecham hurled "Ingrate!" at her niece, pushed past the pair, and stomped from the castle.

Mercy's face crumpled, and she choked back a sob. Sydney drew her to the shelter of his arm.

"Come in and close the door," commanded his sister, well aware of the footman who was staring at them.

Sydney guided Mercillia into the parlor and kicked the door shut. "What in God's name was that all about?" he demanded.

"It was my fault," Mercy babbled. "I should never have come, but Papa wanted me to know my kin—thought I should enjoy a cousin the same—"

"Age? Rot!" said Sydney. "Charlotte, she cannot stay in that household. I won't allow it."

Fearing that her brother might make further reckless statements, Charlotte said, "Not tonight, anyway." She glanced at Auntie Emilie, expecting she might say something to the point, but Auntie merely nodded, folded her knitting, and tactfully sidled from the room.

Mercy was escorted upstairs by a duke's daughter to a cheerful yellow room which did not look down upon the Dower House, but across artistic gardens.

"You must feel perfectly safe and welcome here," Charlotte told her. "This door next to the wardrobe opens to my dressing room, you see, and I am just beyond. Will you have supper here, or come down to us? We will be dining informally."

Mercy, who would have liked to hide her embarrassment within this pleasant room, said bravely, "Of course I must come down when you—and Sydney—are so kind. Papa would say one must not wallow in shame. May I apologize just once for causing turmoil in your family?"

Lady Charlotte said staunchly, "No, you may not. You are a welcome guest."

So leaving Mercy to wash her face and brush her thick brown waves of hair, Charlotte went down to the dubious pleasure of hearing her brother rant about the abominable witch that Cousin John had married, and about keeping Mercy at the castle, safe from Mrs. Beecham's ill will. He did not mention Cleone. Charlotte hoped this meant his eyes were fully open to the self-centeredness that would make Cleone a bad risk for matrimony.

The evening passed pleasantly with no more mention of the Dower House.

In the morning, before Mercy came down for breakfast, the duke told his sister that he had lain awake a long time that night and "thought things through."

"I have come to the conclusion that I must offer for Mercy, so that she need never go back to that household."

"Oh, Syd. Do not be hasty. Her parents may return any time."

"Yes, and they may not."

"We have no kinship, only a connection," she protested.

"But we *will* have. I think I must ride over to see Sir Roland and find out how one proceeds."

Charlotte, who had long ago abandoned any objections to Mercy as a person, whom, in fact, she thought charming, said no more, deciding to rely on Sir Roland to direct her brother to what was right. She had been in command at Heritage for so long, guiding her brother in all matters, that she had come to think herself incapable of blunders. What folly! What conceit! Sir Roland would think her a fool.

So he must be allowed to guide Sydney now.

"Speak privately to me as soon as you come back," she said, and he promised.

She went upstairs to see if their visitor was awake.

Mercy's gray eyes were open, but she still lay abed, her hair smoky on the pillow.

"Did you sleep well?" Charlotte asked cheerfully.

"Yes, I did, but now—I am ashamed to tell you this and make more trouble—but my maid—I quite forgot her! She's alone down at the Dower House."

Of course, the woman was not actually alone in an empty house. Charlotte understood that Mercy meant friendless, and she replied immediately, "But it is my fault. I should have been the one to remember her. I will send a boy down in a gig to fetch her. We will decide about luggage later."

"Will I stay here?" Mercy asked doubtfully. "I must only be a worry to the duke."

"You will be a greater worry if you do *not* stay," Charlotte replied.

"Papa and Mama sent me to Aunt Maude's care."

"Much care she provided!" scoffed Charlotte, but lightly so as to not upset her little visitor. "If you would like me to write a note to your parents, pray give me their address."

"I have one for Athens, which I will give you if my maid thinks to bring my journal. They may not still be there. The only other address I have is the embassy at Paris."

What a muddle.

Charlotte wondered what was passing at Sir Roland's home.

"Do get up," she said cheerfully. "When Sydney returns he will want to tell us what we must do next."

Charlotte was not accustomed to Sydney's telling her what to do, but she realized that Mercy looked to him as to an oracle. Such trust must be quite heady to a gentleman of only nineteen years! Well, this might test his mettle, might make a man of him. Besides, he himself was looking to Sir Roland for leadership, and there could be no better leader than their neighbor.

As it happened, the duke returned before Mercy had quite finished dressing, meeting Charlotte on her way down the stairs. There was a touch of color on his cheekbones and an exhilaration of manner that told a great deal of what he had not yet spoken.

"Come into the library," he said.

Liking Mercy very much, yet apprehensive at his tying himself in matrimony while still not twenty, much less twenty-one, she followed slowly. What could she say?

Very little was required from her.

"Sir Roland said, 'Go ahead. Marry the girl, if you are set on it.' I think Mercy appeals to him as much as to me. Why, he spoke of her serene manner as being just like yours. Haven't I admired that in you? The fact that Sir Roland sees this quality in Mercy supports my view of her. He says—subject to your agreement—I may make her an offer, and if she accepts, then all the pounds and shillings will be hammered out by my trustees and Mr. Pope."

What could Charlotte say? She was surprised that Sir Roland had yielded so readily. "Did he think Mercy *suitable* for you? Did he speak only of your being engaged, or did he anticipate a marriage sometime soon? I must be told to what I am agreeing."

"Then you *are* agreeing? Oh, this is great news!"

She managed a half-smile and said, "Not so fast, my buck! We must not forget Oxford. Are you to enter into an engagement only?"

"That all remains to be agreed with Mr. Pope. Actually, Sir Roland said my having Mercy with me at Oxford might make me study harder. Shall I promise that? Oh, do say you agree to my choosing Mercy to *complete* the happiness that has come with my having you for my benevolent dragon!"

"Dragon!" cried Charlotte, but she was not offended. "I thought I was your Mother Hen."

"Well, anyway, you have been a wonderful sister. Send Mercy down to me now, hmm?"

So it was going to be an engagement! She did not think Mercy would refuse him, and it seemed obvious that Mercy was enraptured more by a bond to the amiable Sydney than by the prospects of being Duchess of Audley and a peeress of the realm.

She kissed Sydney lightly on his cheek and went upstairs.

Mercillia was just turning from her mirror, looking sweet and clean (though it was a second day on her dress) and lovable.

"Sydney is waiting in the library. He asks if you will come down," Charlotte said.

"Oh, yes," replied the girl. "I expect he wants to pull out more books. I am glad to be of use." She smiled guilelessly and went away.

Going through the connected dressing room, Charlotte passed to her own bedchamber and hurriedly cast off her sprig muslin frock to drag on an old and comfortable riding habit. She really did not care how she looked, was anxious only to get away.

Then down a rear stair she flew to the long hallway which opened to the stable yard of Heritage. Pucket spied her coming and whistled for her horse. In no time at all she was leaving the castle and troubles behind, cantering smoothly across meadows where she and Sir Roland had ridden, then entering the woodland, slowing as the climb grew steeper. For Prince, with Lady Charlotte on his back, it was an easy trail that brought them to Audley Knob.

She slid from the saddle and fastened him to a juicy shrub, which he could munch as he waited. From there she followed the walking trail around and up the knob, rising higher than when her friends had come there with her. The tiptop of the knob, which she had vowed some day to reach, was rough rock, so that she had to climb cautiously. Yet ultimately she reached the pinnacle and sat upon it, waiting for a feeling of achievement which did not come. Her world stretched out emptily in all directions.

Where should she go now? What was she to do with herself?

Mercillia Pope, she believed, was going to step into her shoes. Oh, not at once, but someday soon, Heritage would have a duchess again . . . quite a lovely duchess whom everyone would welcome and embrace. Just as Sydney had been bred and born for a dukedom, she had been born to give place to another, her work of rearing her brother was done, and she must find another focus for herself . . . if one existed.

There was a slight stirring in the woods below.

Then Prince whinnied, and another horse answered.

Sir Roland rode into view.

"How did you find me?" she called down.

"You vowed to climb to the top some day," he reminded, dropping to the ground and fastening his horse loosely. "Is something wrong?" He walked to the base of the rocky knob and stood with hands upon his hips, looking up at her.

"Sydney is making Mercy an offer, or—rather—has done so, for I left him with that intention—and Mercy was going down to receive it."

"It will work out well, Charlotte," he said solemnly. "She is a dear creature—"

"Yes."

"And just think, my girl! No more worries about the Cleones of the world."

Charlotte gnawed her lower lip. "There is that, of course, but"—her voice wavered—"I must not hang upon them. W-what is to become of me?"

It was the first sign of weakness he had ever seen in her.

"You can come to me," he said huskily.

"To—to run your h-house?"

"No, to be my wife." He did not smile, only stared at her intently. It seemed very odd. She could not think he wanted a wife. But he held up his arms and said, "Come."

Mesmerized, she stood shakily and began to thread her way down among loose rocks, peeking at him from time to time, looking for a smile that was not there. At the last bit of trail she slipped badly and tumbled into his arms.

"Oh, God," he whispered against her hair. "I have wanted you for so long! Am I too old?"

She uttered a muffled sound which was meant, and taken, as no. His right hand detached itself from her body and raised her chin so that his lips could reach hers. They made her more dizzy than the altitude of the Knob. Then he whispered into an ear, saying, "I am only a baronet, love, nearly twice your age, not what a duke's daughter should have, but will you—"

"Yes," she gasped. "Don't talk. Kiss—"

Sir Roland gave a shout of laughter and obliged.

Sydney and the castle had been her point of focus for many years, and she could understand Syd and Mercy better now, but she really did not have time to think of them, because she was soaring above Audley Knob, and because the most wonderful man in the world wanted *her.*